There's
Lovely

Johnny Morris

There's Lovely

An Autobiography

— • —

J. M. DENT & SONS LTD

London

First published 1989
© Johnny Morris 1989

This book is set in 11/12½ pt Sabon

Printed in Great Britain at The Bath Press, Avon
for J. M. Dent & Sons Ltd
91 Clapham High Street, London SW4 7TA

British Library Cataloguing in Publication Data
Morris, Johnny, *1916–*
    There's lovely: an autobiography
    1. Great Britain. Entertainments. Biographies
    I. Title
    791′.0924

ISBN 0–460–04775–2

Contents

———— • ————

Contents

List of photographs

— • —

The soldier's return

—— • ——

'Tis said, I know, that the memory plays tricks. Maybe so. But the tricks usually come along later in life. A child's memory records carefully and with wonder, for it is recording for the very first time the things that astonish, bewilder, frighten and delight. It is recording on a blank sheet, a sheet on which nothing has been etched. There are no criss-crossings of doubt and anxiety, no nasty scrawls of revenge and hate, no curly-whirls of passionate emotion, no forked lightning of temper and rage. The sweet secret of life is being painted right before your innocent little eyes.

Some secret. For soon all will be revealed. But what will be remembered, and why, is a mystery. I remember back to the time when I was not quite two years of age. I didn't know, of course, that thousands of people were being killed in France in the trenches but I did know that there were far more women about than men. The house seemed to be full of women. A man was a bit of a rarity. My mother, my brother, sister and I had gone to live with my Aunt Annie, a spinster in Bridgend in Wales. My father was away at the war but I didn't know that. I had never seen a father, well not mine at any rate. I knew my grandfather, my mother's father, he sat most of the time in a black Victorian chair in front of an enormous, black, cast-iron range that glowed red through spring, summer, autumn and winter. Grandfather only moved away from it to go to bed or to go out and buy a newspaper. He sat there silently smoking a pipe and spitting into a spittoon. He was quite a good shot for his age and never missed the bullseye of the polished brass cuspidor. My

Aunt Annie cleaned it out and polished it every morning for him to spit into.

That beautiful brass dish, with a hole in the middle of its sloping sides, pointed out to me one of life's awful truths – unfairness. Oh cursed cuspidor, through you I learned of disillusion. Well, my Auntie Annie and my mother Fanny were washing up in the scullery, Grandfather was sitting in the black chair beside the black range, I was playing with some building bricks on the rug. I saw that Grandfather was getting ready to spit. It was a slow process – the pipe taken out of the mouth and held well away to the left, the cheeks sucked in and blown out, contorting into the spitting position, and then splat. Bullseye. I had watched the operation so many times but it had never occurred to me to do it as well. But that morning I went over to the cuspidor and spat into it. It wasn't a very good shot, my shower of infant spittle splattered over the freshly polished brass. Certainly it was nothing to be proud of. I was concentrating on sucking up some more spit when my grandfather shouted at me, 'Don't do that.' I looked him straight in the eyes. He was smart enough to read the disbelief on my face.

'You're not to do that, it isn't nice.'

And then he called out to my mother, 'Fanny, this lad of yours has learnt to gob, look.'

My mother peered at my little collection of cuckoo spit on the spittoon and said, 'That's very dirty, you mustn't gob like that.'

I spent a lot of my day playing on the rug right beside an old man that never stopped gobbing and now I was being ticked off for one little gob. That presented me with the most unfair situation I had yet encountered. Briefly they could do things that were dirty and I could not. I couldn't possibly analyse their muddled reasoning, I knew perfectly well that not only did my grandfather spit but most of the sadly depleted male population spat too. It was a macho gesture to gob. And if you chewed tobacco, and there were many in those days who did, then you gobbed great brown gobs like an intermittent garden hose. The pavements outside public houses were awash with tobacco chewers' gobs. I couldn't possibly know that my grandfather's and my mother's reasoning was that if I was permitted to spit then I would use the technique for all the wrong reasons. It was like giving a young child a 12-bore shotgun. I would spit in defence, I would spit in attack, I would spit out of spite. Yes, it seemed so unfair.

Then my sister Nell came in and we all forgot about the spitting incident. Nell had only just gone off to school and now quite suddenly she was back in the kitchen. Why wasn't she at school? She said quite simply that my elder brother Reg was coming up the road with a soldier. Now, you could be sure that anything little Nell said had more than a grain of truth in it. Her pronouncements could be a little obscure but they certainly could not be ignored. It was always the policy of my grandfather and Auntie Annie to keep all bad news away from my mother. It was silly really because she always heard about it in the end. 'Don't let Fanny know for goodness sake, it'll kill her.' Trust little Nell to blow the gaff. Once she had come home from school with an astonishing but strangely garbled bit of information. She had said to Annie, Fanny and Gramp, 'Do you know what? Kitchener's sister's fallen in the water.' Aunt Annie and Grandfather made faces at her to shut up. But there was no stopping little Nell. 'It's true, Kitchener's sister's fallen in the water.' It was all confirmed in the papers when they arrived. Kitchener had gone down in the cruiser *Hampshire* – his sister had said that she was sure he was still alive. The difference between going down to the ocean bed in a warship weighing several thousand tons and just falling in the water is quite considerable but little Nell had picked up the essential that Kitchener was in trouble in the water. So when she came and said Reg is coming up the road with a soldier – everyone stopped in their tracks.

'Is it your father?' mother asked. Little Nell didn't know. And then the soldier came in through the front door holding my brother's hand. He was draped in tin cans and water bottles, and the dust of the desert puffed out of his tunic when my mother ran to kiss him. Everybody started crying except for Grandfather, who was spitting every few seconds, it seemed. What on earth was going on? I'd never seen the bloke before yet they said it was my dad. He came over and looked at his youngest son. I'll never forget that look. He leant back on the kitchen dresser. His face was ecstatic with love, relief and thankfulness. No wonder everyone was crying. Then he picked me up and crushed the breath out of me. I pushed myself away. The soldier wasn't playing his cards at all well.

The next day he took me down to the town with him. We went to a gentleman's outfitters. I had never been in one before, I had only been in ladies' dress shops and haberdashers and milliners. But a gentleman's outfitters – this was something. My father bought a trilby hat, a suit of clothes, socks and shirts. He was still in his dusty uniform. The new clothes were packed into a large parcel, the trilby put in a bag and I was asked if I would like to carry it. Oh yes I could manage that. It was a sunny hot day and on the way home we were suddenly shrouded in a great swirl of dust. It only lasted a few seconds but we were both left coughing and choking. My mouth was full of dust, I had to get rid of it. Using Grandfather's technique I held the trilby hat high out to the left, leant forward and spat. It was a pretty good effort, but I instantly thought, 'I shouldn't have done that. Now I'll cop it.' I looked up at my father, who was leaning against some railings shaking with laughter. Well, he'd just come back from the desert, he was an old campaigner, and his little son was behaving like one too. His over-familiarity of the day before was forgotten. The others said I mustn't spit and that was unfair. My Dad thought it was funny. Now that was fair, very fair indeed.

Life in the desert

— • —

You know there are many fine theories in this world but when you come to think of it they are derived from practical experiences and from common sense. In my view that's how they began. The trouble with theories is that they become law, they become tight and fixed, they will not bend or adjust to varying circumstances, they become set and solid like cast-iron with no pity and no generosity. Nowadays, when a life has been disrupted it needs rehabilitating, so they say, and so rehabilitation has picked up a theory as you pick up a leech. It leeches itself on to a situation and feeds on it. It sucks its blood until the theory grows bigger than the circumstance whose blood it sucks.

My father had been away at the war for some years and he didn't know his children. My brother Reg was eight, my sister little Nell was four and a bit, and I was just over two. He didn't know us. He knew my mother, of course, but he didn't know us and we certainly did not know him. But the presence of a strange man in the home was perhaps not as disturbing as it turned out to be. Now why was this? It was no doubt due to the fact that we were our father's children. He was a most good natured and tolerant man and so perhaps his children were most good natured and tolerant children. But he was also a man who knew perfectly well his own mind and had strong ideas of what was right and what was wrong and he certainly knew the codes of good behaviour. What he did not like, we all soon found out, was that he thought his children were suffering from over-feminine exposure. We had lived far too long in a world without men.

He did not say so but he was of the opinon that his children were just a little bit cissified.

There was little doubt that he had learned a lot by being in the army. From being a civil servant he and thousands like him had thrown away the shackles of convention, the patterns of proper behaviour, and had become gipsies who lived off the land, cooked their own grub, and never missed a trick at nicking this and that. So to break away suddenly from such a free-and-easy chase-me-Charlie life was clearly not going to be easy. My dear Dad needed rehabilitating. I don't think that the word had really been invented then. My Dad knew that he needed rehabilitating, and so did his children. The problems were enough to blot out the sun. On present-day values those problems would have made a rehabilitation counsellor talk earnestly and long for weeks on end. My Dad should have been sent to a rehabilitation centre, if there had been such a thing, to stop him from being a gipsy and to learn to become an honest and respectable nine-to-fiver. But no such theory had clamped its dreadful jaws on such innocent people who had all but been destroyed by the stupidity of governments and generals. There was no rehabilitation. You simply had to pick up the threads, carry on where you left off, don't let it get you down, put on a brave front, pack up your troubles in your old kit bag, you know you can do it.

The way my dear Dad rehabilitated himself and his wife and children was really inspired. He secretly resolved that we should be taught to survive, for not only was survival satisfying in that you became an individual, but it was very enjoyable. And so one day he came home shortly after his return from the desert and said that he had got three weeks leave before he resumed his work as a civil servant and that we were going on holiday. We were all very excited. Where were we going, what were we going to do? You'll soon find out, came the answer. We did, for standing at the front door was a great big gipsy caravan. It must have weighed tons. It was solid wood from the bulging domed roof to the iron-bound wheels. The wood was carved, fluted, bevelled and painted. It was a glorious vehicle. And there was a horse to go with it. Are we all going in that? The old horse nodded his head. No, we weren't going a-roaming, we were just going somewhere to be left in the wilds.

The man with the horse and caravan said that we'd better get going because he had to be back in Bridgend with the horse by late afternoon. We set off in that tremendous gipsy caravan, the bands on the wheels crunching on the rough old roads, and went to the sandhills, lovely tumbling sand dunes that swept up with tuffets of coarse grass on their heads and seemed to stretch for miles and miles. I didn't know that they were sand dunes at the mouth of the River Ogmore, I didn't know that the sea was but a few hundred yards away. But I could smell it.

When the old campaigner, my Dad, lit the fire from firewood that he'd gathered in a jiffy, the smell of the sea and the wood smoke was so incredibly honest and lovely that I have never ever forgotten it. And there was nobody there. It wasn't quite like the old campaigner's desert, but not far off. Dad was back in the same kind of environment where he had resolved the problems of this wicked world. My father simply exuded the perfection of what life should be. He had been away for years, so that suddenly, from a state of anxiety, tension, longing and heartache, there we were all alone in the sandhills with the smell of the sea and the wood smoke, a gipsy caravan and the old campaigner in his seventh heaven smoking his old pipe and radiating the love and contentment that countless generations have expected to receive from the great image of Buddha. If this was rehabilitation then the old campaigner knew a thing or two.

Dad made the fire every morning after we had collected the wood. From a gipsy tripod hung a black gipsy pot wherein burbled a murky gipsy stew. We didn't have stew every day. One day the old campaigner said we were going to have dabblegrish. Goodness knows where he got the word from, no doubt from an Egyptian scrawling on an old tomb or a tram. Anyway dabblegrish was a fry-up of scraps – old potatoes, sprouts, leeks, carrots, cabbage, all mashed up and fried in a pan. Dabblegrish he called it. But to make a proper dabblegrish you needed some fat for the frying. The old campaigner had some sausages. Fry the sausages first, they produce the fat, and then pound in the dabblegrish. He got the frying pan and slapped the sausages in army-style. They sizzled and spat like spiteful cats. The fire was just a bit too hot. Suddenly the whole frying pan burst into flames. The sausages were on fire. We screamed and rolled about in laughter. The sausages were on fire. On lord, oh lord, oh lord. We didn't know that sausages could turn themselves into torches. The sausages were on fire. Dad was roaring with laughter, he simply jabbed the flaming pan into the sand and the sausages squealed and died. Life in the desert was truly marvellous.

Back to normal

———— • ————

Everything grows in the right environment. In days of yore, to play any sort of musical instrument was considered a bit of an achievement. Nowadays many young school children play two, three or four instruments. They have been given the chance to try. Who knows, we may all of us be excellent bagpipe players had we been given the chance. Think of the ghastly row that would have been – but preferable to the ghastly blasts that come yelling out of the loudspeakers in pubs nowadays.

Dad gave us all the chance to develop our musical talents if we had any. Little Nell was sent off to a piano teacher, big brother Reg was dispatched once a week for lessons on the cello and I went to a music shop in Newport where an eccentric and very funny little man rented a small attic room where he tried very hard to teach little boys and girls to play the violin. Now to live in a house where three young children are learning to play musical instruments is pretty good agony for everyone and having to listen to a beginner on the fiddle is probably the ultimate in torture. So it could have been in self-defence that father decided that he, too, would explore the dark mysteries of his musical abilities. He bought himself a cello and decided to take lessons from a teacher who had once upon a time been a cellist in the Hallé Orchestra in Manchester.

We were all absorbed in music. My dear mother, too, had musical abilities. She had a fine natural voice and sang like a pretty bird most of the day. When I think of the concentrated noise that we generated in that little terraced house in Newport we would nowadays have had a notice served on us for disturbing the peace. But we weren't the only ones, oh no. The Clarks next door were all singers. Mrs Clark was a soprano, Mr Clark was a baritone, and like us they had a piano. Talk about musical soirées. The Clarks had got pretty good voices but they thought that the louder you sang the better it was. Everything had to be triple forte and no messing about. To hear them singing 'All alone by the telephone waiting for a ting a ling, all alone every evening waiting for a ting a ling a ling'! If there *had* been a ting a ling they would never have heard it, not in a thousand years. When the Clarks got into overdrive Little Nell, my Dad and I would pitch into Mendelssohn's 'War March of the Priests' on piano, violin and cello. This was probably the worst bit of music Mendelssohn ever wrote and boy did we help it on its way. People used to stop outside our front room window and gaze in at us butchering the music — Little Nell with her right foot firmly clamped down on the loud pedal, Dad with a Half Nelson on his cello and horse hairs swishing from my bow. We traded decibel for decibel with the Clarks.

Moving day

— • —

We weren't moving very far, less than a half a mile, I suppose, but we were moving. After all, we had been in the same house for ten years. The same house, the same street, the same iron lamp-post just outside the front door, the same old lamplighter that came to light the gas lamp every evening, the same neighbours with the same children. I never thought about it all being the same until my father came home one day and said that he had bought a detached house that stood in its own grounds.

I never dreamt that we would live in a house that stood in its own grounds, for we lived in a street. There were streets everywhere with all the houses joined together. Streets with tiny front gardens with iron railings that looked at the tiny front gardens on the opposite side of the street and back gardens that backed on to the back gardens of the next street. You could hear the neighbours on either side of you. You could hear them poking the fire, coughing, laughing, arguing, screaming, fighting, moving the furniture, putting up pictures, taking down curtains. And there was always a badly brought up dog that barked and barked. It barked at shadows, it barked at earwigs, it barked at horses, postmen, coalmen and paperboys. And now we were going to leave all this and move to a detached house that stood in its own grounds.

We were all taken to see it. It had a magnificent bay window that looked over a large front garden. Well, it was going to be a garden sometime, but at the moment it was a heap of builders' rubble. The back garden was going to be beautiful because right behind it was

Beechwood Park. This really was a house. Life was going to be entirely different. We were going to get away from the land of same to a place where things were different. It's true the trams ran along right in front of the house and that made a bit of a noise now and again. But to have trams groaning away outside was different, to look out of that great bay window at the trams and at the shops on the other side of the road was different. My Dad had the keys to the new house, he opened the front door and we tumbled in. It was a wonderful house. Mum and Dad were going to have the big front room, my brother and I were to have the big back bedroom which looked out over Beechwood Park, and little Nell would have the small back bedroom also overlooking the park.

'When are we going to move, Dad?'

'Oh, not for some time yet, the gas is not connected, the electricity is not connected and we'll have to get curtains made. There's a thousand and one things to be done, you must be patient. It will be weeks and weeks before we are able to move in.'

'Not weeks and weeks.'

'Yes, weeks and weeks.'

Oh dear, weeks and weeks of still living in the land of the same and not being able to get into the land of the different. It was then that I had an idea. The windows of the new house were, as the windows of new houses are liable to be, very dirty with great dabs of white on every pane to show that there was glass in the window frame.

'I tell you what, I could come up here after school in the evenings and on Saturdays and clean the windows.'

'Mmmm, think you could manage it?'

'Course I could.'

And so after school and on Saturdays I went up to the new house to clean the windows. I had a step ladder, a bucket of water, a cloth and what was called a 'shammy' leather. Now it was not a chore. I used to take the keys of the new house from a hook on the dresser in the old house in the land of the same, let myself into the new and different house and clean the windows. I didn't actually enjoy cleaning the windows all that much but I just loved being in the new house even though it was full of echoes and the hollow footsteps of the electricians and gasmen manipulating wires and pipes. But bit by bit I got those windows to shine.

Now to clean the outside of the bedroom windows without a long

11

ladder required a special technique. It was called 'sitting out'. Some housewives could 'sit out', some could not, for it meant that you had to have a bit of a head for heights. I did have a head for heights – the result of walking high walls, climbing tall trees, and playing about on scaffolding after the workmen had gone home. 'Sitting out' was dead easy. You simply pushed up the sash window from the bottom and sat on the window sill with your back facing the street, then you pulled the sash window back down across your legs so that you were safely held in position and you cleaned the outside bedroom window. I 'sat out' on all the upstairs windows. And then Dad said that we were moving on Saturday week when he didn't have to work and could supervise things.

Now it so happened that my mother had paid one and three for me to go on a school outing to Barry Island on Saturday week. One and three was quite a lot of money. One and three then is what we call six pence today. And so I would not be in on the move. I wanted to help with the move but I desperately wanted to go to Barry Island in a charabanc with all my pals. My father decided that he and the removal men could do without my help on Saturday and I would go to Barry Island on Saturday. I had still two more windows to clean at the new house – I would finish them on Friday evening. I took the keys from the dresser in the old same house, let myself into the new different one and cleaned the last two windows. I was in a dither of excitement. I tipped over my bucket of water and had to clean it up. Thank goodness I had finished all the outside bedroom windows, I don't think I could have 'sat out'. I understood now why some ladies couldn't 'sit out'. I had never known such excitement. Tomorrow we would all be living here in the new different house with the trams and the shops and tomorrow I was going to Barry Island. I had never known a tomorrow like it. When I came home tomorrow afternoon we would be in the new different house having the same old tea.

On Saturday morning the charabanc left before the removal van arrived. We sang all the way to Barry Island. We paddled in the sea with out boots slung around our necks. We had just one ride on the roundabouts with the steam organ honking, blowing and crashing in the middle. We sang all the way home. But I was going to a different home. The charabanc dropped us all off at the collecting point, which was about a quarter of a mile from the new different house. My face was stinging with the sea and the sun. All my pals were going home to their old homes. I wasn't. I was going to bed by the park

It all looked rather still, there was no one about. I looked in through the great bay window. There was nobody there. The house was empty. Oh heavens. Not long ago I had been trembling with excitement, now I was trembling with panic and fear. I turned and ran back through the old same streets to the old same house. I knew as I stumbled into the kitchen that I had done something awful. The kitchen was bare, no furniture, just five chairs. Four pairs of brown eyes looked at me with the most appalling scorn. It was left to my father to speak.

'You, no doubt, still have the keys.'

The keys. The keys. Oh gosh. I felt in my trouser pocket. I had taken the keys of the new house with me on an outing to Barry Island.

My father went on, 'Short of breaking one of those windows that you cleaned so beautifully we thought it best to complete the move tomorrow. The van is all but loaded save for our beds.'

I caught sight of little Nell. She was sniggering. Sniggering at my shame and suffering and my face burnished by the sun and now absolutely crimson.

'It is fortunate', said my father, 'that the men don't mind working tomorrow and that we haven't far to move.'

Yes, less than half a mile but we were moving. I handed over the keys and on the morrow, the sabbath, we moved.

Use your initiative

———— • ————

Use your initiative was one of my father's favourite expressions. It was a very handy expression because it allowed him to get out of all awkward corners when he was asked awkward questions.

'Dad, my bicycle pump won't work, what do I do?'

'Use your initiative.'

'Dad, for homework tonight we are asked to write a short essay on what would happen to the earth if all friction stopped, what do I do?'

'Use your initiative.'

And so brother Reg, sister little Nell and I were brought up to use our initiatives as far as our little minds would permit.

One gloomy summer day when the sky seemed made of lead and a sea mist hung like a muslin curtain, little Nell and her little brother were forced to use their initiatives. We were on holiday at Weston-super-Mare, where we often went. It was easy to get there. You took a tram to Newport Bridge, and there waiting at Newport Bridge was a magic paddle steamer hissing and straining away at the ropes simply dying to get over to the other side of the Bristol Channel. Those paddle steamers were our escape routes to glorious freedom and rough-and-tumble. The *Ravenswood* and the *Westward Ho* used to tie up at Newport Bridge to paddle the tired and weary to Weston and to Ilfracombe and back again for the matter of a few pence. We didn't know how lucky we were. Paddling down the River Usk, the dirty coffee coloured River Usk. Under the cats cradle Transporter Bridge. From the distance the Transporter Bridge looked to me like

14

a flying stork – a stork flying along with a napkin in its beak holding a baby. It was a great privilege to sail under the Transporter Bridge – it was the only one in the world, well, perhaps not in the world but there were only about six or seven others and Newport had got one of them.

From the Transporter Bridge it wasn't far to the open sea. We called it the open sea but you could already see Weston-super-Mare on the other side. There was so much to do on the *Ravenswood* and the *Westward Ho*. You could spend a half an hour looking at the engines that spun those thumping great paddles. There were windows that you could look down through and watch the shining steel connecting rods being pumped in and out by the pistons. I had a model steam engine at home and this was simply a giant version. There was a beautiful bar down below that always seemed pretty busy for it was not governed by the licensing laws and could serve drinks whenever it liked. We would go up to the prow and watch them tie up when we arrived at the old pier at Weston. The old pier was alive with entertainments. There was a water splash. You got into a boat that held about a dozen people, you were towed up to the top of a tower and then let go down an almost vertical slope to hurtle down into a lake at the bottom. You screamed your head off and got soaked for just three pence. Dear Weston-super-Mare.

We normally went there for just a day but now we were going for two weeks. I don't quite know how it all happened or why, but brother Reg couldn't come and neither could our father, so instead Mother, little Nell and I went with my Aunt Laura and her daughter Marie. We were going to stay in a boarding house. The *Ravenswood* bumped us off on to the old pier at Weston and we took a taxi with all our luggage along the seafront. There were the sands, the donkeys and the boating pool and I just couldn't believe that this would be free to us all for two weeks. And then the taxi turned inland away from the sea and he went on and on and on. We were now going away from heaven. What sort of a hell was he taking us to?

We were nearly on the outskirts of Weston before he stopped at a big Victorian house. Quite a nice looking house, quite a well furnished house and quite a nice mother and daughter running it. But they could provide no food for us. It was their rule. The guests had to go out and buy the food and then the mother and the daughter would cook it for us. It meant that the mother and daughter suffered no loss through waste. Now this was done quite a bit in those days, and when you think about it as a system it seems very fair, but it certainly didn't seem fair to us at the time. Every morning, almost as soon as the shops opened, we all went out shopping with baskets and it took hours. My mother and Aunt Laura were both pretty shrewd ladies and they would walk half a mile to find tomatoes that were a half-penny cheaper than anywhere else. We straggled on behind. To the butcher, the fishmonger, the baker, the grocer, the greengrocer. Should we buy a cucumber? Well, Aunt Laura liked cucumbers but they didn't like her. They repeated on her. It was something that I didn't understand. Cucumbers repeated, radishes repeated, onions repeated, broad beans repeated. I didn't understand it.

What I did understand was that all this ghastly fiddle faddle took hours and hours and hours. Then we took our food back to the boarding house to explain how we would like it cooked – not too much salt in the potatoes and please don't make the gravy too thick. And then it was a good twenty minutes walk down to the beach. We never got there much before midday. We had just about half an hour there before we had to walk all the way back for lunch at one o'clock. It wasn't funny because at first high tide was 3 o'clock, which meant that we never even saw the sea in the morning as the tide had gone out and at Weston when the tide goes out it goes right out of sight – you can't even see the sea. Now tides get later and later every day and by the second week of our holiday high tide was round about seven o'clock, which meant that our chances of seeing the sea before we went home were very remote. We wouldn't be there in time for the morning tide and we would be having supper for the evening tide. So we used our initiatives.

It was half past two in the afternoon. Aunt Laura and Mother had settled themselves in deck chairs on the sands when little Nell, her little brother and cousin Marie set off across the golden sands into the brown oozing mud ploughing off towards the sea. If the sea wouldn't come to us then we most certainly would go to the sea. Well, we were going home in a couple of days. It was a pity that a great blanket of sea mist dropped silently like a shroud over the whole scene. Out in the mud we weren't the slightest bit worried, we couldn't see anything much, but if the worst came to the worst all we had to do was to follow our little footsteps back to the sandy beach – using our little initiatives.

But back on the beach things were happening, although we didn't know it. When the sea mist came down Mother and Aunt Laura started to cluck and croak just like chickens. We had vanished. What had happened? They had lost their children. They started scurrying about the beach asking everyone if they had seen three children. Within ten minutes the wild rumour had spread all along the beach that three children had been drowned and that search parties were being organised.

Half an hour later an ambulance was standing by on the beach, a fire engine came clanging along. Out in the mist-shrouded mud we heard the bell of the fire engine. Something exciting was happening back on the beach so we found our way back by retracing our little footsteps which were very clear in the mud. We emerged out of the mists on to the golden sands. There were lots of men in uniforms, an ambulance, a fire engine and large clumps of people. Mother and Aunt Laura came running over to us and then something hit me on the side of the head. Bang. I knew what it was, it had happened many times before. My Mum hit me. She had got one heck of a clout. It was a left hook as fast as lightning. 'You little wretches,' she said, 'you little wretches'. The girls didn't get clouted, it was I who got the fourpenny one.

Life is very strange. One minute you are presumed dead, the next minute you are resurrected and bang, you cop a super fourpenny one. So should you feel like using your initiative, for goodness sake use it at the right time and make sure that it is the right sort of initiative.

Cocoa tins

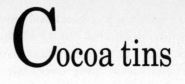

Human beings are like cocoa tins. Well, cocoa played a very important part in my life in those days. Warm sweet cocoa was the ultimate bliss. Human beings, like cocoa tins, are more or less the same to look at, some a bit battered, some with faded labels, some with the lids missing. If you had a lid missing, of course, it meant that you were barmy, but most human cocoa tins had their lids firmly hammered on and you never knew exactly what was going on inside.

I mean take the great cocoa tin in which Mrs Evan Llewellyn was locked away. She would come and sit in our front room and moan away to my mother and my aunt for hours, it seemed. 'Yes, well it's twelve years next week now that my Evan died. I was only saying to Mrs Morgan last week twelve years week after next that my Evan died. He was a very good man in many ways but like a lot of men he didn't show no consideration for others. Why he done away with himself I shall never know – not a letter, not a note, nothing. My sister up in Merthyr always said he was a cruel man and she was right. Fancy doing away with yourself and not leaving a note. Very cruel was Evan at times, very cruel.' Mmm, I wonder what went on in Mr Evan Llewellyn's cocoa tin. Something pretty awful to make him do away with himself. Could have been Mrs Evan Llewellyn, of course.

Oh, the human cocoa tins were very strange and very secretive. There was Walter Wade whose cocoa tin had something inside it that made him laugh as he spoke. We called him Uvee Uvee because that was the noise he made when he talked and laughed. 'Well, I was standing there in the door like you know, uvee uvee, when along he came like you know with this pound of sausages in his hand, uvee uvee, by where shall I put these he said, uvee uvee, well I could tell you I said like you know, uvee uvee, but I'm too much of a gentleman, uveeuvee.' Uvee Uvee had got funny things going on in his cocoa tin.

Very peculiar the human cocoa tins. I longed to know what was going on inside them. For I was inquisitive. Inquisitive to the point of being downright nosey. So were my father, my brother and my sister. All very nosey. Perhaps that is what prompted us to mimic people, we wanted to experience what it was like being someone else. The way they walked, the way they talked, the way they ate. We were particularly fascinated by the way people ate. We often had people to tea on Sundays and my sister was very quick at spotting the different eating techniques. Well, some people were so keen to impress on others the fact that they had been nicely brought up that it affected their eating. They ate with the slow, precise manner of a placid dairy cow rolling the bottom jaw round very slowly and viewing my father with great respect. Others had no inhibitions about eating at all, they just nibbled rapidly like ravenous rabbits. Then there were those who employed very strange eating techniques. As my father used to say, 'Goodness knows where they'd been brought up, quite revolting'. And it was.

My sister spotted the revolting eater right away. I noticed that before she had even started on her slice of cake her big brown eyes focused on the opposite side of the table. There sat a young friend of my brother eating in the most extraordinary way. He was a slosher. The slosher method was as follows. You filled your mouth with cake and then took a copious swig of tea so that your mouth was about ninety per cent full of dry cake and wet tea. Then you pursed your lips, blew your cheeks out and sucked them back in very rapidly. You flapped your cheeks violently and made a sloshing noise. Slosh-sloshsloshslosh. You turned your mouth into a liquidiser. I have long held the view that liquidisers were invented by a slosher or a whole family of sloshers. You couldn't tell that a slosher was a slosher if you saw him walking in the street, for his slosher habit was safely sealed up in his cocoa tin, but ask him to tea and you've got him. So the human cocoa tin was not as watertight as all that.

Bit by bit, little and sometimes very big bits of information escaped from the human cocoa tin. My father taught us how to gauge the

19

contents of the human cocoa tin by the way it moved, by its size, by its length, by its breadth, the way it ate, the way it coughed, the way it laughed, the style and condition of its clothes, whether it washed and brushed its hair, the impurities of the skin and the blackness of the nails, the way it sat in an upright chair, the set of its head, the colour of its eyes, the tone of its voice. Oh, you could learn a lot about cocoa tins by considering these points. Beyond that, a few quiet questions and you'd got a good idea of what was in most cocoa tins. People were beginning to ask me questions. Daft questions. Well, well, well, he's grown, hasn't he, yes, yes and what are you going to be when you grow up? What was I going to be when I grew up? How could I possibly know, I hadn't the faintest idea.

I had never dreamt of becoming what I was at the age of 26. On Christmas morning I was feeding the cattle. Yes, feeding the cattle on a very large farm. Well, apart from the milk cows we always ran a bunch of Aberdeen Angus steers through the winter. They did pretty well on the Wiltshire downs, the tough indigenous downland grasses kept a lovely sheen on their coats but they did need a mouthful of hay to keep them up together. It was a nice country saying, 'keeping things up together'. At the end of haymaking or harvest it was always very comforting to say, 'Well, things are pretty well up together'. And it was nice to see the cattle up together, the pigs up together, the horses up together and the ploughing and hedging up together. And this Christmas morning I was riding on the trailer doling out a pitchfork of hay every yard or two, the black Angus steers strolling and trotting along behind.

Go a bit quick, Bob, they're getting up in a bit of a heap. Bob the tractor driver opened the throttle a shade and that spread the following steers out a bit. As Bob always said, 'They treads in more hay than they eats'. It certainly did seem that way. There were always a dozen steers or so that followed close behind the trailer. They smelt every pitch of slightly mouldy hay that I tossed out and then came running after us. They were sure that I had something better to offer. They couldn't believe that I couldn't whistle up something a bit better than the dusty rubbish I was lobbing out. When they saw that the trailer was empty and that we were heading back for the gate they were devastated. Each of them accused me personally. I don't know if you've ever been accused by a cow but it's an expression that you will never forget. It says, 'Look what we do for you and what you do to us. We give for nothing – don't forget that, for nothing – our milk, our meat, our leather, our children, yes, even our children, all for nothing. And what do you give us? Rubbish, a load of rubbish.' Cows can make you feel exceedingly mean. But they always finished the rubbish I fed them, for it was a strict rule 'You don't want to give them no more than they'll finish up'. Well, that'll do for today, because today is Christmas Day. A grey Christmas Day with a steady drizzle.

Even as a little child I was always rather disappointed by Christmas Day. You may think that's a pretty rotten thing to say. But from a child's point of view there is such a long run-up to Christmas Day of rejoicing, singing, thankfulness, praise and glory. Surely there was no mistaking our feelings about the birth of the Son of God? We weren't hypocrites, we honestly and truly meant it. 'Tis true that *part* of the joyful celebrations meant that I would be getting a steam engine from my Mum and Dad. My sister tipped me off, she'd seen it in mother's wardrobe. Quite an expensive one, judging by the box. Well, that was marvellous, because I really wanted a steam engine. But apart from that, singing our little hearts out and finally mastering my one line as fifth shepherd in the nativity play, what happened? Nothing. Nothing. There was no recognition or a sign of any sort to acknowledge our devotions. On Christmas morning the sky should be lit with a thousand rainbows and the sound of heavenly music should come drifting in on the breeze in a thunderous and glorious crescendo that reached its climax around lunchtime when my father poured us all a glass of port. That was a supreme moment. But how we had to wait for that moment.

My father was a civil servant and he worked in the post office. But in the dear, dead days loyalty and devotion to duty was the sentiment of all honest men. The post office sorters worked right through the night of Christmas Eve until dawn of Christmas Day. Every parcel, letter and card of outgoing mail was cleared out of the sorting office. Nobody went home until the sorting office was absolutely cleared. You could post a card for local delivery on Christmas Eve and you knew it would be delivered on Christmas morning, for the sorters worked all night. So did my father and he usually got home at about half past five on Christmas morning and went to bed. He would not get up until lunch time, which meant that my brother, sister and I would have to be quiet. Dad must sleep. When he got up we would have our presents. It was agony. All the other children in the street were already out playing. Trying out their new roller skates, peg tops, hoops, skipping ropes, pedal cars and, for one lucky devil, a new bicycle. It was now nine o'clock and Christmas lunch was four hours away. It was an eternity.

You can see why Christmas Day was always just a little disappointing. But then Dad would get up and do an imitation of an old lady who complained to him that she'd sent two pounds of laverbread to her nephew. It was wrapped in brown paper and the counter clerk exploded the whole black mess when he drove his date stamp right through the volcanic morass of laverbread. It wasn't too long before we were all laughing. The presents stacked up on the sideboard. Mother brought the chicken in. We had chicken twice a year, at Easter and Christmas. Chicken and port wine and Brazil nuts and walnuts, and we chattered and chattered and laughed and laughed. Five cocoa tins chattering and laughing. All the same, but all so different.

The cat's whisker

——— • ———

It was the coming of the cat's whisker that magnified even larger the fact that we were all the same and yet so different. The cat's whisker was the very clever name given to the little bit of wire that you probed around the bit of crystal that was the heart and soul of the crystal set. The cat's whisker was nothing short of a miracle. And what did it cost? Just a few shillings. Pretty well every magazine and newspaper that you picked up carried articles on how to build a crystal receiving set with diagrams of step by step construction. And every time you went into town you noticed that another shop had opened selling the bits of wire and terminals and crystals that you needed to make a crystal set. As I remember, there were no factory-made sets, and I don't suppose that anyone had had time to adapt a factory to make wireless sets. If you wanted a wireless set you had to make it yourself.

There is nothing very new about Do It Yourself shops as they all must stem from those very early wireless shops. My brother, who was a good deal older than me, scrounged enough bits from one of those shops to build a crystal set. The simplicity of those primitive little sets was truly a little gem of home-made magic – a silver cradle for the crystal, a crystal the size of a pea, a little silver rod on a pivot with a little ebonite handle at one end and the little curly cat's whisker at the other. But it was the terminals that I remember. Well, two people cannot build a wireless set, there isn't enough room and all I could do was to play with the terminals. They were beautifully machined, you only had to flick the round nut and it spun and scuttled around the threads of the little bolt and stopped at the bottom. Then you only had to flick it the other way and it would surge up the bolt and fly up into the air and spin down to the floor.

I was not a lot of help to my brother building the crystal set. He made it on the lid of a wooden cigar box. Wooden cigar boxes were extremely valuable things. Well, you could keep marbles in them and lead soldiers and my brother made a phono fiddle out of an old wooden cigar box and it worked. I wondered if the crystal set would work. I remember he allowed me to put the headphones on to the terminals and tighten them down but he was going to have the first 'go' at listening in. A face concentrating on sound and sound alone has a quality all of its own. My brother's face was just like a spiritualist medium that had gone off at last into a trance. He was straining hard to contact the spirits way out beyond – pricking and probing away at the crystal with the little cat's whisker.

'Can you hear anything?'

'Sssshhhh!'

'Can I have a go?'

'Sssshhhh!'

And then a peaceful bland look settled on his features. A faint smile spread a little.

'Got anything?'

'Sssshhhh!'

Well, a crystal set was very clear but very faint and it could only support one pair of headphones – we called them earphones. I just had to sit and watch his face and try and guess what the spirits were saying to the medium. I did get a go in the end and then they brought out headphones that you could take apart so that you could have an ear each. And then along came valves. A friend of ours had built a one-valve set, a rather complicated affair. You had to be able to use a soldering iron to build a set with a valve in it. But valves needed batteries, tremendous dry batteries that I could hardly lift and almost equally heavy wet batteries that needed charging almost once a week. In garden sheds all over the country little men equipped themselves with the mysterious electrical equipment that was needed to charge a battery. Whenever you went out shopping you met people carrying batteries, taking them to be charged or bringing them back from being re-charged. The tram cars carried scores of people carrying batteries. So did the buses, and every other person you saw on a bicycle would have a battery swinging to and fro on the handlebars.

It did occur to me one day that it would be a good idea if you could plug your wireless set into the mains electricity and do away with all this fetching and carrying of batteries. Well, I was always allotted the job of getting the batteries charged and it was a real drudge. And the clever human animal is for ever seeking anti-drudge devices. The ban-the-battery campaign scored its triumph eventually but it took quite a time before a wireless set arrived on the market that operated without batteries and you could just plug it in and turn up the wick regardless. There came wireless sets with as many as seven valves, there came wireless sets fitted with super-hets, whatever they were. There were no more headphones or earphones, there were loudspeakers instead. Great trumpets blossomed, blooming and booming in every kitchen in the country. Wireless aerials sprouted in every back garden, high poles, long wires and a tremendous copper lever screwed to the window frame so that you could throw the master switch to save you from being struck by lightning.

Wireless sets were now very definite status symbols and the first of the factory-made symbols came from America. They were massive vulgar lumps of furniture. The fronts of some of them were like stone cathedral windows all covered in toffee. If you wished to let the world know that you had a bob or two you bought one of these ghastly things and bunged it in the front room along with the cocktail cabinet and the three-bar electric fire. It was the open boast of a rich friend of ours who had bought one of these Americal vulgarities that if he was to turn the volume right up you would not be able to stay in the room with it – it would blow your head off. It was the popular criterion – as it was with some singers – that the louder the noise the better it had to be. The germs of the disco were already infecting the blood stream. There was a man in the next street who bought a seven-valve wireless set and he used to switch it on in his kitchen and take a chair to the bottom of the garden to listen to it.

It was a most astonishing period in my young life although I didn't know it. Well, it was as though all the people living in the world has almost overnight grown great donkey's ears, for one of the five senses had suddenly grown out of all proportion to the other senses. We take our senses very much for granted – that is if they are working reasonably well. With the sense of touch, we recognise hot and cold, rough and smooth at once. Taste and smell go almost hand in hand. The scent and flavour of fried onions register simultaneously with the scent of the fried onions just a nose ahead. Our eyes are often astonished by a flaming sunset or the orange dish of a harvest moon. But the poor old ears are perhaps the most reluctant of all the organs, for most of the stuff that you heard you did not wish to hear. Especially when you were a child, your ears were constantly telling you 'No'. A thousand times a day you heard 'No', as well as all the tirade of variations on the theme of 'No'. My mother, when she was at her wits' end cleaning, washing and cooking for five energetic, boisterous people, could turn in a variation on the theme of 'No' that we all got to know by heart. 'If I've told you once I've told you a thousand times, heaven knows, I work and slave day in and day out, week after week, scrubbing and cleaning, and what do you care? You come in tramping mud all over the place – one of these days when I'm dead and gone you'll remember my words...' No, you didn't want to hear that perpetual reproach and the drone of most conversation was boring and predictable.

There was almost no need for ears except to listen to music and there was precious little of that about save the music we made ourselves. So when the wireless came along we were just about bowled over by it. For the microphone was of course like the microscope, it magnified. It magnified noises and rammed them into the head. What an incredible world whistled and whooped and sang and played and yammered away out there. Until the wireless smashed its way into our homes we knew practically nothing of what went on in the world. Our heads had been boxed in with sound-proof boxes. As yet we hadn't really heard a thing. Of the five senses that were designed so that we may survive in this wicked world the sense of hearing was suddenly made to work as it had never worked before.

And wasn't it wonderful? My young ears went into training and practised and practised every day for as long as I was allowed to stay up. But even after bedtime I used to sneak to the top of the stairs and listen in the dark. Sometimes I was allowed to stay up to listen to the song of the nightingale broadcast live from a wood near Pangbourne. The late night dance music would be interrupted from time to time when the little bird was in full song. The nightingale was singing full blow accompanied by a lady playing a cello from a wood near Pangbourne. I know the first time we heard it my mother cried and my father sucked very hard at his pipe.

For me sound had got the cinema licked. I did not need pictures, for sound had its own individual way of prompting the imagination. The biggest shock I ever got from sound was when I first went to look and listen to a talking picture. I was absolutely shattered when I heard the noise those glorious looking American film stars made. On the screen you would be looking at a dewy-eyed beauty simply tempting you to give up everything for her and her alone and yet the noise she made was enough to make you want to cut and run for it. No, I could do without pictures.

The dear little cat's whisker had given me donkey's ears. Big eavesdropping donkey's ears.

Time to think

———— • ————

One thing about life on the farm before the war is that you had plenty of time to think about things. There were some jobs, of course, where you had no time to think at all, like loading sacks of wheat, barley and oats on to a lorry. A sack of wheat weighed two and a quarter hundredweight, a sack of barley two hundredweight and a sack of oats one and a half hundredweight. We grew about a thousand acres of corn a year and it averaged out at something like ten sacks to the acre, so during the course of the year there were ten thousand sacks of grain to move about. Not just once but several times – from the field to the harvest cart, from the harvest cart to the rick, from the rick to the threshing machine, from the threshing machine to the barn, and from the barn to the lorry that took it all away. It was all done with muscle power. There was no other way.

To exist in the farm world in those days you had to have shoulders, arms and legs like a shire horse. Anybody with a bad back was told to try and get a job in the drapers or the grocers. The men, who were built like cart-horses, could not be daunted. The sight of half a dozen six-ton lorries rolling into the farmyard to be loaded with 36 tons of wheat worried them not one little jot. As the lorries pulled up, someone would shout 'Right ho, me boys, the time has come for a bit of savage entertainment'. And a bit of savage entertainment it was. They raced each other to see who'd get their lorry loaded first.

The word macho was not in popular use in those days but if ever there was a bunch of macho boys it was the boys that worked on the farm where I was known as manager. Even during their dinner hour they would vie with each other as to their physical prowess. One favourite trick was to carry a sack of wheat up a ladder. I could manage a sack of wheat on my back on the level with hard going but never up a ladder. There were also lots of tricks with 56 lb weights. There was one quite dangerous one where you held a 56 lb weight in each hand and then jerk-lifted them above the head. Should one wrist weaken slightly then you could knock yourself out stone cold. I never tried that one either. But the macho boys did in their dinner break. Their dinner was bread, cheese, and an onion which they ate like an apple. If they weren't doing their strong-arm stuff they would play pitch-and-toss with pennies.

These were the days when everyone had to work in a gang. Such a time was threshing, when you needed at least eight men. Three men were on the rick, two on the threshing machine – one cutting the bonds and the other opening up the sheaves and fanning them into the drum. One man bagged up the grain, one looked after the chaff, and two or three baled up the straw. We used to spend weeks in the winter threshing. I often joined the gang for this and attended to the wheat sacks as they filled up at the back of the machine. It was one of those jobs where you could think if you wanted to or had anything to think about. A sack of wheat takes on many human characteristics. Watching a sack fill with wheat was like watching someone get stupidly drunk. It was quite all right to start with, but as it filled itself up it would suddenly do a nasty lurch. Hic. Now come on, haven't you had enough? I'm quite all right now, don't you worry, I am quite capable of looking after myself, I'll just have one or two for the road. Meanwhile while you've been struggling with that drunk there's another one on the back of the thresher filling itself up and looking very unsteady.

Haymaking, harvesting and threshing were all gang jobs. But there were a lot of solitary jobs where you were more or less alone for days on end – in particular, driving a tractor up and down a great field of stubble, pulling a plough or a set of harrows, or riding on a binder. The binder was designed originally to be pulled by horses but was adapted to be pulled by a tractor. A most remarkable machine was the binder. It cut the corn, made it into a sheaf, tied it up with binder twine, tied a knot in the twine and chucked it out on the ground. It has the Heath Robinson quality of a steam organ, with clappers and hammers suddenly coming to life and banging and clapping and becoming inert.

For me it was always a bit of a sad time riding the binder. Well, it was a beautiful crop of wheat standing up straight. It was a shame to cut such a good looking bountiful crop. You'd known it all its life from the seed that you'd sown to the little green shoots that perked pale green in thin lines. And it grew to dark green leaves that waved to you when the wind blew and suddenly someone would say, 'That wheat's in ear, that's early'. Sure enough the little heads of wheat were showing. Then it was only a matter of weeks before the binders were ticking and clacking around the fields of wheat, barley and oats. The tall stalks and heads of corn would fall in thousands on to the canvas rollers that carried them up to be bound and knotted and chucked out just a few feet away from where they had spent their short glorious lives. Of course it was a bit sad. But then you had time to think about things. All the time in the world to watch the world. Just trundling up and down a field rolling the young spring corn.

The moment you started rolling the field the lapwings more or less told you where their nests were as they flew around and shrieked alarm. A lapwing's nest is just a little hollow in the ground and the camouflaged eggs look like stony ground. You cut a stick from the hedge and stuck it in the ground to mark the nest and drove around it. All our tractor drivers did that. All our tractor drivers knew where the partridge and pheasant had their nests, they knew about the bird life and the animal life and indeed the human animal life. They knew every car that passed by the field where they were working. If you wanted to know about the movement of a particular person you asked Jimmy who was ploughing or Doug who was harrowing. They would know. 'Seen the Guvnor go by, Jimmy?' 'No, he ain't been by. The doctor's been by and that 'ooman who's just moved into Myrtle cottage, but I haven't seen the Guvnor. You know they've come for the barley?' 'No.' 'Yes, the lorry went along five minutes ago.' Wherever you are in the country there's a pair of eyes watching you. The place may *look* as empty and forsaken as a wilderness, but you may be sure there's a pair of eyes on you. A pair of eyes that has time to think and to watch.

But there are occasions when you've no time to think at all. Like when the barn got struck by lightning. I can't quite remember what we were doing but I know that the rain was absolutely belting down and we all made a dive for cover into the big thatched barn with black tarred lap-boarding. We were watching this tropical rain when suddenly there was a heck of a bang. It sounded as I always thought Big Bertha the German Gun would sound. No one was hurt but the thatch began smouldering. The roof was on fire. 'Ah, the rain'll soon put 'ee out.' But the rain didn't put 'ee out. In fact the rain was rather unhelpful for it stopped as suddenly as it had begun. And the sun came out. The thunder storm was soon pounding at the nearest town, Marlborough, some miles away. We found four buckets, got a long thatching ladder up to the roof and formed a bucket chain. Jimmy, Harry and Doug were on the ladder while the Guvnor, Little Siddy and I ran to the water trough filling buckets and running back to the ladder. The water trough was at the back of the barn and so we had to run through the barn with the empty and the full buckets of water.

Little Siddy stood four feet and a few inches and wore a large cap. He had a very angry face with beetle brows and fiery little black eyes sunk deep in his face. You could never be sure where he was looking or indeed if he could see anything at all. His clothes were given to him by kind-hearted country gentlefolk. But as there were very few kind-hearted country gentlefolk down to four feet and a few inches, Siddy's clothes were not just big, they swamped him. He kept his trousers up with string and concealed their true length by stuffing them in leather leggings which came up to his knees. To say that his appearance was comical was a grave understatement. Little Siddy was not on the permanent staff. He was called upon when we were a bit short-handed. He was very willing but very surly. He ran with the full and empty buckets as fast as the Guvnor and I. But the fire was taking hold, wicked little waggles of flame popping up here and there. At the top of the ladder Jimmy shouted out, 'Look, we got no time to hand the empties back, chuck 'em back down'. Unfortunately Little Siddy didn't hear the command. He was just coming out of the barn with a full bucket when an empty one came down and hit him right on the top of his head. Little Siddy spun around a few times, his face a cross between Ben Turpin and Chester Conklin. He fell about like a punch-drunk boxer, slopping water all over himself.

After a few minutes Little Siddy came to and glared up at me like an angry little Rumplestiltskin. 'Ere is no use going on like this.' Clearly it was no use going on like this. The Guvnor started to laugh and got into his car. 'Where are you going?' 'Hahah, to ring the fire brigade and get my camera.' Meanwhile back at the barn we decided that water was not the answer. Isolate the fire, rip the thatch off. As we started to do so Doug unfortunately ripped off a bit of thatch that was smouldering, and as it fell to the ground it caught alight and nestled comfortably against the tarred lap-boarding. This was just what it had been looking for. I've never seen a fire go so mad. Talk about wildfire. The barn was quickly ablaze and so was the ladder. We had to jump for it. And then with an awful roar the barn consumed itself. We watched as it reduced itself to a smoking black skeleton. Little Siddy said, 'I arn't half got a bloody great lump on my head, and 'sno use going like that, we should have ripped that thatch off in the fust place.' Mmmm, perhaps we should, but we didn't think about it. That's the trouble with farming. Most of the time you've got time to think, but at other times you've got no time to think at all.

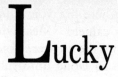Lucky

—— • ——

On my very first day at school, when I was four, I was run over by a bullnose Morris motor car. Well, not run all over, just over the foot. Here's what happened.

My sister of eight, who went to the same school, was commissioned to take me there. The entrance to her part of the school had 'Girls' chiselled on it, while on mine it said 'Boys'. By then I'd had four years of learning simple physics. I knew very well about the force of gravity. It exerted a firm control on your exuberance and enthusiasm. I suppose it was the hardest bit of simple physics to learn. The scabs on your knees registered the fact that you'd gone crashing to the ground very frequently. Little boys did not qualify for long trousers. You wore short 'nicks', as they were called. You were not accorded the protection of long trousers. You were put into long trousers only when you were in your teens. I'd got another ten years of short trousers to go. Ten more terrible winters of trotting to school in short trousers and purple knees, the short serge trousers acting like coarse sandpaper on the tender little legs.

Your two legs were like a couple of big chilblains – and we had those too. Every night I treated my cracked and angry little legs. But you didn't make a fuss about it. Course not. It was part of the process of growing up to have badly chapped legs. Every night I got out a little cardboard box on which was a picture of a flaming brazier in a snowscape. It was called 'Snowfire'. Snowfire knew all about little boys with chapped legs. I think that Snowfire kept the tradition going of no long trousers until you're thirteen. Snowfire was a soothing balm. It looked like a stump of a candle. You warmed it gently before the fire to soften it a little and then you smoothed it into your little sandpapered legs. It was heaven. The angry stinging pain seemed to be lifted away and absorbed by the Snowfire. I got hooked on it. I always checked at the weekend that there was enough to last through to Monday so that Mum could get me some more if necessary. And Snowfire really worked. All the little boys at school were hooked on it. We never questioned the stupidity or the cruelty of the parents who kept us in short trousers. They gave us warm hats, thick coats, thick boots, woollen socks and serge short trousers. Why? Well, you just weren't old enough for long trousers. Don't be silly.

And now on my first day going to school I was run over by a bullnose Morris. I wouldn't last long at this rate. I was soon surrounded by children who were going to school. 'Cor, look at your foot.' 'That's the tyre mark.' 'Cor, does it hurt?' 'No, not a thing.' 'Cor, aint you lucky.' 'Mmm.' 'Hey, we'd better tell Miss.'

We all scurried up to the playground where Miss was standing with her brass hand bell ready to ring at nine o'clock.

'Miss, Miss, Morris has been runned over, look Miss, there's the mark on his boot.'

Miss looked at my boot and then at me. 'When did this happen?' 'Just now Miss.' 'Whose fault was it?' 'It wasn't his, Miss.' 'You're new aren't you?' 'Yes Miss.' 'You're a very lucky little boy, a very lucky little boy.' I didn't know what luck really was but it may have had something to do with what happened as we went home from school. Leslie Chard attached himself to me. He was older than I was. He said, 'Now look, don't rub that mark off your boot'. I wasn't going to. 'Now come here.' We went into the sweet shop that faced the school. It was kept by two gaunt spinsters who dealt in a hap'orth of aniseed balls or penny gob stoppers or liquorice sticks. The taller, gaunter of the two spinsters looked down on us from behind the bottles of boiled sweets.

'Yes please, what do you want?'

'Look, my friend has been runned over.'

She looked at me hard and long. 'What are you trying to tell me?'

'Look, my friend's been runned over, there's the tyre mark on his foot.'

The tyre mark had by now faded quite a bit. The long spinster came from behind the counter and looked at my foot. 'Does it hurt?'

'Not so much now.'

'Well, run along home right away and tell your mother. You're a very lucky little boy, very lucky.'

And then came the moment that Leslie Chard had schemed for. The spinster gave me a sherbet sucker. 'There now, run along.' Leslie Chard and I shared the sherbet sucker, but a sherbet sucker between two doesn't last very long. We'd finished it long before we got to the grocers, where Leslie Chard pulled the same trick again for a few broken biscuits and at the fruit shop where we got a very small bruised banana. They all said the same thing, 'You're a very lucky little boy, very lucky'. I honestly didn't know what luck meant or how it worked or who controlled it. If someone did control it then it was a mass of contradictions or at any rate you could interpret what had happened just how you liked. I was unlucky to be run over by a bullnose Morris but lucky not to be killed.

I was very lucky to get a job when I left school, but I got a very unlucky job. I was a junior clerk in a solicitor's office. Lucky my foot. It only took me a few days to realise that I was not a junior clerk but a dogsbody. An errand boy. A little skivvy. Oh, I was lucky all right in having a job, but it was entirely without prospects. Prospects – you expect prospects. Well, that was more or less the standard philosophy of the early 1930s. Expect nothing and you will not be disappointed. Well, I certainly could not expect to be a solicitor. That cost a lot of money and the firm already had one articled clerk who crouched under the sloping slate roof on the third floor. I don't know what he did all day. Then there was Mr Forbes, who did all the engrossing. Sometimes Mr Forbes the engrosser would make a mistake and say, 'Oh damn and blast'. He only did it about once a week when he was not as engrossed as he should have been.

Mr Forbes the engrosser, Miss Travis and I shared the downstairs clerks' office. The flowing signwriting on the door said Clerks' Office. I had a tall mahogany desk with a brass rail around the top. There was a tall stool to go with it. It was from this desk that I tried to balance my post book. Every letter that was sent out from that office had to be entered in that book – Name Evans, Address Merthyr Tydfil, price three ha'pence. I was given one pound to buy stamps. At the end of the week I had to balance the post book. It was examined by the chief clerk, Mr Bumstead. It took some time to balance the post book – after all, you could send out 160 sealed letters for a pound. The Clerks' Office was like a mortuary. It was full of black tin boxes with beautifully written names in copper plate white. T.Llewellyn Evans deceased, Morgan Jones deceased, Archibald Prothero deceased, William Williams deceased. Their bones lay elsewhere but their manipulating, fiddling and jiggery-pokery lived on in those tin boxes. They were as dead as nits and yet they were still earning money wherever they were. No doubt where dead William Williams was he used to get a quarterly cheque from United Smelters. Mr Bumstead was always tending the tin boxes, tending the graves in the black tin box cemetery. I was left alone in this cemetery every weekday from one to two. I went to lunch from twelve to one and the rest of the office staff went to lunch from one to two.

Quite frequently Mr Bumstead would call me into his office just before he went to lunch. 'Look, I want you to type out these depositions.' A deposition, by the way, is the written evidence of people involved in a court case. 'I want you to type out these depositions. I simply can't ask the girls here to type out this filth. Get it done before they come back and put it in my drawer. They mustn't see this filth.' Well, I was barely sixteen – I'd got long trousers, it's true – but what was this filth that the girls mustn't see? The *girls* had to be protected but it seemed I was sufficiently a man of the world at sixteen to be strong enough to take this filth. No doubt about it being a sort of filth but it certainly made my lunch hour from time to time. It was quite fascinating what went on in the Welsh towns and valleys. I'd never heard of such things. And what about that case at Abergavenny? And Abergavenny was supposed to be a pretty posh sort of a place.

I'll never forget riding home from work that evening. There were lots of others going home from work. Had they ever done the things that I had typed out during the office lunch time? I watched them very carefully. Yes, now he could quite easily have done it. Phew, you just don't know what people will get up to. My father was in the garden. 'Hello. Hello. Had a good day?' (Did he know what I now knew?) 'Yes thanks, quite a good day.' 'Interesting work?' 'Oh yes.' 'Good, stick at it, you're lucky to get a job, you know, very lucky.'

Not everything

— • —

There are many things in this life that I don't want to be explained away. Consider the game of chess. It seems to me that chess is a reflection of the human condition. I don't want to know who invented chess for I would rather believe it came out of the heavens. Check, checkmate, stalemate. You're done. If you are but a pawn in the game of life, who moves you around? I have never made a positive move in my life as far as I know. Something has just shoved me around. I was unlucky to be run over by a bullnose Morris but very lucky not to be killed, I was very lucky to get a dogsbody job in a solicitor's office but very unlucky to only get £2 a month. I was still in my teens but the opening gambits had been made. Checkmate or stalemate was half a century away.

The first moves were made and whoever was playing my game of chess rather cunningly moved me to Hallam Street in London, where I was a time-keeper on a building site. It was a move that was all too familiar in those days. And of course the pull of the great cities still goes on. How did I get to London? Ah well, somebody put in a word for me. My wage was £3 per week – quite a sum in those days. But the cost of keeping body and soul together was quite something. Bed and breakfast 23 shillings a week, lunch and a meal in the evening you could manage for about 25 shillings. Not much left of your £3. There were bus fares to get you to work and that wretched gas fire simply gobbled up shillings. But I was lucky. Oh, very lucky. I'd got a job in London. It may not have looked a very spectacular move on the chess board of life but I was at the centre of everything, wasn't I? No longer a little solicitor's office boy in South Wales. I was right in the centre of the Empire.

Now if I learned a little of the facts of life at the solicitor's office, typing out depositions of disgusting happenings, what I picked up on that building site was enough to earn me a certificate in life's great temple of knowledge. I was a time-keeper on a pretty big building site. I had a little wooden hut on the ground floor with a telephone, one stark staring unshaded electric light bulb and a very battered copper dish that was supposed to reflect the heat from a pale electric element. You could tell by looking at the dish that it knew it was a failure. Its stupid round dish of a face lacked confidence of any sort and the dents all over it showed that it had been kicked by boots that had nothing for it but contempt. But I was lucky, I was in the dry, in the warm. I could have been out there with the brickies or the chippies or the iron fighters. The site or the job, as it was called, had only just begun. The steel erectors or iron fighters had got up to the second floor and the brickies were catching up with them pretty quickly.

Now all around this mass of metal and bricks was a wooden hoarding. It was put there of course to stop pedestrians falling down into the basement. It also marked the frontier 'twixt us and them. Them of course were a totally different race from us. Them rode about in taxis and large motor cars, they wore fur coats, tottered along with pekes and pug dogs and believe it or not they were called toffs. Yes, toffs. 'Watch what you're doing, you don't want to spill that concrete all over them toffs out there.' 'Mind your language, there's toffs about.' They were the toffs and we – well, I'm not sure what we were except that on our side of the hoarding on the job life was as it must have been in the fourteenth century. To start with, there was no sanitation. Add to that the smell of wet concrete and the eternal smoke of the fire that smouldered all through the day.

The tea boy made the fire to make the tea. This tea boy seemed to me to be well over sixty and every day he made the tea and what tea it was. He collected all the off-cuts of wood that the chippies left lying around and made a fire. The wood was always wet and it did not want to burn at all. It just gave off a heavy, lazy, black smoke. A smoke that knew it had no chimney to go up, so it roamed around the ground floor, looked at the toffs on the other side of the hoarding, went groping around my little wooden hut office, lurked behind the paper sacks of cement and twined itself around the old tea boy as he made what he called tea. It was very potent tea.

The tea boy had a big black bucket that spent a lot of its life sitting on the wet wood that made the smoke that had nowhere to go. In this bucket a couple of gallons of water would slowly get warm as the sad wandering smoke stuck its tongue into it for hours on end, licked round the big black bucket, liked the flavour of itself, stayed out of the way as the tea boy approached with a quarter of a pound packet of tea. Into the water that was still slowly getting warm in the big black bucket went one quarter of a pound of tea, a whole tin of condensed milk and a pound of granulated sugar. All this was stirred around with any lump of wood that was handy. After half an hour the tea boy would stick a fag-stained finger in the dreadful brew to see if it was hot enough to serve. Talk about warming the pot first of all. When he could not bear his fag-stained finger in the brew then the tea was ready. And he came like a ghost out of the smoke with the big black bucket.

Now everybody had an enamelled mug. It was always left in a handy place. Mine was left on my three-ply desk. A brickie's mug was left on the wall he was bricking up. It was left on the bricks and the wet mortar. The tea boy simply took the brickie's mug with mortar sticking to it and dipped it in the black bucket of tea. The mug came out full of dark brown tea and shining clean. The mortar just turned to slurry in the big black bucket of tea. We were served this incredible drink three times a day at ten, twelve and four.

I didn't realise at the time but, looking back, if it hadn't been for that dreadful tea I would never have been able to walk the joists. Oh yes, in those days everybody walked the joists. You could not avoid it. You had to walk the joists – or girders, as some people call them. The joists were part of the steel frame of the building. The steel frame was of course put up first of all and, bit by bit, the floors were filled in and the brickwork built up. But there were often great gaps with no floor and no brickwork. So you had to walk the joists. If the phone went and someone wanted to speak to the foreman you had to go and get him and if he was supervising the steel work erections on the fourth floor then you had to go and get him. This meant climbing ladders and walking joists with nothing between you and the basement floor forty feet below.

As a little nipper I was always pretty good at wall-walking. On the way home from school there were certain stretches of wall that I used to run along. All right, they were only about five feet above ground level but wall-walking was a fascinating and fairly dangerous thing to do. Walking the joists was altogether a very different business. And I swear that I would never have been able to do it had it not been for the dreadful tea that the tea boy used to serve up. Consider the ingredients: condensed milk and sugar, which were stimulants, and mortar which was not a stimulant but just clogged the brain. I believe that all of us who walked the joists were as high as kites and thick in the brain, all on tea.

There were stories of all sorts of accidents but nothing awful ever happened on any of the building sites on which I worked, although the conditions would have made any representative of the British Safety Council swoon away. Which perhaps goes to show that if you are aware of the dangers that surround you, you will be alert and look after yourself. For in those days survival was a very personal thing, you were responsible for your own safety, nobody else was and neither should they be. We were all very alert. Of course, you could get killed when you walked the joists but we didn't – well, after all, most joists were eight inches wide. Now that's a very wide tightrope. If you couldn't walk a ten by eight then you weren't a lot of use. The steel erectors, the iron fighters were quite brilliant at it. Week after week they were poised in mid air with absolutely nothing to hang on to.

The joists and the steel stanchions were riveted together. Not bolted, riveted. And the riveters were a real dare-devil bunch of characters. As you know, the most effective way of joining two lumps of metal together is to drill them and rivet them together with white-hot soft rivets. Yes, they need to be white-hot, then you hammer them in and they cool out hard, firm and solid. This riveting operation was carried out in mid air a thousand times a day, it seemed, and you always had to keep one eye on the sky and watch for falling white-hot rivets. Well, that's what used to happen. The riveters used to establish themselves on a lofty platform with a blacksmith's furnace. The rivets were made white-hot in the furnace and simply thrown to the riveters. When they were white-hot in the furnace the thrower would take a rivet in a pair of tongs, swing it over and over, and let it go. It was caught in a bucket down below by a riveter and hammered in. The thrower of the rivets and the catcher had to be very accurate, like a bowler at cricket and a wicket-keeper.

There was a story of a rivet thrower and a catcher. The thrower threw a rivet and in cricket terms he bowled a wide, the wicket-keeper couldn't stop it and it went like a meteor curving in a fine arc down to the ground. Unfortunately it never hit the ground, for there was a carpenter in the way. He was bending over a trestle marking a plank of wood. The rivet landed on the back of his neck just about where his back stud might have been. The shock made him stand upright. The rivet dropped down inside his shirt and burnt its way out through the seat of his pants. The shocked carpenter looked around to see that he'd laid a white hot rivet. Well, he was unlucky.

I was lucky, I was never hit by a flying white-hot rivet. I never fell off a ten by eight joist. It never occurred to me that perhaps my chess men were being manipulated. Well, not then. It's taken a long time. I may be wrong, but then I don't like everything in this life to be explained away. Not everything.

A good start

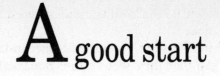

The most important thing in this life is to get away to a good start. How do you get off to a good start? Well, it depends who your parents are. Mine were wise, happy and loving, with a variety of interests. My mother was always singing and laughing, my father loved woodcarving and playing the cello. He arranged for his three children to play musical instruments. My brother played the cello, my sister the piano, and I played the violin. We always seemed to be laughing and playing. I was the youngest, which also helped me to get off to a good start: if you're the youngest your parents don't worry over you, for they have done all their worrying on the older children. Also being the youngest you have that extra drive of keeping up with the others. And so life for me and for all of us was very happy. We had nothing to be resentful about, nothing to be envious of. We accepted that you had to work for a living. And we all did.

My brother married, so did my sister, and I left the happy home to walk the girders on the building site in Hallam Street, London. The site was very close to the BBC, and one day I saw Clapham and Dwyer going into that great new building. Over the door was written 'And nation shall speak unto nation'. And what terrible things they do speak. Hitler was screaming his lungs out pretty well every evening, it seemed. Things did not look very good. But I'd got off to a good start and nothing could depress me. Even life in a bedsitter in Victoria with no shillings for the gas fire could not depress me. The boarding house was full of young people and we all got on very well and one young chap said to me one day, 'How would you like to go down to the country and spend a week-end at my brother-in-law's place?'

That weekend in Wiltshire I met the brother-in-law Willy and his wife Gwen. To say that they were rather remarkable would be an understatement. They were extraordinary. Willy had spent most of his life at the Stock Exchange until he saw the threat of another war. He said to me, 'There is going to be another awful war, we are going to get bombed to blazes, the country will need all the food it can get, farming is the thing to do, farming, me boy.' Now Willy knew very little about farming except what he had read in books and he had bought a great lump of Wiltshire getting on for 2,000 acres. It was not real farm land. All this land had done in the past was to provide grazing for sheep. There were no fences, very little water and no electricity. He was starting from scratch. But Willy was a very practical and thoughtful man. He'd made his money by thinking about money and he was determined to make more money by thinking about *farming* and money. He showed me the plans of the farm as it was and plans of the farm as it was going to be. He was going to build cottages, barns, a big farm house, piggeries. There was a lot to do. Could I help? And so I went to help on the farm.

There was a certain amount of office work to do and the wages to make up, but most of the time I spent driving tractors and getting ploughs and harrows repaired at the blacksmith's. It was at the black-smith's that I first met George. George was a tenant farmer, as big and tough as they come. He had enormous feet, tremendous hands and a face that looked as if it had been hacked out of a walnut tree. 'Ow be getting on, then, along with the stockbroker?' 'Oh, all right, I think.' 'I hope you're not going to plough that bottom bit of ground alongside the road there?' 'We were thinking about it.' 'Don't you dare do that, that's as wet as muck, that'll turn over, dry out and bake out like a lot of bricks, and you won't be able to do a thing with it. Don't you dare do that. Now look, boy, if you wants a bit of advice I'll give it to you. I don't want to poke my nose in but stockbroker Willy is going to get into one hell of a mess if he's not careful. What are you going to be at tomorrow?' 'Well, we were going fencing and we've got some cattle to move.' 'What else?' 'Well, I'm not sure.' 'Listen, boy, you've got to be sure. If you like I'll come and have a look around this afternoon and see what you be at.'

And so began the strange but most profitable association between

Willy, George and me. Every evening George came to the farm to look at what we had done and plan what we should do tomorrow. He'd been farming all his life except for several years of hell in the trenches in Flanders. I was fascinated by his physical strength, by his genuine desire to help and by the simplicity of his directions as to what should and should not be done. For me George drew back the curtains that had so far obscured many of the wonderful qualities of this dear old earth. What I'd learned in the solicitor's office and on the building sites in London seemed quite trivial to the great vistas that were being revealed week after week. You are controlled by the seasons, you are entirely at the mercy of the weather and you are dependent on the generosity of the animals and the earth for everything. The basics of farming are very simple. You simply provide your animals with the best possible environment and the best possible food. You provide that little seed of wheat with the seed bed that suits it best so that it can lie there and work its own little miracle for the benefit of the bakers and brewers. Organise it and do it.

At the begining of the war we were classed as a C minus farm, the following year we were A plus. This was almost entirely due to the stern directions that George gave to Willy and me. After the war started in September 1939 Willy built the piggeries, the cottages, a foreman's house and a fine farmhouse with views across the downs. Willy, Gwen, the cats and the dogs moved into the farm house and I moved in as well. The phoney war, as it was called, suddenly exploded in the spring of 1940 and in no time at all it seemed the Germans were just on the other side of the English Channel. The Germans had got it all their own way, they couldn't go wrong in this wonderful weather. It was sunny, dry, just right for warmaking and haymaking. That was the farmers' outlook. Just right for haymaking. And that's what we did.

We started work at 7 o'clock. It was too damp to pick up any hay yet so we got the tackle ready, sharpened the knives of the grass cutter, oiled the hay rake, filled the tractors, fed the cattle and horses. And then, at 9.30, we all had what was called lunch – dinner was at midday. Well, on this beautiful haymaking day I went back to the fine new farmhouse for my lunch. It was in a fairly isolated situation and outside the front door were several motor cars that I did not recognise. Willy's car was there too. I went in through the front door and there, looking most menacing, were six policemen. In the sitting room were at least six more boys in blue and one with a lot of silver pips on his shoulders. Heavens, they'd come for Willy and Gwen. This was terrible. Not only terrible but most embarrassing.

I said, 'Oh, excuse me, got to get on with the hay', and made to go back out. But my arm was taken by a policeman who said, 'We want you to get in there.' I was led into the sitting room. It was one of those moments when what you see suddenly enlarges itself and is so sharp and poignant that you know you'll never forget it. Willy's face I will never forget. He looked like a spaniel who'd been expecting a bone and received a boot in the ribs instead. Gwen's face bore a look of aristocratic indignation. And they were both looking at me. Accusing me. Without a doubt they were saying 'What the hell have you been playing at?' Well, I hadn't been playing at anything enough to warrant one policeman calling, let alone twelve.

A policeman came over to me where I stood wondering by the baby grand piano. 'Just empty out your pockets will you, please?' I emptied out my pockets on to the top of the baby grand piano. They thought I was a spy. No, they thought that Willy was a spy. And then Willy came over to me. 'Have you done anything that you shouldn't have?' 'No nothing, have you?' 'No, but from what I can gather we have been denounced as spies.' 'By whom?' 'I don't know, the police are here to search the place and we are under house arrest. Have you anything in your room that might incriminate you?' 'No, nothing.' 'They have authority to search the whole farm.'

And they had started. They were opening drawers, looking in cupboards and chests. Coombes, the local policeman from the village, was actually helping them. What were things coming to? Coombes drank with all of us down at the local pubs, we were friends, he could shift a pint quicker than anyone I knew. He saw me watching him as he opened a drawer in a lowboy. He instantly closed it without looking inside and hung his head. He was a jobsworth. By now I had arrived at a point where it was absolutely essential for me to go to the lavatory. I moved towards the door. Coombes stood in the doorway. 'Where are you going?' 'To the lavatory.' 'I'm afraid that I shall have to come with you.' 'Why?' 'You may put something down the pan.' 'But that's the object of the exercise.' 'I mean something incriminating.' Incriminating. I was steeped in crime.

Suffice it to say that Coombes came with me to the lavatory. When I was ready to leave, Coombes said, 'You'll have to hang on a bit, I want to go myself now.' Have you ever been forced to stand in a lavatory with a policeman sitting on the seat going slightly pink in the face? I looked out of the window at the downs. Things were going barmy. We could all get put in the nick, for Regulation 18b stated that you could be held in jail without trial at His Majesty's pleasure. Well, it might give His Majesty pleasure but we could be for it. I could be coming to a sticky end. Pity that, because I'd got off to such a good start.

An old pond

——— • ———

You know, I often think that memory is like an old pond, covered with a fine green weed. And like an old pond it just lies there. All the junk and rubbish that you've tossed into it lies deep down in the silt hidden by the fine green weed. You have to take a stick and stir about in that pond and just wait and see what you dredge up. That business with the twelve policemen came to nothing, but not before they had gone over the farmhouse and the whole 2,000 acres of farm with a fine-toothed comb. They were looking for transmitters, detonators, bombs, code books, anything that would incriminate. They found nothing. Of course. We weren't spies. We were straightforward British People. Our records showed that. But nobody had thought of looking into them for we were at war and the war had so suddenly exploded and brought the Germans so close to our front door that there was more than a whiff of hysteria in the air. We were unknown locally. People didn't know who we were or what we were up to. We were building all sorts of buildings, developing large lumps of land, Willy had a beard – which was very rare in those days – and he drove a German Opel motor car. We were preparing to receive several divisions of German paratroops. No doubt about it.

Hysteria of course blots out reason and those twelve policemen and those that controlled them had ceased to be reasonable. We were asked to make statements and we were all under house arrest for some days. The police kept watch day and night outside. It was sad to see PC Coombes out there as six o'clock in the evening came around. We both should have been in the local by then. But gradually the hysteria and the tension died down and the police went away. We were still under suspicion, and we weren't the only ones. Our next-door neighbour owned an aeroplane. Very fishy that. He was given a very thorough going over. Another neighbour out shooting on his own was alleged to have taken a pot shot at a low-flying British bomber. And he was the son of H. G. Wells and everyone knew what a free thinker he was. He was done too.

The Home Guard was formed – Dad's Army. Willy's application to join was ignored and so was mine. We were under suspicion. PC Coombes and I still met in the local and had a pint or two together but we were under suspicion. George still used to come in the evenings to see what we had done on the farm and to plan what we should do on the morrow. 'Look, boy,' he'd say, 'coming up here just now I noticed that fifty acres of winter wheat was winter proud.' Nice expression, winter proud. It meant that in the spring of the year the wheat was too far advanced – winter proud. 'Yes, boy, that's winter proud, what be going to do about it?' 'Well, I'll wait for it to get a little drier then I'll turn the cows out on it.' 'Yes, that's it, boy, but not too long and don't let 'em puddle it down, you got the right idea, boy, you got the right idea.' You had to have the right idea with George around otherwise he would lash you ruthlessly. And in the main I was getting the right idea.

Willy left the farming more and more to me. He spent a lot of time thinking. He thought about money and farming. He thought about money and silver and money and antique furniture and money and impressionist pictures. He also acted on his thoughts and bought silver, furniture and paintings. It's quite extraordinary what went on in spite of the war. Willy went to London every week for a couple of days. He went to the salerooms, he went around the silver shops and the picture dealers, he bought and he sold. He wasn't dealing, his taste was varying and changing and so he bought and sold. I used to drive him to the station, perhaps on Wednesday, and he'd say, 'I'll be back on the six o'clock on Friday – bring the estate wagon, I won't come home empty-handed.' And he certainly did not come home empty-handed. I knew exactly what to do. Park the estate wagon at the station exit and take the lumbering old station trolley down to where I knew the guard's van would pull up.

In came the six o'clock hissing and puffing, bang on time. Willy always got a seat close to the guard's van so that he could help me load his week's buyings on to the station trolley. He comes tumbling out of the carriage. 'There's quite a bit to move, duckie.' Duckie. No, I must explain the duckie bit. Willy and Gwen addressed almost everyone as Darling. Darling so and so, darling this and that, even the vicar was darling. But to closer friends and intimates their form of address was duckie. Willy always called me duckie. There was nothing suspect about it, I absolutely accepted it – I was duckie. I was often reminded that it might sound suspect, as it did when Henry Moore, the sculptor, came to stay for the weekend. Willy had commissioned him to do a piece of sculpture for the new farmhouse and Henry Moore fetched up at the station and I met him there and took him to the farmhouse. When we arrived, there was a hearty shaking of hands. The down-to-earth man from Yorkshire meeting the hard-headed man of the Stock Exchange. They were going to get on. They understood each other. No messing about. No subtleties. Cash in the hand for a lump of stone with a hole in it. Couldn't be better. We were standing outside the front door and Willy said, 'Nice of you to come, Henry, er will you bring in Henry's bag, duckie?' It was as though a bomb had exploded. Henry Moore looked quickly from Willy to me, from me to Willy. To the man from Leeds to hear one man call another 'duckie' could mean only one thing. It may have been the reason why Henry Moore never carried out his commission. Anyway, the piece of sculpture never materialised, which was just as well in a way as it would never have suited the new farmhouse. But that was the sort of man Willy was. He thought and thought. He thought of money in relation to all things. Money and sculpture, money and pictures, money and silver. 'There's quite a bit to move, duckie.' The station staff knew Willy pretty well, they were quite used to 'duckie'.

Right, then, what had we got in the guard's van tonight? Well, it's a bit of a mixed bag. There was one picture attributed to Fragonard, there was another attributed to Manet, there was a Corot, there was a Fantin Latour.

Fantin Latour, who was he? 'A very famous painter, duckie, very famous.'

Then there was a box of silver. George II mostly. 'Some of it's a bit dodgy, duckie. I'll knock it out next year, bung it in the wagon.' I'd been moving pigs about that day and the estate wagon smelt to high heaven. The picture were not wrapped up or crated, we just shoved them into the old straw in the estate wagon. Now this operation happened pretty well every week. And it also happened in reverse. Lots of works of art went back to London and lots more works of art came down from London. Until now I knew nothing of pictures or silver or antique furniture. But there's nothing like a good practical education. I was not a scholar, I just humped the works of art about and looked at them and got lost in some of them.

If the memory is a dark pond covered in fine green weed then Knowledge and Experience must be a clear sparkling lake, everything that you toss into it reflecting back at once. I was getting to know the painters, the silversmiths and the periods of furniture. There were lots of reference books at the farmhouse which were referred to quite a bit and, as the burglar said when he stole the Rembrandt, I know nothing about art but I know what I like. Sometimes when Willy came back from London he would stand the new lot of pictures up in the hall. 'Right, duckie, who painted this one?' 'It's not a Modigliani, is it?' 'You're right, duckie, there's not mistaking that, is there? 'Er, no idea.' 'Well, believe it or not, it's a Daumier.'

Now Daumier was one of my favourites, I loved his wicked ways of taking the mickey out of lawyers and judges. But this was a landscape. 'I know, very rare, duckie, very rare.' But I never really liked it – well, you can't take the mickey out of the countryside. Just then George turned up. Spending money like water again, what are you going to be at tomorrow then? 'We are going to drill the hundred acres.' Yes, there was one field of a hundred acres that we were going to drill with wheat. 'Got it well worked down, have you?' 'Any couch grass?' 'Just a bit at the top end.' 'No good drilling it if there's a lot of couch there.' 'No – there's very little.' 'Mmm, I don't know what you see in all these blessed pictures. Give me a good herd of dairy cows any day.'

As you can see, my sparkling lake of knowledge was reflecting a thousand images every week but then I was only a young feller, me lad, before the lake had started to turn into an old pond covered in fine green weed.

Full of surprises

— • —

Life on the farm was fairly full of surprises. There was so much that could go wrong. We had five milking herds and a lot could go wrong there. We had 2,000 pigs and an awful lot could go wrong there. We had eight or nine tractors and they were always going wrong. Day after day we were innovating, tinkering, bodging, adapting, helping the vet deliver a calf, helping the blacksmith shoe the horses, patching the fences that the cows had broken through. 'Guvnor, guvnor, Charlie's tipped his tractor over.' 'Jump in, we'll get some ropes and pull him pright.' They always said pright in that part of Wiltshire.

It was much easier to adopt the local terminology – to go downhill was down it hill and of course up hill was up it hill. So you had down it hill and up it hill. You didn't back a tractor, oh no, it was always back back a bit. You had to learn the special skill that it takes to make a tractor and trailer back back. Sometimes it was, 'Look, you'll have to back back backwards.' Back back backwards – you simply could not confuse that with forwards. I liked back back backwards. Another one was emp. Yes, emp. It meant to unload, to empty. It you had a trailer stacked with bales of straw you took it to the barn and emped it. But over the years that had developed into unemp because it had crosssed its lines with unload. So you unemped a lorry, you unemped a trailer, you unemped a bucket of water. No, there was a lot of dirt in that bucket of milk, I unemped it. On a farm there's a lot of unemping to do. You unemped a trailer till there's narn a bit left.

Narn was a good word. It meant not or none but it was better than either. Narn was a mean word, a barren word. 'Look, I bin here since seven o'clock this morning, I've had narn a crust of bread, narn a mouthful of water.' It paints a picture of the Sahara Desert. 'I've had narn a crust of bread and narn a mouthful of water and I can't quilt.' 'You can't quilt?' 'No, I can't quilt.' Quilt meant to swallow. 'There's something up with that cow, 'er can't quilt', and you knew perfectly well that if a cow couldn't quilt it had something up with it. I've never tried to find out how the word quilt came about. I like to think that the physical effort of saying quilt was very expressive of having difficulty in swallowing. You simple cannot swallow when you are saying quilt. When a cow couldn't quilt you had to catch her. 'Oh, ah, I caught her and we went scortin about all over the place.' Scortin about roughly means going hither and thither in a disorderly fashion. 'Scortin about all over the place in the end I let 'un went.' I let 'un went. I let un go is what it means, of course, but it's much more final than let un go. Let un go is when you've just released the animal from your grasp and it's still fairly accessible. But let un went means that it's gone out of sight over the horizon and you don't wish to know anything more about such creatures.

The young lad that was sent to catch a bad-tempered cockerel came back and said that he couldn't produce the cockerel. 'Well, I catch 'ee, 'ee peck I, so I let un went.' No good to tell him to go back and try again. 'Oh no, I let 'un went you.' You means you and nobody else. 'That baint no good you' means that the remark applies to you and not to the world in general. It is intimate in a way, but definite. 'I let 'un went you so don't ask me to try again. I'll only get myself in a caddle.' Now you never want to get yourself in a caddle, won't do you any good at all. Caddle speaks for itself. Flustered, off balance, unable to reason properly, irrational. Oh no, no good getting in a caddle. And sometimes, especially at haymaking, we used to get caddly weather. Caddly weather was when it didn't know whether to rain, shine, blow or snow. Proper caddly gets you going round nt round. Round nt round is like up it hill and down it hill. 'How do you want me to harrow this field then to and agen or round nt round?' To and agen or round nt round. To and agen, that'll be a bit differenter. Quite a bit differenter. The two chaps putting up a wooden rail fence stood back to view the horizontal rails and Harry said to Bill, 'Hey, Bill, one of them rails aint parell'.

No, they wasnt parell they was differenter and they both knew that they ought to be parell. And of course it only needs one of the rails not to be parell. The ways of communication were simple, effective and surprising.

You scarcely hear these words and usages nowadays, they're slipping away. The old people trot them out now and again and some of the very old use words that we don't understand and they are unable to explain. A local doctor was rung not so long ago by a woman who was in a bit of a caddle. 'Is that you, doctor?' 'Yes.' 'I wonder if you could come and have a look at mother.' 'Yes, I'll come around after surgery. What's the matter?' 'Well, she says she's weamish.' 'She says she's what?' 'Weamish.' 'All right, I'll come around once today.' Once today is reassuring because it means a definite promise. Once today.

Well, the doctor went around once today and there was mother sitting in a chair by the fire. 'Hello and what seems to be the matter?' 'Well, I be weamish.' 'And tell me, what does it feel like to be weamish?' 'Course I'm weamish, me waters all spuddly.' The doctor, a quick and wise man, could only guess. He administered an antibiotic. His was a good guess, for the waters became unspuddly and the weamishness and the weams went away. She let un went.

As I say, these words were used by the older people. And two such people that were the centre of much amusement were Little Siddy and old Danl. They looked very much like Mutt and Jeff. Little Siddy was four foot and a bit. His face bore an expression of enraged ferocity. I knew Little Siddy for years yet I never saw him smile once. He obviously had a grudge. Could have been on account of his size, could have been on account of the strange life he led. He was always prowling around the farm and I could usually find something for him to do. He was no good for humping sacks or heavy work and he had not the slightest ability with machinery so most of the time he worked with the rabbit trappers. I know, I know, the trapping of rabbits is a fiendish business. The fact that it happened nearly fifty years ago does not excuse it but what does in part excuse it is that our farms were infested with rabbits. And I mean infested. Look at the downs, the downs that billowed away just above the 100 acre field that you'd just planted with wheat. The downs are a pale, pale green but there's that dark brown patch of several acres in the middle there. Fire a twelve bore in the air and that brown patch will move and vanish. It was thousands of rabbits. One bang from a gun and they would scamper and disappear underground. Their warrens were vast. It was wartime and we were instructed to grow more and more cereal crops. But the more crops we grew the more rabbits we created. The borders of every field of wheat, barley and oats were bare, eaten by rabbits. Sometimes those bare borders would be many yards deep. Every field that we ploughed from pasture to cereal crop would be infested overnight. We had to keep the rabbits down. On our farm alone we caught three hundred rabbits every night. A lorry picked them up every morning. Food was very scarce, so we lived on rabbits.

Little Siddy helped the rabbit trappers and he lived in a tiny tent until some dear lady in the village offered him a tumbledown crooked cottage on the outskirts of the village. Well, not to Little Siddy alone, for there was old Danl too. They could share the cottage. An excellent arrangement. Little Siddy and old Danl were both bachelors. Washing and shaving were not part of their daily routines, so they were ideally suited to each other. Old Danl was a mild sort of creature but he was all alone and he had, as they say, let hisself go. That was the excuse that was applied to any dirty old man. It was a sympathetic and generous judgement. He was not disgusting or revolting or filthy, he'd just let hisself go. He hadn't went. Not yet. He'd just let hisself go. Little Siddy had also let hisself go to up to a point, but he had a grudge. Well, if you are created a foot shorter than the shortest of men it's understandable.

I have a strong feeling that it was Little Siddy who was responsible for the dreadful atmosphere that settled in that crooked cottage. The two old men lived in hatred of each other, a sullen negative hatred, the hatred that breeds demarcation lines. Well, there was a little staircase in that crooked cottage and it got to a point where Little Siddy walked up his half of the staircase and old Danl walked up his side. Little Siddy would sweep down his side of the staircase and old Danl would sweep down his side. They never ate together. They prepared and ate their food separately at different times. There was no sharing. It was carefully studied non-cooperation. If Little Siddy was first up in the morning he would light the fire, make a pot of tea, have a slice of bread and plum jam and then he'd pour the kettle of water on the fire to put it out so that old Danl would have to make his own fire and his own tea. Old Danl did the same. Total obstruction by both parties. At times it was comical.

It was autumn and the harvest was gathered and the evenings

drawing in. I had taken a tractor and trailer with a load of yealms along to the thatcher. Yealms were the neat bundles of straw that we used for thatching ricks. The amount of thatching that went on in those days was pretty staggering. We had dozens and dozens of corn ricks and hay ricks and they all had to be thatched and fenced in. And you need a lot of straw to do it and a lot of fencing. I was driving back quite close to the village when I spotted a man at the side of the road waving me down. I knew him well, he worked on a neighbour's farm. 'You got a minute?' You got a minute – now that means something important. You got a minute means that a cow has died or Charlie's tipped his tractor over. 'You got a minute?' 'Yes, I got a minute, what is it?' I could see he was smiling. 'I've just come past Little Siddy and Danl's place – go up and look through the window.' So I walked up to the little old crooked cottage. Mustn't be long, it's getting dark. There was a light coming from the crooked cottage. It was an old oil lamp oozing out a yellow glim. It was placed in the middle of a fairly long old table in Little Siddy's and old Danl's downstairs room. At one end of the table was old Danl having his tea. He'd got a half a loaf of bread and a pot of plum jam and a brown pot of tea. At the other end of the table was Little Siddy and guess what he was doing. He was skinning a fox.

Charming. As I say, life on the farm was fairly full of surprises. All sorts of surprises.

Education

—— • ——

Education, they say, is a very fine thing. Perhaps it is, but it does depend on how you are educated and by whom. There are also some who say that education does more harm than good. They could be right. But as far as my education was concerned there was absolutely nothing I could do about it, for life at the farmhouse with Willy and Gwen was in itself an education. Willy's deals in pictures reached a point where we had nowhere to hang the pictures and so they were often just stacked in the hall. Willy said to me one day, 'Would you like to change the pictures in your bedroom, duckie?' 'Well yes, I wouldn't mind.' 'Help yourself.' I'd got a David Wilkie – very nice – an Etty study of a nude and a doubtful watercolour attributed to Constable. I swapped them for a small Renoir of a young girl, a drawing by Picasso – which looked as though it had been done in about ten seconds and probably had been – and a very nice Corot. A small picture, but it sat very nicely above the mirror over the wash-basin in my bedroom. As I washed and shaved every morning there was that Corot picture of a farmyard. It was a lovely way to start the day – it was such a calm, quiet picture. There was all the time in the world in that little painting.

The stack of pictures in the hall fluctuated quite a bit as Willy went up and down to London buying, swapping and selling. It was always a fascinating stack and it held a tremendous fascination for the dogs. Willy and Gwen had two big standard poodles, one black, one chocolate. They were both good-natured dogs and they were house-trained and clean except when they sniffed around that stack

An early family photograph of (left to right) my sister Nell, my brother Reg, my mother and myself

The soldier's return: my father in 1919

As a schoolboy in Monmouth, aged 10
(front row, second from right)

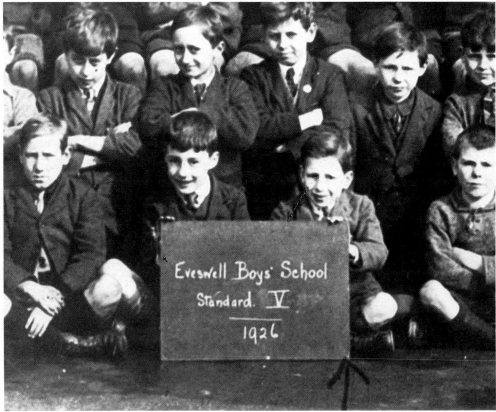

Eveswell Boys' School
Standard. V
1926

On holiday with my parents and sister, Exmouth, 1933

My first film: with Harry Carter in a Thomas Hardy story, *The Secret Cave*, late 1950s

Plapp and I, St Martin's, Scilly Isles, late 1950s (*Photo copyright Tony Soper*)

At home with Eileen, 1962 (*Photo copyright D. C. Thomson & Co. Ltd*)

The Hot Chestnut Man, BBC TV, 1962 (*Photo copyright BBC*)

In pensive mood at Bristol Zoo, 1962

With Dicklow, my pet mynah bird, early 1960s (*Photo copyright Woman's Realm/IPC*)

With a chimpanzee at Brighton (*Photo George Douglas*)

of pictures. Some of the frames were quite old so they must have carried some alluring smells. The one or two that had been smuggled out of France a few weeks before must have had most exciting smells, for the dogs simply could not pass those pictures without cocking a leg. They were so clever about it too. They never did it when there was anyone about as they knew very well that they would be given a severe ticking off and a smack to go with it. There was one picture, a Utrillo, a street scene with white houses. Heaven knows where it had been and where it had come from, but it really suffered badly for exciting the dogs so. That poor Utrillo was doomed, I'm afraid. One Saturday night during a party it got rather badly damaged.

Now we worked on the farm seven days a week all the year round but when darkness descended on Saturday Willy and Gwen always gave a party. They still had a fair stock of wines and spirits and were very generous in the way they dished it out. At times things got just a little bit out of hand. We invented quite an exciting game which usually happened around midnight. There were a couple of bicycles in a shed at the back of the farmhouse. The game was to ride the bicycles around the interior of the farmhouse. Starting in the boiler room through to the kitchen, around the kitchen table into the dining room, around the dining room table across the hall, around the sitting room and back. It took quite a bit of doing for there were some very tight turns and for quite a lot of the time you were practically stationary. You needed to have just the right amount of alcohol to complete such a nerve-racking course. Sometimes it all became hysterical and there were some agonising spills and on this particular night I was riding bike number 2, following close behind bike number 1, which was being ridden by quite a famous painter. I'll keep his name quiet because he had a bit of an accident in the hall. He hesitated, wobbled and fell. He went one way, the bike went the other and the pedal of the bike went through the Utrillo. It was a nasty noise and there was Willy smiling in the doorway. 'Think nothing of it, duckie, think nothing of it. It can be repaired. I'll take it up next week, think nothing of it.' And so the Utrillo, looking as though a bomb had hit its sunny street, went up to London from whence it came. It often think of that Utrillo and wonder where it is now. It must surely now hang on a wall that keeps it well out of the range of things like bicycle pedals and poodles' pee.

Willy now more or less left the farming to me. George came along every week and as we drove over the fields and walked through the cattle and pigs he told me where and what I had done wrong.

'Look, boy, I thought you'd have this field planted by now with winter wheat.'

'Well, it would have been but we had an order from the Ministry of Agriculture to say we've got to grow forty acres of flax.'

'Forty acres of what?'

'Forty acres of flax.'

'Cor, I've never growed any in my life.'

'Neither have I, but we've got to grow forty acres of flax and twenty acres of potatoes.'

Planting both crops was the easiest part of the operation. Harvesting was a very different matter. We simply ploughed the potatoes out of the ground and picked them up by hand. Twenty acres of potatoes at ten tons to the acre made two hundred tons. Flax, ah yes well, the harvesting of flax will drive the calmest, sanest creature off his nut. Flax can become two things. The stalks can become linen and the seeds can become linseed oil. If you consider the quality of these two materials you've got some idea of the nature of the beast. You pull flax up by the roots. There was a special machine that you could borrow. It pulled up the flax for a yard or two and then got bunged up, for the dreadful flax wound itself round everything. Every wheel was wound with flax, every cog was clogged with flax, everything that moved was strangled with flax. When I drove that flax puller I was sure that I would in the end be throttled to death by flax. It was like wading though a field writhing with snakes. So when we finished the field of flax I was singing as I went back to the farmhouse. 'What's that you're singing, duckie?' 'It's from the Tales of Hoffman "Oh joy beyond compare" or something.' 'Mmm, you know a lot about music, don't you, duckie?'

Now that was one hole in Willy's cultural make-up. Pictures, furniture and silver he knew. Music not so much. So a few days later he came along with a thick gramophone catalogue in his hand. 'I'd like you to order some gramophone records, duckie.'

'Oh, what would you like?'

'I leave that to you, duckie. I ought to know more about music, so you choose what you think I ought to listen to.'

'Well, it's unlimited.' 'All right, duckie, order around a hundred quid's worth.'

'A hundred quid's worth?'

In those days a pint of beer had risen to the crippling price of nine pence a pint. You can always judge the price of living with the price of a pint. Beer nine pence a pint. In other words if you handed today's five pence piece over the counter you got a pint of wallop and three pence back. Beer now is roughly a pound a pint – 240 pence a pint in the old currency – so beer has gone up 25 times like everything else. So Willy's hundred pounds for gramophone records was the equivalent of £2,500. 'I should start at A, duckie,' he said, 'and go through the book.' Well, I didn't spend anything on the As. Adam, Albeniz and Arne I didn't think would appeal to Willy. But B – ah, now you're talking, B for Bach, Brahms, Beethoven, Berlioz. I spent a fair bit on B, quite a bit on C (Chopin and one or two bits of Chabrier because I liked him) and I went slowly though the catalogue. I spent lots on the Vs – Verdi and Vivaldi – and then came the Ws.

Now you could have spent a thousand pounds on the Ws and it was over Wagner that I had to make some heart searchings. Wagner turns me into a wall banger. I hadn't a lot of money left so I found some overtures, some extracts from the Siegfried Idyll, and that was about it. Except that there was another W – Wieniawski. Wieniawski. Wieniawski was a violinist and not only that, he composed many pieces for violin. I remember as a little boy when I played the violin I played a piece by Wieniawski. It was a showy piece, quite difficult to play, with bags of double stopping which I could just manage. It was quite a touching sight – a little boy in short trousers whacking away at Wieniawski and slamming in slabs of double stopping. My mother and father came to the concerts where I performed and generally sat in the first row.

It was not easy learning to play the violin – I don't mean the actual playing, I enjoyed that – because my violin teacher lived on the other side of town and to get to him meant that I had to walk through a pretty sleazy area. Now to be seen carrying a violin case in those days was asking for trouble if you were a young boy. For the playing of violins was considered to be more than effeminate. As I entered the slum streets with my fiddle case the kids playing hopscotch and skipping would leave their games and come dancing around me going daa di daa di daa. Quite often there would be a scrap. I'd put my case down and start swinging away at the leader of the gang. Going for a violin lesson was like riding shotgun with John Wayne. You had to fight like an angry stoat to bite your way into the tough sinews of culture.

There was another hazard of which I was not aware. Warts. In those days conditions seemed to be favourable for warts. They came and went and then came back again. I didn't like my warts, nobody did, but you got 'em. My mother said to me, 'Look, for heaven's sake go to the chemist and ask him to give you something for those dreadful warts.' The chemist gave me a styptic pencil and I rubbed it into the warts morning, noon and night. On the Sunday evening of that week I was engaged to take part in an evening concert. Quite a few famous local artists would be obliging as well. I had decided to play a piece called Mazur by Wieniawski. It was a well-equipped hall with a good selection of spotlights. The stage manager decided to light the little fiddle player in a single pool of white light. My Mum and Dad were down in the front row.

I often used to get nervous but tonight I was not so much nervous as keen. I walked into the pool of white light and swirled away into Wieniawski. It was going really rather well. Mum and Dad would be pleased. I glanced down to where they were sitting in the front row. I couldn't believe it. My mother's face instead of wearing that divine look of adoration was aghast with horror. What had I done, left my trousers off? Oh yes, it was as bad as that. But my mother was following with some sort of terror the movement of my bowing hand. I glanced at it as it came up into vision. The chemist's styptic pencil had turned my bumper crop of warts black. A white and black spotted bowing hand flashing about in that bowl of light. It was like some daft surrealist joke. Nothing I could do about it – slam into the double stopping, black warts and all – you have to learn not to be put off.

The educator was at work. On the farm Willy was educating me about pictures, silver and antique furniture. I was educating Willy about music. George was educating me on large-scale farming. As I say, education is a very fine thing but it does so depend on how you are educated and by whom.

Crossroads

— • —

It has been said that there comes a time in everyone's life when you reach a crossroads. May be so. But the trouble with crossroads is that you don't recognise them as crossroads until you're gone past them. Looking back, you can see that you wandered off down the turning that seemed more attractive at the time. The less attractive one might easily have done you just as well. But those innocent turnings weren't as innocent as all that. As things turned out, some of them were the most tremendous crossroads. One way could have taken you to slow and certain death, another to the foundations of a career. Well, I was working on a building site in London as a timekeeper. I really quite enjoyed it at first but then I became revolted by it. And so I started looking around for another job. And I got one – as a teacher of languages in Germany.

There were certain formalities to be tied up first of all. The man at the agency to whom I applied was most helpful. 'Now, have you any qualifications?' 'No.' 'Well, that doesn't matter, in fact it's a help because the pupils you will be teaching will only be speaking English. Clarity of diction is what we are looking for and you clearly have that. Now all I need is a photograph to send to our office in Germany. Can you bring me one?' 'Yes, of course.' Well, today was Friday, I promised to take the photograph on Monday and for the week-end I was going to stay with a friend of mine at his brother-in-law's place in the country. It was that weekend that I met Willy and Gwen.

I'll never forget the look that Willy gave me when I said that I was going to work in Germany. 'In Germany? You must be barmy, there's going to be one hell of a war.' 'But Neville Chamberlain has said peace in our time.' 'Neville Chamberlain my foot, there's going to be one hell of a war, no question about it and it could happen at any time. You go to Germany, you'll never come back.' So I didn't go.

Now if ever there was a crossroads that was one, but I didn't realise it at the time. I most certainly would have been locked up in Germany for the duration had I gone along that road. I went the other way, to work on a farm. Now if life on the building sites was tough, life on the farm was at times almost torture. Well, Wiltshire is an extremely beautiful country, it is but lightly populated, it has rivers, forests and downs. And it was on the downs that Willy developed his farm, 2,000 acres of rolling tumbling downs. Now living and farming in Wiltshire was a farmer with some revolutionary ideas. His name was Arthur Hosier and one of his revolutionary ideas was to develop and improve the downlands and make them really profitable. It truly was a beautiful theory.

The quality of the downlands varied quite a bit. Part was really poor chalk land, what was called marginal land, part was light and dusty, and part was clay and flints. In the past these billowing downs had been grazed with sheep. But the new theory was to graze them with milking cows and to milk them in the field where they were grazing. A stunning theory, wasn't it! The cows grazed the grass, they manured the land and they gave milk, hundreds of gallons morning and night, which was collected in churns every day. You were making money on the milk and improving the quality of the land to bring it into corn production. A wonderful theory, but in practice it was sheer hell. Arthur Hosier designed a sort of movable milking parlour on wheels which took six cows at a time. It was rather like the starting gate they use nowadays to get the horses racing.

What I'm getting at is this. There were many, many things that could go wrong – and did go wrong. You were dealing with sixty or seventy cows, a petrol engine, an electric fence, a vacuum pump, yards of chromium and rubber pipes, a coal-fired boiler, a cat's cradle of ropes and pulleys, and a horse. These open-air parlours were called bales and Willy bought five of them. They were dotted here and there over the 2,000 acres. That meant 350 milking cows, five horses and all the complications of internal combustion engines, five times over. The men who worked these bales – there were two to each bale – had to understand cows and a strange collection of mechanical appliances. Looking back, I can only marvel that we found men who were so versatile. They had not means of communication, so the only way to find out if they were in trouble was to visit each bale.

Imagine a black February morning, an east wind blowing that practically cut you in half and hurling blinding snow in your face. Driving over a field in the pitch dark. The black-out, of course, prohibited lights save for a small slit in the headlamp of the car. The ground was frozen solid. Listen, yes, that's the petrol engine of a bale. They've managed to get that started, so everything should be all right. You get out and walk towards the noise of the engine. There are the cows in their electric fence corral, waiting to be milked and to have that mouthful or two of concentrated muesli. Standing mute and miserable, their backs into the wind. There's a tiny light showing in the milking stalls. Inside, the old strawberry roan was waiting her turn to be milked and as I watched her she began to produce her calf.

Now most cows when they calve like to isolate themselves from the main herd but this old strawberry roan had had so many calves she didn't, as they say, give it a thought. Just a couple of heaves and the little calf slithered down on to the hard frozen ground. Almost at once it sat up and shook its head as though it was saying Cor blimey what a morning to be born. The old cow licked it over and decided to miss her turn to be milked and before I left the little calf was on its feet and drinking. Our cows and calves weren't pampered and neither were we. The little calf was a heifer, a lovely colour just like her mother, worth hanging on to – had it been a bull calf it would pretty soon have gone to the abattoir.

Calves have crossroads too, if they only knew it, and so do cats and our farm cats were facing a pretty serious crossroads. I suppose we had over a dozen farm cats and they lived around and about the place where we stored all our grain. It was stored in several big silos, six of them in all, each of them holding several hundred tons of grain. They were a great attraction to rats. The poor old rat changed its character and way of life when people started to store grain. Before that it lived on grass and berries and this and that. So you appreciate that cats were essential around the silos to keep the rats down. Now there was plenty of milk for them and fresh rabbit. They were not hungry but nevertheless they had a lean and hungry look. Well, they were a lean breed. They weren't chubby and cosy. They were like Spanish alley cats. They came from a different drawing board from the one that designed the smiling British Tabby. They were looked after by the dear old man that looked after the silos and all the machinery that went with them. He was very fond of his cats. They sat all around him when he had his bread, cheese and raw onion, and cold tea. He talked to them in a high Wiltshire falsetto. 'Ooo what be doing there then, come on want a bit of rabbut then?'

Once when one turned up with a broken leg that dear old man Oliver cut two hazel twigs from the hedge and made the neatest little split for the broken leg. The cat stumped around on it for a few days and then Oliver took it off. 'Isn't that a bit soon, Oliver?' 'No no, he's a lovely young cat, they heals up very quick.' So you see, our cats were well looked after and, most important of all, they were loved. But we had living in the area a Herod – but a queen rather than a king. Herod ordered the destruction of all our cats. She was the boss's wife, Gwen. She said our cats were starving and they were to be put down by the vet. There are some people with whom you just cannot argue. Gwen was like that. She had ordered the executioner. It was up to Oliver and me to head him off, as it were.

Two days before the planned execution Oliver didn't feed the cats and nearly broke his poor old heart and the cats' hearts too. What on earth was wrong? But on the morning of the execution the condemned cats ate a healthy breakfast. We really let them have as much as they could eat at a go. I've never seen a more peaceful troop of cats, snoozing and purring all over the place. They were no trouble at all to put into sacks. One or two got a bit upset but we both talked to them. 'Don't you worry now, my little beauties, don't you worry.' We carried them all to the top of one of the silos, opened the trap door and took them down into the silo and left them there with the bags open so that they could get out if they wanted to. 'They'll be all right there for an hour or two.' 'Start the engine, Oliver.' The engine that drove the silo machinery was an enormous single cylinder engine with a fly wheel that must have weighed a couple of tons. Oliver started the engine. It made one heck of a noise. Like someone hitting a big drum. It only did about seventy-five revs to the minute – dum dum dum dum. If the cats were yowling nobody would hear them. The vet and his assistant came. And went – they couldn't understand it. They'd come prepared to exterminate dozens of cats. Dum dum dum dum. Not a sight, not a sound of a cat, dum dum dum dum.

I think it was the next morning that I had a letter to say that in reply to my application for an audition at the BBC studios I could attend the following week. It was a crossroads. I didn't know at the time but there you are, it applies to calves and pussy cats as well as humans. The only trouble is that you just do not recognise a crossroads when you come to it but do when it's gone by. You most certainly do.

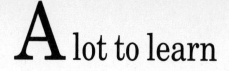

A lot to learn

———— • ————

Living and working on the farm with Gwen and Willy certainly kept me at about half a tone above concert pitch, for I was dealing with things with which I had never ever dealt before, for a start. But the younger the brain the more it will absorb. Willy now left the farming to me. He never had been a countryman. He was a money man. Always sniffing at this and that, seeking out ways of turning the material things of life into financial gain. And he was very good at it.

Willy's collection became quite famous. Dealers turned up with pictures under their arms and more often than not left with the same pictures under their arms. 'Didn't you like that picture, Willy?' 'Looked like a dodgy do to me, duckie, a bit of a dodgy do.' The telephone echoed with foreign voices offering goodness knows what for heaven knows what. 'Tell them I'm out, duckie, tell them I'm out.' Willy was not a man to mess about. And then one day he came back from London and I met him at Hungerford station. 'They're in the guard's van, duckie, in the guard's van.' I knew exactly what to do. I took the station trolley and lugged out five or six pictures. There was one very big one and my first impression of it was that it was a smash and grab raid, where someone had bunged a house brick through a plate glass window, and yet it couldn't have been because whoever had thrown that brick had hit a cardinal right in the mouth and he was screaming with rage and pain. 'Who on earth painted that smash and grab raid, Willy?' 'He's the man to watch, duckie, he's the man to watch.'

'Who painted it?'

'Francis Bacon.'

I got to know the work of Francis Bacon pretty well, for Willy bought many more of them. He bought so many of them and they were so large that Willy had a special studio built to house them and it was called by one and all rather impolitely The Baconry. Many many years later when we had both gone our separate ways I asked Willy what had happened to the Bacons and he said, 'I sold them, duckie, sold them'.

'Must have made a tidy lump on them, Willy.'

'Obscene, duckie, obscene.'

Lots of people came to look at Willy's collection of pictures – and at Willy and Gwen. They were quite outrageous, their language was dreadful and the topics of conversation at times quite unbelievable. Gwen had her own strange little sense of humour and she was often convulsed with silent choking laughter at things that other people just did not understand. On the other hand she was quite conventional at times and used to repeat stories that she had heard but could not understand. I always knew when one of these stories was on its way, for Gwen would always begin to tell a large dinner party her story with 'My dears, have you heard that story about the woman who went to the doctor's? It's wildly funny, it's so funny it'll make you roar. Well, this woman went to the doctor's, you see, it's so funny, well, the doctor examined her and you'll love this, it's so funny, it really is a hoot.' I knew just how they were going to end.

It was an experience to watch the guests' faces turn from happy informality to mild wonder, then to embarrassed horror and finally to bowed shame. Long before the end of the horrific story Gwen would turn to me and say, 'Oh, you finish it, darling, you do it so much better than I do, and it's so funny, you finish it, darling, you know it'. And so I was stuck with this ghastly story to finish. Sometimes a general would be sitting there with his medals shaking or a bishop with his false teeth rattling. I always took a run at the end of the dreadful story hoping that the sooner it was over the quicker it might all be forgotten. You could always tell by their expressions just how many people knew filthy stories.

Willy and Gwen soon made many friends in that part of wild Wiltshire. For example, there was Gerald Brenan and his wife Gamel and they came to the farm house quite a lot or rather I used to collect them from their cottage in the village, for they hadn't a motor car. They were a gentle couple and seemed never to be lost for words. Gwen said to me when I first met them, 'You must have heard of Gerald Brenan, he's a very famous writer, darling'. Well, I hadn't heard of Gerald Brenan. By then I knew a little of painters, sculptors and composers but virtually nothing about writers. And now here was one right before my very eyes. Gerald had a face that looked as though it had just come out of a fifteen round contest at the Albert Hall. The battered and sad face of a gallant loser. He did look as though he had taken quite a pounding. But here was a writer. A real writer. He talked of poets and painters, of writers and craftsmen and I listened and listened. He talked of the Bloomsbury Group – the Bloomsbury Group, who were they? My ignorance was quite appalling. But then everybody around me was at least twenty years my senior. I had a lot of ground to make up, an awful lot of ground.

It so happened that I met another writer. He was a young man who had come to live in the village with a young family. He had written several books and wrote scripts and adapted books for the wireless. We still called it the wireless. His name was Desmond Hawkins. We were both given to laughing a lot and talking a lot and at times drinking a pot or two. We were all very sad when he was appointed as a producer to the BBC and had to leave the village to live much nearer to Bristol. We wrote to each other from time to time and I did mention that in the past I had been an amateur actor, singer and fiddle player and wondered if there was any possibility of doing something as it were on the air.

In those days one thing dear old Auntie would always do was give you an audition. You would have to wait perhaps several weeks but you would get your audition in the end. My audition was to be in several weeks' time. Willy was quite delighted when I told him that I would be away for a whole day doing an audition in Bristol. 'Oh, that's good, what are you going to do, duckie, what are you going to do?' Yes, what indeed. My experience as an amateur actor was extremely limited, but as a boy soprano and fiddle player I was much in demand and seemed to be treading the boards several evenings a week. But what was I going to do? Gerald Brenan was a writer and yet to look at him you just would not have known.

I will never know what prompted me to do it. It was really a very saucy thing to do. But I am inclined to be a bit saucy. I had the sauce to go to the office typewriter and write my own short story which I hoped to read at my audition. It was a story about a man who ran a coffee stall and he had a boil on the back of his neck. He was trying to forget all about it but every one of his late-night customers asked him how his boil was. A slight and flimsy tale but there was scope for mimicry and different voices. I don't know who was looking over my shoulder when I had finished writing but whoever it was said quite quietly to me, 'That's awful, that's not not natural, it's not you, is it?' And I had to say, 'No it isn't, it's forced and phoney.' And it was. You see I had tried to write in a literary way like Gerald Brenan and all the other writers who used to visit Willy and Gwen. They wrote to be read. I was writing to be heard. It had to sound like someone telling a story off the cuff and not like a lawyer reading a document. That's what it sounded like.

I had been pushed into or rather stumbled upon the secret of speaking to be listened to. Listen to yourself first of all saying what you want to say. Nothing fancy, just the bare facts. And then bung it down. I had spent several long winter evenings writing rubbish in the office and it was quite a relief to crumple all those pages into a ball and chuck it on to the fire. Willy was also writing into a large exercise book. Since I had started writing he, too, thought that he would have a go. He was writing a play. He could make money out of paintings, antique silver and furniture, but the only way to make money out of writers was to write the stuff yourself. That's what we were both doing in our different little ways. But we both had quite a lot to learn.

An audition

— ● —

We toddle through life with occasionally an awful feeling of absolute terror and helplessness. Perhaps I can give you some idea of what it's like to present yourself at Broadcasting House and say that you've come for an audition. I found myself sitting all alone in a studio with a sort of small colander in front of me. A microphone. The glass panel on the side wall was screened with thick curtains. They were all in there behind the curtains – the producers, the spotters of talents, the damners of pretentions, those who would control the countdown and blast you off into space or inflict a self-destruct before you even got off the ground. A calm quiet voice came from a loud-speaker in the corner.

'Right, are you ready to go? Take your time, make yourself comfortable and we'll give you a green light to start – it's on the table in front of you, this is it.'

The green light flicked on and off. 'When it goes again it's your cue to start, OK?'

'Yes, OK.'

I had my neatly typed story in front of me. It suddenly seemed to me an utterly stupid story. What were they in there going to think of a story about a man running a coffee stall with a boil on the back of his neck? Noel Coward wouldn't write such a thing. J.B. Priestley would trample it into the ground. There was no insanity in our family as far as I knew. I waited for the green light. Now we were always taught at school that red is the most arresting colour. Red shows up more clearly and presents itself to you more definitely than any other colour. Red rag to a bull, red is danger, red is there to frighten you. Wrong. Green is the frightener, green is the one to scare the pants off you, green is the one that suggests to you that you have lost the power of being able to speak and that even if you could speak and wag that little old tongue about, you probably wouldn't be speaking English. Green strikes dread and terror. Green turned me cross-eyed as I focused on all those holes in that microphone colander. To this very day a green light will make my nostrils twitch.

I managed to start when the green light came on and I had been reading for several minutes – hours it seemed – when I heard them laughing. Behind the curtains they were laughing. I always had a good head for heights and was never much put out by a bad-tempered bull. I just kept on reading and finished the ridiculous story of the man with a boil on the back of his neck. All that was left for me was to slink off back home to the farm. Then the studio door opened and they came in. There was Desmond Hawkins the features producer, Pat Beech the news editor and Rosemary Colley the Children's Hour producer. They were smiling, all of them.

'We enjoyed that very much.'

'You did?'

'Oh yes, it was a very funny story, who wrote it?'

'Well, I wrote it.'

They looked a little surprised. 'Well, I'm sure we'll be able to think of something for you to do.' Having suffered the agony of one green light flashing at me I did not relish the idea of any more green lights at all. I wasn't at all sure that I wanted anything else to do. It was perhaps a strange quirk of fate that the very first broadcast that I was asked to take part in was billed to be transmitted on April Fool's day 1946 and it was called 'Folly to be Wise'. When ignorance is bliss it's Folly to be Wise. It was to be, as most broadcasts were in those days, a live transmission, which meant a whole day's rehearsal and then transmission at 7.30 pm. It was an ambitious programme, to put it mildly. It was a light-hearted revue-type presentation which included a short concerto for typewriter and orchestra. The West of England Light Orchestra was kept pretty busy and they were all present and correct for the great epic that was going to hit the great listening public on this April Fool's evening. Actors and actresses came down from London. Some of them very famous. Norman Shelley, Carleton Hobbs. They were all very casual, calm and abominably confident, but very friendly. They tried to put everyone at ease. I may have looked at ease but inside me was a cauldron simmering away like a badly clinkered boiler. Still there were only ten hours to go. Ten hours of slow simmer to go.

Desmond Hawkins was producing it and it required the use of three studios – the big studio in the basement for the orchestra, a smaller studio where Carleton Hobbs and Norman Shelley were going to read their nonsense poems and jingles, and a very small studio where two young amateur actors were to pop up here and there with the odd line and the odd telephone voice. These two young actors were both making their first microphone appearances. One was called Arnold Tottle and the other was yours truly. We were alone in that little studio. Sometimes you could hear what was going on in the other studios and sometimes you could not. We had scripts, so we knew what should be happening. When it came for us to speak our odd line here and there the dreaded green light would flash at us. Some of the lines were meant to sound as though we were speaking on the telephone, a technique that was very popular in the Tommy Handley wartime programme 'Itma'. We simply spoke into a big pint pot and got the 'Itma' effect. 'Hello, this is Fumpf speaking.'

Now the whole of this large epic was controlled from a control panel that was lodged right up in the top of Broadcasting House. The person in charge of the control panel could only hear what was going on but she couldn't see a thing – save the switches and lights on the control panel. The studios were all on the floors below, so you will appreciate how easy it was for the terrible tragedy to happen. It sometimes happened that if a programme under-ran, or if there was a bit of a gap between programmes, dear old Auntie Beeb would play a gramophone record of church bells. It was comforting to know that the Good Lord was filling in for a minute or two. It was when I heard the church bells during my very first broadcast that I first of all thought it was part of this jokey programme and then I realised that things had gone most horribly wrong. 'Folly to be Wise' had gone right off the rails.

Like all accidents, it's too easy to explain afterwards how and why they happened. Rehearsals had gone very well, perhaps too well. Arnold Tottle and I did our little lines whenever the green light spat at us. We knew perfectly well that we had another ten pages to get through before we had to say a word. We had got to a point where the typewriter and the orchestra were to play their mini concertino. Suddenly our green light winked at us. 'It's not us, is it?' Arnold shook his head. We neither of us made a sound. The dear girl on the control panel had flicked the light of the wrong studio. She should have flicked the orchestra but she flicked us. We didn't say a word, it would have been nonsense. The orchestra and the typewriter didn't play a note or tap a tap. They hadn't had their flick to start. There was dead silence all around. There's one thing that dear old Auntie Beeb loathes and that's silence. The engineer in charge bunged out the church bells. They clanged and hammered away while Arnold and I trembled all alone and forgotten. It was our baptism of fire. Like two little toddlers in nappies and safety pins, we knew not quite where we came from, we scarcely knew where we were and we certainly had no idea of where we were going.

Dismal worlds

———— • ————

We were a very dismal party as we left Broadcasting House that April Fool's evening. My very first broadcast had met with a dreadful disaster. Through a simple mistake a broadcast had come horribly unstuck because someone had pressed the wrong button. Those wretched church bells still clanged in my head. Although people rushed around and got the programme going again, it was a dreadful shock to the system. It was rather like the mourners parting after the funeral of a much-loved friend. The actors from London were staying overnight. Arnold Tottle lived in Bristol and he was just going home and back to work next day in some government office somewhere. I was going back to the farm in the big old Austin twelve-four that I drove over the fields and rough tracks of the Wiltshire downs.

Driving alone at night at a little under forty miles an hour gives you plenty of time to think. It was a speed that suited the old Austin – it liked forty miles an hour. The moment it got up to forty-three miles an hour it began to judder like an old destroyer that's been suddenly slammed into reverse. By the time I got to Chippenham I had been over the entire evening's happenings a dozen times. Poor Desmond Hawkins had struggled so hard to get the programme on the air, but he had been shattered. We were all shattered. Still, a live broadcast was a live broadcast, and if it went wrong there was nothing that anyone could do about it. Heigh ho. Probably be my first and last appearance at a microphone.

I was involved in dismal scenes pretty well every day. A two thousand acre farm is most fertile ground for dismal scenes, especially if it is influenced by people like the owners Willy and Gwen. Well, apart from their interest in pictures, antique silver and furniture and playwriting they were very interested in horse-racing. Willy bought several racehorses, built stables for them and before long there were quite a few tiny little men with broad Irish accents perking up here and there in riding breeches. The horses were trained on the farm under a 'B' licence. We fenced off a good mile gallop for them on the Wiltshire downs. These horses had the best of everything and were generously petted and coddled and patted. They weren't destined for flat racing, they were all hurdlers and steeplechasers.

Now the self-inflicted wound can manifest itself in a thousand different ways and one lightly disguised form is the buying and training of a racehorse, especially a steeplechaser. If you find that you simply cannot live without excitement, mad elation and ghastly disaster all around you then all you have to do is buy a racehorse – a steeplechaser. For you will find concealed in a steeplechaser all those ingredients. You will find yourself cheering wildly and drinking yourself silly to celebrate a storming finish and a breathtaking win. Just as you will find yourself with tears running down your cheeks as you wait for the bang from the vet's humane killer to put the poor horse out of its misery. The dreadful gloom that a broken down steeplechaser presents to its owner and trainer is enough to drive them to drink. And so they drink to drown their sorrows. You drink if you win, you drink if you lose.

Now there are certain people about who are natural judges of horse flesh. Willy was not, Gwen was not, and I certainly was not. So it is easy to see how we became putty in the hands of the tiny men in riding breeches. They professed to know everything, they were always giving advice and the advice that each and everyone gave was different. 'This horse, sir, is still very green. I doubt if he'd get a mile.' 'You want to get this one going as soon as you can, sir. In a couple of years he'll make the Grand National. He wants forcing on.' 'Take your time wid him, now take your time.' 'This horse, sir, if you want my advice, needs to have the Hobday operation.' 'Hobday my foot, he's just got a bit of a cold. He'll be as right as rain in a couple of days.' 'That vet is no good, sir, he's all right for cats and dogs and things like that but no good for horses.' 'The finest vet you'll ever find, he's treated all them Derby winners, hasn't he.' And because the advice was so conflicting I shudder to think of the number of good horses that we may have ruined and the number of bad horses that we may have made worse.

Willy soon tired of the racing world but Gwen pursued it with a sentimental vigour. She had one horse that was called Colonel Bagwash. She turned it into a family pet and it was very popular on the race courses although there were some that objected to a fine looking horse bearing a sort of pantomime name. I heard one very dignified old gentleman say to another dignified old gentleman in the paddock one day at Kempton Park, 'Damn shame, you know, calling a horse like that Colonel Bagwash.' Colonel Bagwash won a few races, but like so many race horses he was always a source of trouble. His breathing was at times very wheezy, his legs were not to be trusted and he had a wonderful knack of picking up a virus of some sort. Well, that was the vet's explanation more often than not. But Colonel Bagwash was a most endearing horse. Gwen called him Darling Baggles. The tears of joy and sorrow that were shed over Darling Baggles would have topped up Lake Windermere in a severe drought. I quite often drove Willy and Gwen to the races when Darling Baggles was running.

Of all the places in the world a race-course is just about the last place that I would wish to go to. I grew to hate race-courses. It wasn't the horses or the people, it was just the ghastly atmosphere of vicious greed. It gave me goose pimples. Everyone was there for money. An atmosphere of grasping avarice is a most uncomfortable atmosphere. You had only to look at them, their crafty, crude faces painted by Pieter Bruegel. They knew everybody, they knew the horses, they knew the form. What they did not know was who was trying today and who was not trying today. The moment you showed your face on a race-course they would slink up to you. 'Are you trying today?' 'Are you trying today?' If you weren't trying but just giving the horse a bit of an outing for experience then they knew that they could cross you off the possible winners list. If they knew that you were trying then they would simply match your horses' form against the others that were trying. I always had a stock answer to the question 'Are you trying today?' 'Everyone including Darling Baggles has been instructed to do his best according to the rules.'

I did my best to avoid the race-courses but it was difficult. Willy always liked to have me close at hand, for outside the boundaries of his own Wiltshire estates he was shy and ill at ease. Very often we would be approached by a character that looked like a cross between Rocky Marciano and the Pied Piper of Hamelin. I knew who he was, but Willy hadn't a clue. After a short sharp exchange when we were left alone Willy would say, 'Who the devil was that?' 'You know, it was Bertie Barnstormer.' 'Oh, do I know him?' 'Of course you know him.' 'Oh, do I like him?' 'No, you hate his guts.' 'Oh, do I?' Ten minutes later Willy would be abominably rude to a race-course acquaintance whom he liked very much. 'You tore him off a strip, Willy.' 'Of course I did, I don't like him, do I?' 'Of course you do.' 'Oh, too bad, too bad.'

Sometimes Willy was really eccentric. He was more than eccentric one harvest time when his young children by a previous marriage came to spend a few weeks with us. They were charming, intelligent kids and very fond of their father and Gwen. Now amongst the strange collection of horses there was a sturdy little cob-type pony called Jenny. Willy often used to saddle her up and ride her around the farm. He enjoyed it. One day he saddled Jenny up for the children to ride. 'I'll just give her a little gallop myself, just in case she's got a bit too much steam – back in a jiffy.' And off went Willy and Jenny.

Little Johnny and Jill and I watched as Willy worked Jenny up to a smart gallop. Suddenly Willy, all arms and legs, cartwheeled through the air. He lay there out to the wide. We all jumped into the old Austin and drove over to him. A stirrup strap had broken and Willy had taken a pretty hefty clout on the head. We got him home, put him to bed and drew the curtains. He came round but he was badly concussed. His speech was muddled and confused. He was slightly off his chump and kept asking me if I had burnt the straw behind the combines on a certain field. 'Not yet, Willy, we've got to clear the sacks off the field first of all then I'll burn it.' 'Go and burn it now, burn it now, got to get it burned, got to get it burned.'

I left the children with their father, rang the doctor and went off to see a man about some pigs a few miles from the farmhouse. I remember looking into the sky at a great black cloud of smoke which was billowing high and enormous. The pig man said, 'That looks like your place, doesn't it?' 'There's no doubt about it. Look, I'll come back later.' The old Austin worked itself up to a dreadful judder but we weren't in time to save the field. It had gone up in flames by the time I got there. Black and smoking. Forty-five acres of charred wheat straw and in the middle a great four-wheeled trailer loaded with sacks of wheat smouldering and sullen. I knew what had happened and then they came out of the scorched hedge. The little pets – Johnny and Jill. 'Daddy told us to do it, he made us do it, isn't it awful?' 'It's a very dismal scene, very dismal.'

Life in the farming world, the racehorse world and now the broadcasting world could be very dismal at times.

Crisis

—— • ——

There comes a time when you get so used to dramatic events and horrible happenings that if a day goes by without a dreadful crisis then life seems a little bit empty. On the farm Willy and Gwen could create a crisis in a matter of a few minutes. Willy was a dab hand at it.

It was some years before we were allowed to join the Home Guard – Dad's Army. When we were allowed to join I was made a lance-corporal and all the men in my platoon were the men who worked on the farm. And a smart lot of little old boys they were. They were cunning countrymen. They never missed a trick. They were all of them brilliant weather forecasters. They could spot a rabbit crouching in a squat and catch it with their bare hands. They were never short of food, even in times of strict rationing. They usually had a pheasant or two hanging up in the shed, they were crack shots with the twelve bore, they were as furtive and smart as the ferrets they kept for rabbiting. They all kept a pig or two and a dozen or so chickens. What little artificial manure there was about in those days they nicked to improve their vegetable gardens. Every square inch of their gardens was crammed with purple sprouting, primo, January King, curly kale and Brussels. They loved turnips and swedes and most of them brought with their bread and cheese for dinner a large raw onion which they ate like an apple. They were as crafty, careful and watchful as cats. Had the Germans ever landed in our part of Wiltshire I know they would have had a bewildering time, to say the least.

Around the farm were miles and miles of leafy country lanes and in the verges of these lanes completely shaded by trees, the military decided to store petrol in jerry cans and ammunition in big boxes. Shells, mortars, machine gun bullets.

What was of interest to kind friends one and all was the petrol in the jerry cans, for petrol was strictly rationed and very hard to come by. As the military could not afford the personnel to guard the ammunition and the petrol, it was left to Dad's Army to guard these miles and miles of priceless leafy lanes. There were thousands of gallons of petrol there, under no lock and no key. Of course it was a sitting duck. My platoon of crafty little old boys was detailed to patrol the lethal byways and apprehend any person or persons that we found nicking petrol or six inch shells. During the hours of daylight of course nobody came near the petrol and ammunition dumps, and at night it was patiently guarded by Lance-Corporal Morris and his bunch of clever rogues.

Of course we never caught anybody. Well, there must have been over ten miles of winding lanes to travel around. Everybody in the village always knew exactly where we were on patrol so they came across the fields in the pale moonlight, nicked a couple of five gallon jerry cans one in each hand and walked back across the fields to their little thatched cottage to sleep, content in the knowledge that they had enough petrol to go to Sunday cooked dinner with Auntie Lil who lived in Swindon. The Dad's Army petrol patrol cruised around the lanes and stopped now and again to see if the jerry can nickers were about. In the early hours of the morning we would pull into a field and snooze for an hour or so and shortly after first light we'd go home for breakfast, change back into our rag-tag and bobtail clothes and get on with the harvest.

Now Willy, I believe, was one of the first men to start the straw-burning system which is nowadays the scourge of the countryside. He had a mania about it. There was always a distant, slightly mad look in his eye when he went off to burn up a sixty acre field of straw. He used a simple but terrifying system. He tied an old sack soaked in paraffin to the back of his car, set it alight and drove around the outside of the field. Within a matter of minutes the field was a blazing, raging inferno. Now a raging inferno on its own is frightening enough. But a raging inferno in the middle of thousands and thousands of tons of petrol and ammunition still makes me feel slightly faint every time I think of it. Whenever I saw Willy going off on one of his straw-burning pranks I always rushed about and got as many of my Home Guard platoon as I could and rushed them over to wherever Willy was creating his own hell's fires. Willy always said, 'It's quite unnecessary for you to rush about, duckie, and bring the men over here, it would take a hell of a heat to explode that ammunition or set that petrol alight'.

'But Willy, it *is* a hell of a heat.'

'Go away and take the men with you.'

But we always hung about and there were many close calls when we had to wade in with wet sacks and beat out the dry grass that had caught alight and was creeping around the bombs and shells and petrol.

Willy and Gwen both liked a good crisis. Some, like the straw-burning, they created themselves, but very often crisis-makers attract all sorts of peculiar happenings to their homes. At Christmas time Gwen always liked to give a children's party. She had no children of her own and she was very fond of little pets. She always put an enormous Christmas tree in the corner of the big entrance hall. She decorated it herself and packed parcels of presents. Frills and tinsel she draped by the yard, coloured lights twinkled, little stars shone. Gwen's Christmas tree was always ready at least a week before Christmas in the corner of the big hall.

It was a few weeks before Christmas that Gwen acquired another dog. She already had one dog, a big handsome black standard poodle whom she simply called Poodly. Poodly was a nice dog and we were all very fond of him. He wasn't a brilliant dog, for there was no set pattern to his life. He was just a bit daft at times and sometimes just slow. It worried Gwen. She said at lunch one day, 'You know, I think it would be a good idea if I got a companion for Poodly, it would give him more of an interest in life. What do you think?' Well, she soon learned what Willy and I thought of it.

Two dogs together in the country are, or at least can be, a terrible menace. There is a saying, 'Two dogs are worse than one ever knew how to be'. Why? Well, they develop between them a crafty under-standing. They wait for the opportunity, and slip away together. And the great temptation is handed to them on a plate. Or rather in a fenced field. A fine flock of sheep. They'll chase them – it's lovely fun and the chase excites them and from way back in their primitive days the killer instinct will come surging back and in a matter of minutes you've got a half a dozen dead sheep lying around. Poodly had had a companion before, an Afghan hound, and they had both been on a sheep-killing rap. The magistrates had ordered the Afghan to be destroyed, Poodly was let off with a caution. So you see, both Willy and I had to say, 'For goodness sake don't get another dog'. Which was probably why Gwen went out and came back with another poodle, this time a chocolate standard only a few weeks old.

It was a beautiful puppy, as bright as a button and as hungry as a hunter. I've never seen a dog eat like it. Four thumping meals a day. Consequently it had to be taken out walkies quite a lot. But it was a most attractive little puppy and when the children arrived for the party the little dog was a great success. They played with him, fed him biscuits and cakes and goodness knows what. His stomach was like a barrel. After the presents were opened the children played hide and seek. The farm house rambled about a bit and there were all sorts of nooks and crannies in which to hide. You could hear the dear little feet pattering along corridors, thumping about upstairs.

The little dog was forgotten. No one knew that he was hiding under the low sofa. No one knew that he'd been a naughty little boy or rather a naughty big boy behind the Christmas tree in the corner in the hall. And one of the favourite places to hide was behind the Christmas tree in the corner of the hall. The awful truth dawned on me when I opened the kitchen door to get some glasses. What was this on the door knob? It couldn't be. It is. And not only on the door knob, everywhere. It had travelled at the speed of little pattering feet. We quickly rounded the children up. Oh dear, those lovely party dresses! There were tears, sobbing and snivelling. The party was ruined. All the little dears had to be taken to the bathroom and washed. We did what we could. But as you will appreciate, there is not a lot that you can do with this commodity when it really gets about. The house would have to be cleaned up, we would have to face the parents when they came to collect the children.

Some people enjoy a good crisis but nobody enjoyed this one. And underneath the low sofa the little chocolate poodle was hiding. He knew very well that he had created this crisis.

Back to normal

——— • ———

The war had been over for more than two years. The meat ration was still, as far as I remember, just two ounces per person per week. We were still living under wartime conditions and fighting to get back to normal when the country was hit by one of the worst winters that anyone could remember – the winter of 1947. It started one evening when I was driving back from Bristol. It was the 12th of January. I had gone down to play a small part in a radio programme and had taken with me a local character who had a very broad Wiltshire accent and was not at all afraid to speak up and be heard. He too had a small part. We were driving back through Marshfield when it started to snow.

'I don't like the look on't,' said the old Wiltshireman who was known as Pelly, Pelly Barnes to give him his full name. Pelly had many sons and many daughters, all fine strapping lads and lasses. They formed a sound traditional village family. 'I don't like the look on it you, I don't like the look on it.' How right Pelly was. It snowed and froze from the 12th of January until the third week of April. Three solid months of solid Arctic weather with howling east winds to whip us into shape. In places the farm roads were blocked with snow as high as the telegraph wires. The entire farm force of about twenty men dug the road clear so that we could get about to feed the cattle, the pigs and horses and get the milk down to the main road.

That dreadful east wind cleared the fields of snow and piled it up in the narrow roads and lanes. It was easier, where you could, to travel the fields. The tyres on my old Austin were bald, in some cases they were down to the canvas. Travelling the fields in snow with bald tyres is pretty good fun if you like that sort of thing. I was in a perpetual state of skid. It was like being in a boat without a rudder. It was a great way to learn how to handle a motor car.

I used to go down to the village most evenings and call on Eileen. Eileen was a most beautiful girl who had been evacuated from London with her two little boys. They lived in a very pretty thatched cottage. She knew but very little of the way of village and country life, having lived all her life in London. None of the conventional courting gifts like flowers were available then. Sweets were still severely rationed too. But, when you come to think of it, a gift should be something that you value and that is highly prized by the recipient. Something rare, something very difficult to get hold of. I knew exactly the commodity. A string of onions.

Eileen and I still laugh about it now, but forty years ago onions were like gold. No onions were being imported and, like bananas, they were worth a fortune. We had a nice few onions on the farm and one bitterly cold winter evening I turned the old Austin in the direction of the village and slewed and skidded over the snowy fields and turned up in Eileen's sitting room with a string of onions behind my back. 'I've brought you a present,' I said, my voice trembling a little with subdued passion.

'Oh, have you?'

'Yes,' I said, bringing out the string of onions from behind my back.

The effect was quite astonishing. Eileen had a laugh that was, to say the least, a bit on the lusty side. She gasped a few times and then broke out into laughter that had more than a hint of hysteria in it. I was dumbfounded. I shouldn't have been. For true love to manifest itself in a string of onions was ludicrous. To plight one's troth with a string of onions was ridiculous. It took me several minutes to realise what Eileen was laughing at. Eileen had a very keen and lively sense of humour and we spent a good deal of our courtship laughing. It's marvellous what a string of onions will do, if you use them properly.

One beautiful May morning we both roved out in my old Austin and were married by an old registrar who got everything wrong. Our names wrong, our ages wrong, our parents' names and professions wrong. It took a lot of putting right. Eileen called it the string of onions wedding. We laughed all the way home to her little thatched cottage. There was no honeymoon and I went straight back to work on the farm.

Willy had not entirely lost interest in farming for he was still very keen on straw-burning, but his enthusiasm for the good earth had more than dwindled. He spent quite a lot of time writing his play, which was a complicated and awkward semi kitchen sink affair that I found almost impossible to understand. 'You're too young, duckie, you've got to learn a thing or two first, it's just a bit above you, duckie, a bit above you.' It certainly was, it was so much above me that it was obscured by low cloud. But Willy was a very kind man and most understanding when he wanted to be. He always encouraged me when I asked for time off to take part in a radio programme now and again. 'Make the most of everything, duckie, make the most of everything, you must always do what you feel is the right thing to do, never waver, never waver.' Well, I was wavering just a bit. News editors and feature producers rang me quite often and it became clear that I would have to follow on with farming or give it up and become a freelance journalist or whatever. I stopped wavering and became a freelance journalist. Willy said, 'I think you're doing the right thing, duckie, let me know if you need any help.'

And so I left Willy and Gwen and settled down to married life as a freelance in a thatched cottage in a small village in the downs. There is much to be said for life in a Wiltshire village and most of the villagers had a lot to say about it. Everybody knew everybody and what their grandfathers were and did. You know so-and-so's grandfather was so mean he dug a sixteen acre field with a prong rather than pay for it to be ploughed. Oh yes, we knew who the mean ones were, we knew the ones that were just a bit light-fingered betimes, and we knew the ones who would 'run word'. 'Don't have anything to do with 'ee, 'ee runs word.' That means he wouldn't stick to his bargain. We also knew those who could be trusted and those that would lend a helping hand. And in a country village you certainly need a helping hand now and again. We certainly needed a helping hand once a week.

The subject matter of this help is perhaps a little indelicate. There were many dwellings in the village that had no plumbing of any sort. Water was drawn from the two village pumps or from just a stand-pipe outside the back door. It was no hardship if you'd done it all your life. Take a bucket and fill it up, wash the dishes and sling the dirty water back out on the garden. No trouble at all. Toilet facilities were at the bottom of the garden in a little sentry box. Not all that comfortable but at least you were very much on your own as you needed to be. We were pretty lucky, we had running hot and cold water. The waste water gurgled into a soak-away in the tiny little garden. But, and it was quite a big but, we had no sentry box. Instead we had, as so many people in the village had, a chemical closet in the little bathroom in the cottage.

That chemical closet needed emptying at least once a week. For just two shillings a week old Charlie would call on us, take the closet away and empty it. We never knew where. We never inquired. Old Charlie was as regular as clockwork. He came every Wednesday, covered the closet with a sack and took it away. Half an hour later he came back with the empty closet still covered with the sack and we were safe and sound for another week.

Imagine our panic and dismay when one Wednesday, instead of Charlie, Missus Charlie showed up at the cottage to say that Charlie was in bed with a bad back and he wouldn't be coming this week and perhaps not next week but he hoped that we would get on all right. It was a bit of a blow but I went to our neighbour Bill. Bill had a very big garden and he was the carter on the manor farm. He was a proper old farm carter. About six feet tall, very good looking with great clumping boots that walked twenty miles a day behind a team of shires. The squire at Manor Farm was much respected. He still kept his horses and a carter. Carter Bill loved his horses and he kept them in wonderful condition. They glowed a polish to match the brasses that dangled around their necks. He was a most courteous and gentlemanly carter. He understood our plight immediately. 'That'll be all right, I'll be around once tonight.' That was the country way of putting it.

Just before the sun went down that evening the old carter stood at our door. True to tradition he carried the ceremonial sack to cover up the closet. He took it out through the back door but something worried him. He turned his handsome old face towards Eileen and me. His brow was puckered, his blue eyes were anxious. He was very ill at ease. Looking hard at the sack-covered closet he said, 'I suppose it will be all right to tip it in along of ours, will it?' I suppose it will be all right to tip it in along of ours. It was just about the finest point of class distinction that I have ever encountered and I assured Bill that it would be quite all right to tip in ours along of theirs. And so for three weeks he tipped ours along of theirs until Charlie's back got better and things got back to normal again.

Fools rush in

———— • ————

Fools rush in where angels fear to tread, so they say. It was quite extraordinary, but when I decided to become a freelance actor, writer and broadcaster the phone stopped ringing and the postman seemed to walk past the door without slipping anything through the letter box except horrid little bills. Sometimes not so little. I waited for the orders to come in but they didn't come in. Well, not thick and heavy, just thin and light. All new businesses need building up, it takes time, but time can hang extraordinarily heavy. I had a typewriter and was adroit at the keyboard but just did not have an idea in my little old noddle. I had thrown myself off course.

Now the best thing to do to stop yourself rushing in is to do a bit of bricklaying. The therapeutic quality of bricklaying is extremely gentle, steadying and calming. Eileen and I had moved from the little thatched cottage into a little Queen Anne house right next to the village pond. It was a little gem of a house. Unfortunately the wall enclosing our tiny garden had suffered a nasty shock from several bad frosty winters and had fallen down. The old mortar that held it all together had shrivelled in the cold, but the bricks were still good and so I decided to put the wall back myself. I cleaned off all the bricks and started with a good strong foundation all ready for the bricklaying.

Now the sound of a trowel pinging on a brick is very attractive. Some of the bricks needed chipping in half and I must say I found the whole business absorbing and quite compelling. And I was not short of help. Well, not exactly help but advice from kind friends one and all who happened to be passing by. When I started bricklaying in the morning I knew that Little Siddy and old Dan'l would be along by about ten o'clock. They had long since retired from work and although they hated each other they wandered around the village looking at the pond, looking at the brook, looking in on the black-smith to see if he needed a hand pumping the bellows. And so the sound of a trowel on a brick soon brought them to the wall that I was rebuilding.

I had a line which I used to keep the bricks on the straight and narrow but I could quite easily have done without it, for Little Siddy stood at one end of the wall and old Dan'l at the other. Their eyes were bright and keen as they squinted up the wall one at either end and gave a blow by blow account of each brick that I laid. 'That one wants to go a bit more towards Swindon, John. No, towards Swindon, not Hungerford, that's it, a bit more, that'll do.' ''Ee aint right, John, bit more towards Marlborough, Marlborough, that's it, that's it.' I tapped the bricks in the soft mortar according to their instructions and their directions always complied with the taut string of the line which guided my wall into a straight and upright creation.

I became almost obsessed by bricklaying and when I finished the wall I decided to make a small patio of the bricks that I had got left as the wall I had built was not so high as the original. Fools rushing in. I decided to lay a herring-bone pattern floor with eight-eenth-century bricks that were not of uniform size. They varied in length and breadth by as much as a half an inch. I was barmy even to start. It is most important to think carefully and take your time. That is what I did to start with. You measure the work and put a plumb line down the middle and working down the middle you build the herring-bone vertebra, as it were. Everything that you con-struct around this vertebra will reflect its accuracy. I knew that the vertebra was not absolutely accurate, because the bricks varied in size. I knew perfectly well that my master vertebra was veering a bit towards Hungerford when it should have been going straight towards Swindon.

By now the clouds were rolling up and the sky began to present a wet and windy content. I worked myself up into a mild frenzy to try and get the floor finished before the weather broke. A murky gloom came slinking down. It became difficult to see, but I was deter-mined to get the floor finished. I began cutting the bricks to get them to fit. It was fatal. The distortion in the main vertebra was simply magnifying itself as the floor grew and grew. It was twisting itself cruelly towards Hungerford when it should have been heading straight for Swindon. But as the sun went down and the rain came down I finished the floor. I knew it was a mess but would not admit it to myself.

It worried me all night. I was out of bed at four in the morning. The day was bright and beautiful. I looked down at the herring-bone floor from the bedroom window. If ever there was a piece of damning evidence of amateur workmanship there it was. The herring-bone floor had suffered a dreadful stroke. Its whole face was twisted into a ghastly sneer towards Hungerford. I simply could not live with that face leering at me. I would have to hurry, for Little Siddy and old Dan'l might be around soon and they would quickly point out that I was too much towards Hungerford. I got a shovel – the concrete was still green and softish and I shovelled the whole blessed herring-bone floor up, cleaned off the bricks and started again. I got it right second time.

It's always most useful to learn from all this when things go wrong at rehearsal. Generally you don't make the same mistakes twice. And in those days you could not afford to make mistakes too often. You either made it or bust. A small fluff on air was a deadly sin in Broadcasting House. The eleventh commandment was 'Thou shalt not fluff'. One of the great stepping-stones was when I was chosen to play a small part in Desmond Hawkins' radio version of *Far From the Madding Crowd*. It was transmitted live on Sunday evenings shortly after the news. I was allotted the part of Cany Ball. Cany Ball had not a lot to say but he had to sneeze and it had to be a filthy great sneeze. Now that was one thing I could do. You really cannot fluff a sneeze because it has to be an explosion. I shook the studio with that sneeze and I imagine that on the producer's report I was entered as being very good at sneezing. I'm sure that sneeze helped me on my way.

I was getting quite busy, but not busy enough. The standard rate for a bit-part player in those days was just three guineas, which covered all rehearsals and transmission. Nothing extra for mammoth sneezing. You were of course very lucky to get one bit part a week and so clearly I couldn't keep a family on a bit more than three pounds. I had to find other things to do. I must say that I owe a lot to the fact that I was born in Wales. My mother and father came from Gloucestershire but moved to Wales and there I was born. It is very fertile soil in which to be planted. Wales is full of song and over-acting and both those characteristics appealed to me very much indeed. I learned to play the violin when I was about eight and sang pretty naturally from the pure love of singing. I knew that I would never make the grade as a fiddle player but believed that perhaps there was a bob or two to be made in the singing world.

I was recommended to approach a singing teacher in Bristol called Glyn Eastman. He had a very fine bass voice. Would he take me on? The first thing he said to me was 'Open your mouth and let me look at your throat.' I obliged and he said, 'Mmm, you've got a blinking great hole there, haven't you? That's useful, try a few scales.' He sat at the piano and I sang the scales he played. He looked worried, and walked over to the window.

'I'm not good enough, am I?'

He turned and said, 'It's not that, I just don't know what the devil to do with you.'

'How do you mean?'

'Well, I don't know whether you are a tenor or a baritone, you've got a very big range and I don't want to ruin you. There are lots of singers that have been ruined through teachers who have made rotten decisions. Let's try a lesson or two. I am inclined to think that you would make a good lyric tenor, there aren't many of them about, you know. Let's record the first lesson, then we can see how we are getting on.'

That was forty years ago. There were no tape recorders. Glyn Eastman had in his studio a machine that could make a gramophone record. He recorded the first lesson and three months later he recorded my twelfth lesson. 'Now we can compare the two and see if I am making or breaking you. I've got to know for my own peace of mind.' He was a most kind and generous man and I'll always remember his concern over whether he was making or breaking me. He chose the music to sing that he thought suited me and then after about a year he told me that I had better make up my mind whether I was going to become a professional singer as I wasn't getting any younger. 'You'll get plenty of work', he said.

'I'll think about it.' And I thought about it, as I thought about the herring-bone brickwork. I didn't want to get twisted too much towards Hungerford. I didn't really fancy singing the Messiah all over the place night after night. I had to think about it. This time I wasn't going to rush in where angels feared to tread. I might finish up much too much towards Hungerford.

Only ourselves to blame

—— • ——

In this life you have only got yourself to blame and I had decided to become a freelance. Any offers of work that came along I would snaffle up at once. Looking back I realise just how lucky I was to be involved with radio and television in its golden age. In the 1950s most things that we did had never been done before. We were pioneering, experimenting. Not only the freelances and artists but the radio engineers. The radio engineers were discovering all sorts of things and quite naturally they were keen for producers to take advantage of their new discoveries.

One such new producer was Tony Soper. As I remember, he was hardly in his twenties when I first met him and he was very keen on deep sea diving. He persuaded me to take it up and we went on a training course with Captain Trevor Hampton at Dartmouth in Devon. Trevor Hampton had been an RAF pilot and he was an extremely tough cookie. But he was a most kind and understanding man. He knew only too well the apprehension of a beginner going down to thirty feet, let alone a hundred feet for the first time. And he was extremely careful because he knew of the sudden panic that can seize you when you are on the bottom of the sea bed and you find yourself upside down. It can easily happen. I once tried to catch an enormous crab that was lurking in some seaweed under a rock. I got it but in doing so I found myself flat on my back with an enormous crab clamped to my face mask. I managed to stay calm, got upright and the crab slithered sideways away.

Tony and I spent a lot of time in Dartmouth learning to keep calm and collected while we explored the wonders of the deep. We were adjudged proficient at diving using compressed air, oxygen re-breathing equipment and finally the old standard equipment, the old football helmet and the hundredweight of gear, weights and great clumping boots that goes with it. We were taught to work underwater, sawing up lumps of wood, hammering the lumps together again. Fish came to see what we were doing, they seemed fascinated by people sawing up and hammering wood together. They showed no fear, just bewildered curiosity.

Yes, but there was some purpose in all this. Tony had arranged for me to do a live broadcast in a diving suit from the sea bed. I know it's old hat now but thirty-five years ago, it was quite something. They stuck a microphone in my helmet, there was an engineer in a little rowing boat on the surface with a transmitter which transmitted to the land and thence all over the British Isles. Of course it was exciting not only for us but for the listeners, too, it seemed. Shortly afterwards Tony got hold of a cine camera and he decided to make a film about diving. He would shoot the film himself – would I be the learner diver?

We went with Trevor Hampton to the Isles of Scilly, for there the water is very clear as no rivers run into the sea from the Scillies. Tony's camera was powered by clockwork and it only took one hundred feet of film. A hundred feet of film rattles through a clockwork camera in a matter of a couple of minutes. I spent days and days on the sea bed waiting for Tony, who kept going back to the boat to put in another roll of film. Then he had to come back and find me and belt off another roll of film.

I got very used to the sublime peace of sitting on the sea bed with the curious fishes and the waving seaweed. Fortunately I was in contact with Trevor, who operated the fresh air that was pumped down to me. The pump was driven by a petrol engine and one day the exhaust of this petrol engine worked loose and slewed over to the air intake that was coming down to me. I was receiving at a depth of about thirty feet the dreadful outpourings of that petrol engine. Trevor didn't believe me at first when I told him over the intercom that I was being suffocated. But he soon rectified the fault and I was able to breathe freely again. There is little doubt that a moment of danger now and again wonderfully composes the nerves and steadies you up for the next little old wallop, not only in the underwater world but in the animal world and quite frequently in the music world.

It was in the music world that I first met Sidney Sager. He was a trombone player in the West of England Orchestra. And a very slick and smooth performer was Sidney. He had been an army bandsman and a member of the brass section at the Royal Opera House, Covent Garden. Sidney Sager was also a freelance and so we had quite a lot in common. He had a very nice sense of humour and we used to laugh so much that one day a lady member of the staff at Broadcasting House came up to us and said, 'Why is it that you freelances are always laughing? You're always laughing and surely you've got nothing to laugh at?' But we had, we had only ourselves to blame.

Sidney Sager formed his own orchestra which he conducted. They were mostly professional musicians and some played in the West of England Orchestra. If you have any illusions about yourself, get a job with a bunch of professional musicians – they willvery quickly bring you down with a bang to hard reality. Well, they lead quite extraordinary lives. For a good deal of their time they are virtually back in the classroom like naughty children. And like naughty children they are inclined to get a bit bored with the strict discipline that the playing of music imposes on them. They are forever thinking of things to say and do that will relieve the boredom.

I know the feeling well, for a similar situation existed in the acting world, especially in the bit part world where you had little to do. It was extremely boring at times. Some actors sketched on the back of their scripts during rehearsals, others did crosswords or read books and those that were not quite so self-sufficient used to lark about, much to the annoyance of the producer. I knew for a fact that there was a certain young actor of high spirits and a keen sense of humour who blotted his copy book during one rather boring play. And so did I. We laughed and giggled so much during rehearsals that the producer was heard to say to the secretary, 'Make a note never to book those two together again.' We never appeared together again. I know we had only ourselves to blame but then the carefree open road that the freelance travels is peppered with potholes and you do trip up from time to time. But as long as you get a reasonable amount of work and try not to worry, life can be very pleasant.

I very much enjoyed working with Sidney Sager and his orchestra but apart from 'Peter and the Wolf' and 'Tubby the Tuba' there seemed to be no other works for narrator and orchestra and Sidney said to me, 'Look, why don't you write a piece for yourself?'

'Who'll write the music?'

'I will.'

'Thank goodness for that, I couldn't do it in a thousand years.'

It has always been a mystery to me how composers manage to write music, how they manage to get the dots down on paper. I could read music but to write for strings, woodwind, brass and percussion all playing in different clefs and keys was quite brilliant. Sidney was very good at writing mood music. This mood music was used in films and radio plays to set the mood for either what was to come or what had been. So what sort of piece was I going to write for myself? We agreed that it would have to be a piece that would appeal to a family audience and so I went back to the old farming days, for I still had the most vivid memories of one knockabout Laurel and Hardy scene with Willy, some pigs and myself.

We had kept quite a lot of pigs out of doors in old fields that we were going to plough. Now pigs are very difficult animals to contain in the open. They will push their scruffy selves through any old hedge with no trouble at all. You can of course pen them in but that's rather an expensive way of doing it and they need to be moved on every few days and so we decided to keep them in with an electric fence. The fence gives you a very sharp sudden shock when you touch it even though it is only powered by a six or twelve volt battery. The pig is the most intelligent of animals. To call a man a pig is to bestow on him a great compliment. Surround a bunch of pigs with an electric fence and they realise at once that to touch it makes you jump, and they don't like that. But they also knew precisely that when the grass grew and touched the wire, the wire would short out and the entire fence become ineffectual. The pigs would calmly walk out underneath the wire and start to pillage the potato crop in the next field.

One day Willy came after me. 'I say, duckie, those wretched little pigs are out again. I'll give you a hand to get them back in.' We took a mower and cut the grass. The fence sprang back spitefully to shock one and all. We started to catch the pigs. Now just in case you're interested and may one day have to catch a pig the best way to do it is to catch it by the back leg. These pigs were just about half grown and you had to be quick and dive about like a frantic goalkeeper. We had got most of them back when Willy had managed to catch one of the biggest of the bunch and it was just a bit too heavy for him. He had got it by the back leg but he just couldn't get it clear of the shocking wire. The pig's nose was resting on the electric wire and the pig was in a state of screaming shock. Of course Willy was getting badly shocked too – his nose seemed to light up every half second. I went to help him. I too was on the circuit and for quite a time it seemed the pig, Willy and I were all having a shocking party. We all finished up on the ground, the pig squealing and Willy and I helpless with laughter.

You remember such things and so I asked Sidney Sager one day if he fancied writing some electric shock music. He fancied the idea very much. So the story was written about an electric fence and a lot of farmyard animals. It was called 'Delilah the Sensitive Cow'. It was first performed in 1959 at the Colston Hall in Bristol. I remember waiting to go on stage with the orchestra and Sidney. What sort of a reception were we going to get? We'd only got ourselves to blame.

Ordinary jobs

— • —

It so happened that the few odds and ends of radio reporting that I had been asked to do had been appreciated here and there and I was offered a weekly spot of fifteen minutes on radio. I suggested that there were many people doing ordinary sorts of jobs in this world and that it might be a good idea to have a look at them and find out if they were as ordinary as they appeared to be. I would like to do that ordinary job and find out and report. Desmond Hawkins was the producer and he came up with the name for the series. He called it 'Pass the Salt'. And so every week for several years, usually on a Monday, I tackled a different job. The cut of my jib was not at all known in those days and we arranged that the people with whom I worked were to be told that I really was a new hand. Many interesting bits of information came to light.

The thing that struck me first of all was that no matter where you worked you were told in confidence by your mates who were the right so and sos in charge and how to get out of doing the rotten jobs and sort out the cushy ones. But of course in the lonely jobs like a stop and go man your only mate was 100 yards away at the other end of the road works. Road works' traffic lights were not much in use in those days and you simply had a big lollipop with stop on one side and go on the other. Anyone put in charge and having control of any operation, however small, soon realises that they are in a position of power. As a stop and go man you had the power to go and to stop. Once you wore that dirty old mac and flat hat, looking very dingy and drab, there began to grow under that ghastly flat hat the uncontrollable monster of power. 'Right, don't be in too much of a hurry, let this lot through.' You see the way the domineering character works? Let this lot through. You can tell by the way they glare at you that they reckon that you've kept them waiting longer than you should have. All right, be like that but let me tell you I'm in charge here, yes mate, me, I'm in charge here. Who do they think they are, huh? Then there's a bit of gap in the traffic and about 100 yards away comes a well-polished Bentley. He's going at quite a lick. Thinks he's going to roar right through. Right, whip the old lollipop around from Green Go to Red Stop. He slams on his brakes. Got him. 'You'll just have to wait, mate, won't you!' His face is contorted with rage. What he would like to do to me. All right, mate, all in good time. All in good time. I'll think about letting you through, just hang on a bit.

Well, it's just one way, the only way of making a very dull job a little more interesting. With many jobs of course there go little perks. Offcuts of wood, a few bits of chocolate, a slice or two of bacon, little things that nobody will really miss. Interesting to find what perks there really are. Would you imagine that there are any perks attached to the tedious job of litter picking? I worked as a litter picker in the days when you really had a stick with a sharp nail in the end of it. Paper was the only litter. There were no tin cans and lolly sticks and plastic bottles, just paper. Litter picking was a neat and reasonably wholesome job. We litter-picked, in pairs, at the zoo. The zoo bosses were wise enough to realise that to litter pick a whole zoo after a bank holiday would be too demoralising for one solitary person and would take far too long. My litter-picking mate was a dear old man called Bertie. Every now and again he liked to stop and admire the flowers that most zoos seem to grow so well.

At lunch time we went to the litter pickers' rest room to eat our sandwiches. Bertie had a rather smart striped hold-all that he brought his lunch in every day. His missus looked after him well. Cheese and tomato sandwiches, corned beef sandwiches, a thumping lump of fruit cake and an apple. Bertie didn't take long to twist the whole lot back and the smart hold-all was folded and left on the table and we went back to picking up the litter that the dirty thoughtless ones had discarded. We carried on picking away until Bertie said, 'Yes, well, I think that'll do for today, we'll pick our bit of gear up and be off home'. We went back to the rest room to pick up our bit of gear. Bertie's striped hold-all was bulging full on the table – when I'd seen it last it was floppy and empty. I had to ask him, 'What are you taking home, Bertie?' He closed the door. 'Well, between you and me I'm very fond of flowers, and the finest thing for flowers is a bit of camel droppings. I take a little bit home every day.'

Dear old Bertie with his striped hold-all going back and forth to work. I don't know how many full hold-alls went to make up half a ton of dung but it was enough to keep Bertie's begonias in fine flowering form. It was a strange bit of re-cycling, when you come to think of it. The striped hold-all travelling to the zoo stuffed with cheese and tomato and corned beef sandwiches and cake and returning back home bulging with camel's dung. There is nothing to equal the quiet delight of getting something for nothing.

I once worked on a ferry boat taking the fares and issuing the tickets. It was an oldish ferry with an oldish captain at the helm. The ferry crossed a wide estuary in the West Country and there was a pretty strong ebb and flow of tide. But the old captain was a dab hand at slinging his ferry boat all around the estuary no matter which way the tide was flowing or how strong it was. He and his crew's perk was timber. If a plank of wood went floating by he'd go after it. If the ferry boat was full of passengers they'd have to put up with being a minute or two late. There goes a beautiful plank of eight by two, swing the old ferry hard over to starboard full steam ahead. Overtake the length of eight by two and then swing hard over to port and block the plank broadside on. It was quite exciting. Sometimes we almost finished up at sea and really had to fight the current to get back on course again. The regular passengers who were in a bit of a hurry just hoped they weren't being careless at the saw mills higher up the estuary and not dropping too many planks in the drink. The passengers who were not in a hurry really enjoyed the timber chase and often let go quite a cheer when the old captain cut off another plank as it glided down to the sea.

Not all jobs of course carry perks but quite a few do. You get cups of tea if you like that sort of thing or else a tip of hard cash, depending on the sort of people you are working for. As a furniture remover you soon find out the character of the people whose furniture you are moving. I had no idea that it was such a personal business. Moving Mr and Mrs Jones from one house to another is an extremely intimate business. Well, you go into their house, you've never been there before and you take the house to pieces. Mr and Mrs Jones, this really is your sordid life. You dissect them bit by bit, stick by stick – that garish bedroom suite, the fluffy white nylon rugs, the embroidered pictures of horses' heads. The defiant china German Shepherd dog. The shiny dining room, combined bookcase, jam cupboard. Bit by bit you find out quite a lot about Mr and Mrs Jones and when you come to packing up their pantry and have stacked away the last tin of baked beans and the last bottle of tomato ketchup you know them intimately. What I was quite unable to gauge was their stunning generosity. They gave us all a very big tip each.

I worked as a stage hand at Sadlers Wells for a while and it was interesting to hear what the scene shifters had to say about music. Now perhaps it is or perhaps it isn't unusual for the chaps who hump the timps and the drums and the double basses to know quite a bit about classical music. Most of them do and they have strong likes and dislikes. They may say, 'We're doing the Bruckner tonight, don't want to miss that, I'll nip out for my pint when they're scratching away at the Brahms, but I don't want to miss the Bruckner'. At Sadlers Wells the scene shifting force was at work on *The Bartered Bride*. It's an attractive opera, with lots of tunes. It was well produced and well sung and most of us stood about to watch and listen. My mate said to me, 'What do you think of this lot then?'

'Oh, I like it very much, don't you?'

'Oh it ain't bad, not a lot of hard work attached to it. Tosca's the one. I hates flippin Tosca.'

'Oh no, Tosca's very good.'

'What? You wait, there's a set of doors in Tosca weighs over two hundredweight, flippin Tosca, I hates it. Now Madam Butterfly, there's an opera, lovely, Madam Butterfly.'

'But it's by the same composer.'

'I know it is, but I loves Madam Butterfly. Japanese, see! All the scenery is made of paper, everything light as a feather, lovely Madam Butterfly, but flippin Tosca, cor flippin Tosca.'

His was a practical and not a musical viewpoint.

Once a suspect, always a suspect

— • —

It is sometimes true. I don't know how often but for the time being we will say sometimes. We sometimes read in the newspapers that some poor wretch charged with a dreadful crime will say, 'I am innocent, I am innocent, my conscience is clear. I have nothing to fear.' Now although I tend not to believe anyone who says that their conscience is clear I know very well what it is like to be suspected of a serious crime when you are innocent as a baby. This of course happened to Willy and Gwen and me during the war when we were suspected of being spies. And it was not just a momentary thing, it stuck with us for years. We were, in the eyes of the locals, spies. As far as we knew, the police didn't have a shred of evidence that would send us headlong into the slammer. But we were spies. I never felt like a spy, I had no desire to enter into that ghastly world where some people spit their spite and vengeance at the homeland. But we were spies.

I have no idea just how seriously the police considered us. Perhaps our mail was examined, our laundry examined, our past explored and investigated. We never knew. We were never charged or for that matter cleared. We were just downright suspect. And when you are suspect you begin to feel like one. Oh, we were suspect all right and although you are never aware of it you behave like a suspect. If only the police would charge us with something. Spitting on a bus or bill posting. Anything. But they didn't. They remained watchful and aloof. And this went on for some years. Willy and I were not allowed to join the Home Guard. This really upset Willy much more than I imagined because he had been a pilot during the First World War in the Royal Flying Corps.

Some years after the war I bought a caravan. I had taken a few weeks away from the farm and Eileen and I were going down to the deep West for a holiday. We stopped for lunch at a pub somewhere in the Wylie valley. It was a pleasant place and a pretty good lunch. We didn't dally long for we had a long way to go. We were about ten miles away from our luncheon site when Eileen suddenly blurted out that she had left her glasses behind in the pub. Now this meant that we would have to go back ten miles and so I would have to turn the caravan round. It was a large heavy caravan and it did not have all the easy handling gadgets that modern caravans have. But we got back to the pub and retrieved the glasses and once more I had to turn the caravan around, which meant unhitching the blessed thing and lugging it around and pulling and heaving to hitch it up again. I was far from being a happy man.

The trouble with caravans is that they sulk and deliberately plead for more help at the slightest incline and then push you peevishly in the back down the other side. We were swaying dangerously some- where near Yeovil when a police car overtook us and signalled for us to stop. I stopped. The driver of the police car got out and with a very measured gait came slowly to my window. I wound it down and said, 'Good afternoon'. He said, 'Good afternoon, sir, will you be good enough to tell me why you were exceeding the speed limit? Just notice his crafty way of questioning me!

Now he did not know that he was dealing with a long-term suspect. I could have convicted myself in a trice by saying 'I'm sorry, I was in a hurry'. But did I? No, I did not. I was too old a suspect to fall for that rubbish. I said calmly and firmly 'I was not exceeding the speed limit'. There was a long pause as he thought he had me caught and bowled off the first ball of his over. But he had a lot to learn as he did not know that he was dealing with a suspect of some years' standing. I admitted nothing. He took out his notebook. 'Can I have your name and address please?' Eileen and I lived in a dear little old Queen Anne house in Aldbourne, Wiltshire, called Pond House. I said to the policeman, 'John Morris, Pond House, Aldbourne, Wiltshire'. He wrote in his book and although I was looking at his notebook upside down I could see that he had good, bold, agricultural handwriting. And then to my great surprise he said to me, 'Now I will ask you once again, Mr Pondhouse, why were you exceeding the speed limit?' As an old suspect I realised in a tick that he had handed me what they call in Wiltshire 'a lovely plate of dinner'.

'I was not exceeding the speed limit.'

'Now look, Mr Pondhouse, we clocked you doing over sixty.' He made out a ticket as a memento. He wrote my name as John Morris Pondhouse. John Morris Pondhouse, the well-known suspected spy, was picking up a little retribution. It seemed as though I was almost home and dry. But I was not. The summons arrived for me to appear at a Somerset court in the following month. At last I was being charged with something. Too good a charge to miss. How many years had I been a suspect? At least ten or fifteen and never been charged. Now I had been. I made a careful note of the day in my diary and couldn't help wondering if they would call me by that strange name in court. 'Next case, please.' 'Call John Pondhouse.' 'John Pond-house.'

Now the possibilities were endless. I would be fully justified if I remained silent in the court and just looked about me like everyone else wondering who on earth and where the devil was this strange John Pondhouse. The permutations of what might happen and the complications of getting a name so wrong were quite tantalising. Of one thing, though, I was very sure. I would seek no legal advice, for they would surely mess things up. We old suspects are like that. It was sure to be a most interesting day. But the day never came. Things got into an even deeper muddle. I received a phone call from a local police inspector. I was most disappointed that he did not call me Mr Pondhouse. He called me Mr Morris. Blast. He had obviously rumbled the whole mess-up. But instead of matters being straightened out, the police inspector put several new and nasty kinks into the works. He was most polite and proper.

'I understand, Mr Morris, that you have had certain correspon-dence with the Somerset police.'

'Yes, I have had certain correspondence with the Somerset police.'

'May I call and see you this evening, at about six?'

'This evening at about six.'

So far we were both playing strictly by the rules, neither side giving any inkling of which way the mental cogs were turning. Now as a suspect it was important to have no preconceived ideas of what you were going to say or how you were going to defend yourself, for a suspect could remain tacit and mute if he so wished. The only preparations I made were to put a few big glasses on the table with a bottle of whisky, a jug of cold water and a syphon of soda water. I must say the inspector was a most leisurely and easy-going man. He had developed that wonderfully smooth manner to put people at their ease. Yes, he would love a whisky with a lot of water. I poured out a couple of good whiskies and although he was looking out of the window away from me I knew that he could see me in the mirror over the fireplace and check the amount of whisky I poured him. He was not going to get plastered and give the game away.

He sat and we talked. We talked of the heavy yields of barley and wheat that we had that year. We talked of the wonderful quality of the pears and the apples. We both frowned heavily at the dreadful beef prices and of how the poor, poor farmers were being robbed by the Milk Marketing Board. We considered the quality of battery eggs compared with the healthy brown eggs laid by free-range chickens. We bemoaned the dreadful state of Swindon Football Club and both of us really preferred rugby. Yes, he would have a drop more whisky with plenty of water, please. Time tiddled by. He hadn't taken a holiday this year. He'd taken time off, of course, but he didn't go away, he stayed at home and painted the outside of the house and got the garden up together. There was so much to do. Was I going on holiday with the caravan when Somerset police stopped me? Ah, now we're getting warm.

Yes, I was going to take a few days off, well, we all need a bit of a change now and then.

Of course we do, and at holiday time there are a lot of people using the roads. Goodness gracious, the number of cars and caravans has increased enormously. Puts quite a strain on the police force and of course there's an enormous backlog of work to be done by the courts. Did I know, I probably did know, of the new ruling designed to lighten the load of work in the courts? Saves time and money for all parties. If you plead guilty to an offence you do not have to attend the court. In my case quite a journey to make to the middle of Somerset. Of course, if you plead not guilty you have to attend court. Was I going to attend the court? Well, it was worth waiting for. He wants to know how I am going to plead. If I say I'm going to court it means I'm going to plead not guilty. If I say I'm not going to court it means that I am guilty. Was I going to the court? Well, I might and I might not. The harvest was over, the pressures of the year were not quite so heavy, yes I might go to the court, it's always a bit of a giggle, see how things go. I flannelled on for quite a while, giving myself time to think of why he wanted to know how I was going to plead. I could think of no reason. But I was determined not to let the nice inspector know. Yes, he would have just a tiny whisky and lots of water. We both settled back and we went over all the old ground again. The crops, the chickens, the milk, the beef, the football, the rugby, the traffic, the work of the courts, and if you plead guilty you don't have to go. Was I going or was I not going? Probably, could be, we'll see.

It was now after eight o'clock. He was a nice man this inspector. He had been fishing patiently for two hours and the rotten little fish hadn't so much as lifted its head even to smell the bait. He might just as well pack up his rod, take off his waders and go. But before he went he handed me a 'lovely plate of dinner'. He said, 'There's been a bit of a mess-up down in Somerset, a whole batch of summonses were sent out and they weren't signed.' This meant that they were null and void, I wasn't obliged to go to court. He was a nice man this inspector. He did not even ask to see my summons. But that was not the end of the matter. Two weeks later the nice inspector was back again in our sitting room and he had fresh news for me and a proposition to make. The people in authority had found out that I broadcast now and again and were prepared to forget all my alleged offence if I made no mention of it on the radio.

My answer to that proposition was short, sharp and to the point. I would have nothing to do with a sly deal. I would promise nothing. Briefly, if the Somerset police wanted to prosecute, they must stand firm by their own convictions. I certainly would not make a deal. If their prosecution was successful then it was clear that I would have to pay the penalty. But they knew only too well that their case was as wobbly as a raspberry jelly on a hot summer's day. They simply could not face up to listening to the error of their ways in a crowded court room. They could not admit to wrongly naming me John Pondhouse and then forgetting to sign the summons. I still have that summons in my desk drawer and often look at it with much affection.

Once a suspect, always a suspect. You simply cannot but admire the tenacity with which Old Bill hangs on. Several years later I was invited to open a fête in Somerset. I was still driving that big old grey Rover that could pull a heavy caravan at a speed which, according to the police, was far in excess of the permitted speed. It was a beautiful

motorcar. Built like a battleship, it oozed quality, strength and reliabi-
lity. And it had a distinctive number. That number was not only
distinctive, it was also notorious, although I didn't know it. But I
was soon to find out on that Saturday afternoon when I went off
to open the fête in Somerset. It was a lovely afternoon and just right
for a church fête. Eileen stayed at home as she wanted to get on
with the gardening, but she left me with clear instructions to get
a sponge cake at the cake stall. She insists that the best sponge cakes
in the world are to be found at little old church fêtes.

The fête was in a dear little buttercup meadow next to the church
and all the usual trappings were there. A little flutter of bunting,
a clout of coconuts, a whoops-a-daisy hoopla. A jumble of woollies,
a blast of brass band and there we are, a sagging trestle of rock
and sponge cakes. And, would you believe, a real old-world policeman
with a wonderful walrus moustache and a fifty-inch belly. He was
waving me over to where a dozen or so motorcars were parked
amongst the buttercups. He was waving me on with that regular
steady arm-swing that policemen use to persuade queues of traffic
to get a move on. And then I simply could not help noticing that
he was staring at my number plate. He stared and stared until the
long grey bonnet of the Rover stopped right under his nose. He was
still staring at the number plate when I got out of the driving seat.
And then he looked up and his jaw dropped. He looked at me in
wonderment and he said, 'Good god, good god, it's you!' I could
only say, 'Yes, that's right, it's me, you knew my number, didn't
you, but you didn't know it was me'.

It was quite clear that my number had been circulated – one little
slip up and I would be nabbed. But once a suspect, always a suspect,
and being a suspect of course I'm not saying whether that summons
was signed or not.

Lucky again

———— • ————

I have said so before but I must just mention it again. I must have been born under a very lucky star. Or perhaps you create your own luck. I am not a worrier. As a family we were not worriers. We laughed and sang and fooled about, mimicking people and taking the mickey out of each other. We were also very good at spotting people's motives – who was doing and saying what and what was the motive. The tough old world of the cattle market was a pretty good training ground for spotting motives. They were of course very basic motives. It always fascinated me to lean on the rails of the auction ring and watch the cattle being sold. I didn't really watch the cattle at all, I watched the faces around the ring who were watching, judging and gauging. They were a cunning, crafty lot. They had their own special signals for the auctioneer so that other bidders would not know whether they were bidding or not. They were fairly easy signals to read. When Harry Lucas took his pipe out of his mouth that meant he was not bidding any more. When George Cummings scratched his ear he was out of the running and when Charlie Stacey put his stick under his arm he was packing it in. They were thinly veiled secret signals to try to hide from others what you were thinking. But generally the secret signallers were simply telling us all what they had in mind. We knew what they were thinking and of course we knew the motives. To make a bob or two.

It makes life a lot easier and happier if you can spot motives. In the now enormous and confused world of radio and television it is comparatively easy to spot them. Some of course are benign and helpful, quite a lot reek of sulphur. And as the colossal and top heavy administration gets bigger and bigger the motives multiply and spread as devastatingly as lava down a mountainside. The main force in the cattle market was money. The main force in radio and television is power. Power is very heady stuff and there are many who will strive for it with the same greed and tenacity as a bunch of farmers over a cow and calf for money. And as we know very well, if you marry a desire for power to a love for easy money you will create a bunch of gangsters. Mind you, they are awfully well spoken and quite a few have got degrees. But their methods relate to the old Chicago of the 1930s. But of course this was not always the case.

It has been said that the two decades following the war was the golden age of radio and television. If that is the case then once again I was lucky, for I became a freelance in 1951 and enjoyed that golden age. And we all enjoyed the golden age. We cared but very little as to how much we earned and how long we worked. The excitement that radio and television provided in those days was quite exceptional. So many of the things we did were for the very first time. Quite early in the 1950s I was asked if I had any ideas about radio programmes. The Light Programme, as it was called in those days, was experimenting with the news and what followed the news and they wanted just five minutes of light-hearted chatter to follow it. Tony Soper was to produce it. It would be extremely easy to do now but thirty odd years ago it was, as people so often say nowadays, 'a challenge'. We decided that I would walk from Manchester to Torqay and broadcast an account of my adventures, just five minutes, every night. It was going to be a really cheap programme. In those days the BBC was peopled by thrifty, efficient housekeepers who always worked well within their budgets and saved their pennies very carefully. I suppose the whole thing started because the BBC had eventually been persuaded to record on tape recorders and not on wax discs.

The switch from wax discs to tape was an absolute revolution. Making a recording 'in the field' on a wax disc had been a most ponderous operation. To start with, the machine that made the wax disc was enormously heavy. It had to be driven around in a thumping great Humber Imperial. It could only record continuous conversation for something like two and a half minutes and then the disc had to be changed and a new one put on. This, as you can appreciate, interrupted 'the flow'. But that was the way things had to be done until the tape recorder finally elbowed its way through the dreadful brambles that were strewn about by those who opposed it. It was easy to see why the opposition struggled to hang on to the old wax disc method. It wasn't any old Tom, Dick or Harry who could cut a wax disc, for when you cut a wax disc you were plagued with some dreadful stuff called 'swarf'.

Swarf would come spewing out of control and completely ruin the recording. Swarf was a menace and it was always threatening the operator. Swarf was quite simply a long spiral of fine black wax that was produced as the cutting needle ploughed around and around the wax disc. You had to get the swarf out of the way otherwise it would devastate the recording and you did it by pointing a miniature vacuum cleaner at the winding swarf and sucking it away out of sight and swallowing it in a bag somewhere. It took a good recording engineer to deal with a steady stream of twining swarf. Well, so the engineers said, and it was perfectly clear why they said it.

Anyone could operate a tape recorder. No skill was needed, you just switched it on and switched it off. There was no skill needed to 'marry' the end of one disc to the beginning of another. A tape would go on and on and on. A child could work it. I remember the transition from wax disc to tape was one of great concern. The engineers were a worried lot. At coffee time, lunch time and tea time in the canteen there were huddles of engineers crouched around tables discussing and breathing hard about the wretched new tape recorders that were threatening their very lives. There was no doubt about it, there wasn't a machine in the world that could so faithfully reproduce the human voice, the violin, the flute, the singing birds, with the same quality as a black wax disc, swarf and all. The quality of tape recorders was pathetic and the range was appalling. Low registers simply growled and high registers were tinny. But of course the tape recorders won through after quite a ding dong. And it was because of tape recorders that Tony Soper put into action the idea to broadcast 'from the field' the light-hearted account of my travels from Manchester to Torquay every evening after the news.

Now I happened to have in those days a caravan and Tony had a small tent. He was very fond of camping and bird-watching. Eileen and I quite enjoyed touring about in the caravan. And so the operation was a very simple one. Every morning I would set out walking. Tony would pack up his little tent, bung it into the caravan and then he and Eileen would meet me for lunch at a reference point on the map.

Tony was very organised and a dab hand at reading maps. He and Eileen always turned up at the map reference round about lunch time and we did this every day for three weeks, which was the time it took me to walk from Manchester to Torquay. After lunch I like to sleep for about fifteen minutes and then rattle out the day's thoughts on a typewriter.

And then came the real pioneering stuff. We would record the day's thoughts onto tape. Tony would take the tape and the tape machine to the nearest post office that had facilities for receiving and transmitting signals. The post office engineer plugged the tape recorder into a landline that after a bit of manipulation reached the transmitter. Tony had a small portable radio which was tuned to the Light Programme in London. At the end of the news the announcer would say, 'Well, that's the end of the news and now it's time to find out what J.M. has been doing today'. On that cue from London Tony would press the start button on the tape recorder. Meanwhile, back at the caravan, when Eileen and I heard me after the news babbling on about the day's country walk, we knew that Tony had made it to the post office. As we sat and listened it became a sort of secret operation. It was as though we were a trio of spies transmitting signals from a foreign land back to base. Nothing ever went wrong with this little exercise. It worked every night of the week.

There was no doubt about it – it was a very cheeky operation, very cheeky indeed. I have been a freelance for over thirty-five years and so I do not get to know the official pronouncements about what the heads of departments think about cheeky bandits, but there is little doubt that we crossed several demarcation lines and contravened many rules and regulations by operating our own freelance broadcasting system the way we did. I have to hand it to Tony – his attitude was most original. I believe that his unorthodox methods very often caught administration unawares and while it was bumbling away, having meetings and writing memos, we naughty little guerrillas were out in the bush raiding and creating havoc with the rules and regulations.

One of Tony's early ploys, I remember, took the establishment very much by surprise. He had an office in Broadcasting House. He did not spend a lot of time in it as he was out 'in the field' quite a bit. And, I suppose, to make up for the time he was out of his office he turned it into a bed sitting room and slept there. That way he could never be late for work. It made pretty good sense really.

111

He was usually up and dressed, with his sleeping bag neatly folded away in a filing cabinet by the time the cleaners arrived to 'do' the office. I'm sure they must have smelt a rat as it is most unusual for members of staff to be in their offices at six o'clock in the morning, yet nothing was said and no complaint made to the Head of Personnel.

In time Tony became a little careless in concealing from the cleaners the scraps of evidence that clearly pointed to the fact that he was dossing down in his office. One scrap of evidence was quite a big scrap really. It was a herring gull, a live herring gull, but it wasn't very well. I have no idea how Tony got hold of it but it certainly needed looking after – I believe it had a damaged wing. Even the kindest and most understanding cleaners in the world will jib at the sight of a herring gull in an office. The window sills were beginning to look like the harbour wall in a Cornish fishing village and to clean them up far exceeded the terms of their employment with the BBC. Not only that but they did find Tony curled up in his sleeping bag once or twice when they arrived. It took some time for the official machinery to understand, digest and appreciate the cleaners' complaint. Sleeping in a bag in his office with a herring gull with a damaged wing. Never heard of anything like it. Surely Sir John Reith wouldn't tolerate this sort of thing. And so Tony was told to shift his digs elsewhere.

Plapp

—— • ——

The great thing about audacity is that it also promotes adaptability and Tony was a dab hand at adapting. In many ways he was ahead of his time. It was the mid 1950s and we were just beginning to realise the horrors of oil pollution at sea. The sea birds were suffering and dying. It was Tony's idea to make a film about our polluted seas. It was not to be an investigative film. He wanted to make a film that we would enjoy making and that the viewing public would also enjoy. It was going to cost practically nothing and Tony would be the cameraman. The film would be about the rehabilitation of an oiled-up sea bird.

The plot of the film was very simple. I was to be a sort of part-time lobster fisherman who chucked out a few pots every day and pulled them back in a few days later. I was to take the pots out in a rowing boat one day and find a very distressed oiled-up sea bird on the rocks. I rescue the bird, clean it up and look after it, feed it and finally release it back into the wild. Very romantic. The entire cast would be an oiled-up sea bird and yours truly. There were just two people involved – Tony and I. But where would we find an oiled-up sea bird? Don't worry, Tony had acquired a cormorant chick and he was hand-rearing it. It was already as tame as an old spaniel. And so off we went to the Isles of Scilly and landed on the sparsely populated island of St Martin's. Tony pitched his tent on the shore and Eileen and I found lodgings at one of the few occupied houses. It was early May and the weather was brilliant.

The cormorant was no trouble at all. Well, not a lot of trouble, but he could not, as a juvenile, feed himself. He needed fish, pounds of the stuff every day, and we had to find it. Now the sea around the Isles of Scilly is remarkably clear – there are no rivers on the islands and so there are no murky mouths of rivers to cloud up the sea. From a dinghy you can gaze down into the clear depths where the seaweed sways and the fat fish fan their fins and blow kisses to each other. It is child's play really to lower a baited hook in front of a pouting pollack, call out 'tea time' and within a matter of seconds the fish is in the bottom of the boat. Pollack were very easy to come by and so were eels. But there seemed to be no limit to the amount of fish that this cormorant could gulp. He seemed to grow every day. And the more fish we fed him the more he converted it into big black shining cormorant. He earned himself the name of Plapp partly on account of the size of his splayed web feet and partly because of his incredible digestive system which was astonishingly regular and prolific. The more we fed him, the more spaniel-like he became.

He liked to perch on any human arm that was held out to him – just like a hawk. He followed us everywhere. He came out in the boat with us, sitting up on the prow of the boat with his great wings stretched out almost in benediction. It was a most impressive sight. A big black saint blessing the sea and all that in them is. He never attempted to fly, but of course there would come a day when he would take off and we would have to film all the shots that he was in before he took wing. In the wild, cormorant chicks are fed by their parents until they are fit to bust and then the parents simply leave them sitting on a rock and say, 'All right, that's your lot, we're doing no more fishing for you, it's up to you to go and get your own'. It takes a few days for the cruel truth to sink in but eventually the young birds get the message and start fishing and flying. Hunger is a great stimulant.

We watched Plapp every day for signs that he might take off but he was perfectly content for us to pluck pollack from the sea for him to choke back. Little did I know that Plapp had not the slightest intention of leaving us – ever. The sun shone all day from dawn to dusk, the days drifted by, we fished the seas around St Martin's. I started nagging at Tony to get on and start filming. The weather might break, the bird might take off and in the end Tony agreed that if it was fine tomorrow we should start. The morrow was as beautiful a day as the one before. We knew perfectly well that once we had oiled up the cormorant we were committed. We did not of course use black sludge oil – that would have been cruel and an awful mess. We made up our own oil of cold-cream and black make-up mixed together.

Plapp was a born natural acting cormorant. He looked suitably dejected in his black cold-cream make-up, he looked apprehensive when I discovered him helpless on the rocks, he attempted to peck me when I picked him up, he hung his head when I put him in the boat. As I remember, each take in that opening sequence was just shot once. There were no re-takes. Tony's camera, a clockwork Bolex, took 100 feet of film and, fully wound up, would run for something like 20 seconds. Then it would have to be wound up again. It was a most economical way of filming and every shot was concise and to the point, with very little wastage. I find it very difficult nowadays to get used to cameras that are operated electrically, where the camera-man keeps his finger clamped tight to the button and film flies through the camera relentlessly, regardless of expense. You serve a well-ordered apprenticeship working with a clockwork camera. We got Plapp back to Tony's campsite and filmed the beginning of his cleaning up and rehabilitation. The black cold-cream came off much too easily and so we had to draw the operation out a bit, but Plapp didn't mind as long as we fed him pollack between shots.

It wasn't long before Plapp was restored to his former brilliance and we were all very relieved. The tricky part of the filming had gone off very well, we now had nothing to worry about. Well, that's what we thought. I know now only too well that it is sheer folly to try to dictate to animals what you want them to do. You must let them do what *they* want to do and dovetail your own ideas and plans into *their* behaviour and wishes. If you try to force an animal to behave as you want it to you can be sure that you are gradually moulding into the character of that animal a spirit of defiance, reluctance and sheer bad temper. And so we let Plapp behave exactly as he pleased. He just followed us about. We had ample footage of Plapp on the prow of the boat blessing the sea, of him swimming in the sea, of him twisting back whole pollack, of him wandering on the seashore looking as though he was beachcombing. But we hadn't a single shot of him flying. Simply because he would not fly. So how do you get a cormorant airborne?

To cover ourselves Tony took pictures of other cormorants taking off from rocks and flying in the powerful way they do, a few inches above the sea. And he took pictures of other cormorants diving and fishing. Tony took lots of pictures of solitary cormorants flying drama-tically into the setting sun. Nobody would be able to tell one cormor-ant from another. So our film did have a beginning and an end. But Tony was not satisfied. He wanted our bird to take to the air. It had to be authentic. Not only had it to be authentic, the awful truth was slowly dawning that we would have to be back 'ashore' in a few weeks. 'Ashore' is the term the Scillonians use for going back to the mainland. We would have to be as ruthless as dear old mother nature and desert our offspring and leave him to fend for himself.

Unfortunately we could not fly and so we devised a shallow scheme to deceive our overgrown schoolboy. All around the Isles of Scilly there are scatterings of rocks known as 'lumps'. Some of these 'lumps' are very dangerous as they lurk in wait just below the surface of the sea. Other, less dangerous 'lumps' stick well out into the fresh air and can be seen. Our plan was to dump our podgy film star on one of these visible 'lumps', quickly nip around to the blind side and skid back to St Martin's without Plapp seeing us. We planned to use Tony's inflatable dinghy with an outboard motor. Plapp nor-mally travelled in the wooden rowing dinghy but he was more than happy to come in the power boat. Well, he was with friends whom he could trust, for they petted him and fussed him and fed him. He had forgotten that nasty trick with the black cold-cream. We said goodbye many many times as we placed him on that rocky lump and then at full throttle slipped around to the blind side of the island and buzzed back to St Martin's.

Another nice mess

—— • ——

Plapp had enough pollack and eel inside him to last for at least a week, so we were sure that his natural instincts would slowly come into force and he would start feeding and flying and all would be well. We would be able to keep an eye on him. But rehabilitation is not as easy as that. Eileen, Tony and I were sipping tea outside Tony's tent several hours after we had banished poor Plapp to solitary confinement. We were watching some gulls who had found a small shoal of fish and were screaming with delight like a half-tipsy chara-banc party. We did not notice this very angry cormorant come stamp-ing up the beach swearing like a bosun's mate. He'd never known the like of anything such as this in all his born days – call themselves gentlefolk, they wasn't worth that much.

To demonstrate his point he called for corroboration from his diges-tive system. Takes him out to an island all nice and luvey dovey, dumps him on a strange island and then buggers off. Wouldn't treat his worst enemy like that, bloody disgusting, left him to walk two miles home in a filthy choppy sea, how would they like it if someone did the same to them? They'd left him there without so much as a crust while they was back home stuffing their guts with Dover soles and Christ knows what. I can only imagine that this was the sort of angry soliloquy that Plapp was delivering as he stamped and flapped up the beach.

He looked livid and there was no doubt at all that he had paddled back home. He had not flown. He came walking up the beach and we were all confounded. He choked back three pollack as though

117

it was the least that we could do under the circumstances. He had navigated his way back home without a map, compass, traveller's cheques or car phone. He knew where we were no matter where we dumped him.

We were due to go 'ashore' in something over a week's time, so we would have to try the same deceit again. The fact that we once again put him in the power boat did not arouse his suspicions in the slightest, the fact that we put him ashore on a different rock ruffled not a feather, the fact that we were once again sipping tea when he walked back home again produced the same rage and anger. There was no doubt about it – we were stuck with a cormorant. A cormorant that was now an adult who had no intention of fending for itself as we were its social security. It jolly well knew what its flippin rights were. We had well and truly got ourselves a humanised cormorant.

Tony decided that when we went 'ashore' we could do no more than take Plapp 'ashore' with us. The time came, we packed everything up including all the film we had shot and carted everything down to the beach to wait for the motor boat that was coming from St Mary's in time for us to catch the boat back to the mainland. We had packed all the film into a tea chest. There were several hundred tins of exposed film, with one hundred feet of film to a tin – even in those early days of the clockwork camera there was a tendency to overshoot. It was all packed tightly in that tea chest. The glorious surging sea that washes around the Scillies, the white sand beaches, the rocks, the leather seaweed, the lobster pots and the phoney lobster fisherman – all were laced together with the antics of a humanised cormorant. It would make an interesting and unusual film.

Now the beach at St Martin's is a very shallow beach. Tony's inflatable rubber craft could be persuaded to run right up the beach on to dry land but the motor boat that was coming for us could only get within ten yards of the dry land as it needed at least three feet of water to stay afloat. But it was no problem, we had a horse and cart. All we had to do was to drive the horse and cart with all our gear out into the sea and load the motor boat from the cart. You get very resourceful when you take to living a bit on the rough side in the wild. Apart from all the filming equipment, Tony's tent and our personal gear that we had carefully packed, we had also packed up Plapp the cormorant. He was no trouble at all. Tony had packed him in a cardboard box that almost totally restricted any movement and certainly prevented any flapping wings from battering themselves to shreds on the sides of the box. He was virtually in a coffin except that Tony had cut a hole in the end of the box so that we could get Plapp's head and neck through to see what was going on. He could see his dear friends whom he loved and trusted. He could see his dear dear friends who had tried to double-cross and desert him. He kept his beady eye focussed on them. None the less it was a very comical sight – a cardboard box with the head of a cormorant sticking out. It presented a most pugnacious picture. But he was quiet and calm.

All this reminded me of the late Leonard Hill of Birdland, Bourton on the Water, who was a wizard with birds and used to bring back humming birds from South America wrapped in silk with just their little heads exposed. He laid them on a tray and sat them on his lap in the aeroplane. This way he could feed them the precious nectar that they needed several times an hour. They were well fed and calm and I don't think that Leonard ever lost one. On one occasion, though, he very nearly did lose one in the television studio at Bristol. He brought part of his wonderful collection of humming birds to the studio and transferred them into a large cage. This cage was hung with little bottles full of nectar so that these incredible little birds could be seen placing their tiny needle beaks into the feeding bottle and apparently hanging there as though suspended on an invisible thread. The only indication of the tremendous energy they were expending was the faint coloured haze produced by the fantastic wing beats. They all performed very well and looked truly beautiful.

In those days most television programmes were live. What you saw was actually happening before your very eyes. And when it was over it was over, the end really meant the end. The anticlimax after a television show is most dramatic. The powerful lights are switched off, the scenery is wheeled away, all the tinsel trimmings are bunged into sacks and boxes, a howling gale swirls in through the open doors of the scene dock and there is much shouting of the 'Mind your backs there' variety. The whole studio is totally transformed from fairyland to a warehouse in the matter of a few minutes. It was during this dismal and drastic transformation scene that I noticed Leonard collecting up his humming birds in the big cage in the studio. He did it beautifully, so sure and so gentle. A fine net, one quick swoop and each tiny bird was in its little travelling cage. No panic, no hysteria. He had caught them all save one and he muffed it.

It was most unusual for Leonard to muff a catch and most unusual for him to leave the door of the cage just that little bit ajar. In a tick the bright little flash of colour disappeared up into the dark night studio sky. Gone. When you consider the cubic capacity of a large television studio and the minute size of a humming bird you don't need a slide rule to work out the odds against a mere mortal catching one of these deft little darlings. Although I had known Leonard for many years and was well acquainted with his wizard ways with birds, I could not be very hopeful of his ever retrieving his humming bird. But of course Leonard doesn't go all over the world collecting birds to lose in television studios. He had a word with one of the scene boys and he had a word with one of the lighting boys and he waited with his net in hand. The scene boy went across to the florist and came back with a very large and beautiful fuchsia. The lighting boy spotted it up with a very bright light and turned out all the other lights in the studio. There stood that beautiful fuchsia on a low plinth absolutely glowing in a pool of light while Leonard lurked in the gloom with his net.

How long did he wait? Hardly a minute. He simply said, 'Quiet everybody, please!' And in deadly silence we all saw that flash of colour drop out of the black sky and hang suspended by that lovely plant. It was back in its travelling cage in a matter of seconds. Which all goes to show that when you are dealing with animals you must learn to appreciate their basic requirements.

Tony and I had only partly appreciated the requirements of the cormorant Plapp. Trying to get rid of him by taking him away to another location was of course doomed to failure. Of course he was going to go home to the place he knew, the place where he was fed. We should have left him on St Martin's, where he would have probably have stayed as it was Home Sweet Home to him. But he was humanised and vulnerable and so we had a cormorant in a cardboard box with his head sticking out of a hole in the end. He seemed to be saying 'Here's another nice mess you've got me into'.

With Dotty, the ring-tailed lemur, who was then aged 6 months, Bristol, 1960s; named after Dorothy Lamour, Dotty is now in her mid twenties (*Photo copyright BBC*)

With an injured cat in Animal Magic, 1960s (*Photo copyright BBC*)

With a tiger cub in Animal Magic, late 1960s

Feeding sea lions at Bristol Zoo, 1967 (*Photo Mike Wagen*)

A trunk call, London Zoo, 1970s (*Photo Terry Beasley AIIP*)

In the studio with young orangutans and a macaw, Bristol, 1970s (*Photo Michael Martin*)

Showing the size of a tiger, Bristol Zoo, 1970s

Another interest – as Vice-President of the Bluebell Railway, 1970 (*Photo Discourses Ltd*)

Meeting Princess Anne in Jersey on the 25th anniversary of Jersey Zoo

Meeting Prince Philip at the presentation of awards to the Young People's Trust for Endangered Species, mid 1980s; Spike Milligan is in the background

With Michaela Denis, David Attenborough and Desmond Morris, mid 1980s (*Photo Michael Martin*)

With Percy Edwards and Kenneth Williams, May 1984

Overboard

———•———

The sound of the motor boat grew louder. A horse and cart appeared on the brow of a hill and came carefully down to the beach to where we were waiting. The horse and cart were the property of Bernard Bond, a grower of flowers and vegetables. Eileen and I had stayed with him and his wife while we were making the film about Plapp. He had said that he would bring the horse and cart down to the beach when he heard the motor boat. The motor boat was a few hundred yards from the shore.

Now, I only have an impression of what happened in the next ten minutes and I may not be entirely accurate in the details. Bernard Bond and his wife were kindly people and, like most of the islanders, were hard-working and easy-going. Bernard was a biggish sort of man, hale and hearty, yet beneath this tough exterior was a sensitive and slightly nervous character. He spoke in quick sharp bursts, a dozen words at a time all strung together. At times you had to listen hard to hear what he was saying for it sounded like the warning growl of a dog. Several times as we loaded our gear on to the cart we had to ask him to repeat his instructions.

It was a two-wheel tipping cart and it needed to be loaded and balanced properly – not too much up in the front and not too much at the back. It took quite a time to get it right and the rapid gunfire of Bernard's instructions as to what he wanted where clearly began to show that he was just a touch irritable with us. The horse, too, was getting irritable, taking a step forward just as we were loading a suitcase so that it went with a thud on to the sand and not in the cart. Or taking a step backwards when you were going forwards so that the tailboard of the cart rammed one in the midriff. This erratic behaviour from the horse brought a good deal of admonishment from Bernard. 'Stop that.' 'Get back.' 'Woa.' 'What's the matter with ee?'

While Bernard was shouting instructions, Tony and I were adding to the confusion by voicing our own thoughts as to what the flipping horse should be doing. We were in fact working up a pretty effective Laurel and Hardy act. The horse started rolling his eyes and muttering to himself, a vicious metallic mutter as the bit in his mouth clattered on his teeth. 'Bloody idiots, what do they expect me to do next, dance the polka?' Strangely enough it got to a point where the horse did seem to be trying to do just that. The captain of the motor boat did not help matters at all by shouting out from time to time, 'Come on, we haven't got all day, we'll miss the tide, come on'. We were all a bit on edge as we finally clambered on to the cart and drove into the sea.

The plan for offloading the cart and loading on to the boat was simplicity itself. You just did that. But here we were faced with another difficulty – a badly bobbing boat. A backwards and forwards horse and cart is one thing but to try and synchronise that with a bobbing boat is really asking too much. The boat went up and down, the horse went back and forth. On the rare occasions when the horse was back and the boat was up, Eileen, Tony and I jumped into the boat and Bernard tried to pass the gear across to us. I have never been a lover of boats and, like my mother, I grew up with a profound distrust of horses, but here I was with the two most awkward commodities on this planet, and nobody was really in control of anything.

At one point when the boat was up and the horse was back Bernard was about to hand over Tony's tent but the boat went down very suddenly and the horse moved on and Bernard on the spur of the moment simply threw the rolled up tent at the boat. It nearly knocked the captain overboard and he didn't like that a bit. 'You want to mind what ee be doing,' he said and then he added as a warning, 'Come on, it's blowing up'. And it was beginning to blow up. The curtsies and bobs that the boat had been doing got deeper and more obsequious but, to give him a bit of credit, the horse had settled down quite nicely. He had decided he wasn't going to move now unless someone told him definitely and clearly to move on. He stayed quite still as the waves licked his belly. He seemed to have dropped off to sleep. Now was the time to transfer the last item from the cart to the boat. It was the tea chest full of our eight weeks' endeavours.

Bernard was clearly nervous and so were we all. He slid the chest along to the end of the tailboard. The boat went down and came up. Tony was long enough in the arm to hold on to the chest while the boat went down and up again. He said to Bernard 'Next time'. The boat went down, and as it rose he shoved the chest well over the tailboard. I suppose we were all to blame, for as the boat was coming to the pinnacle of its rise we all shouted out 'Now!' It woke the horse up and he plunged forward up the beach. There was nothing that anyone could do about anything. The chest seemed to hover for a tantalising second two feet above the sea and then it dropped and sank. We watched it go, fascinated by the rippling bubbles that came sniggering up at us. There was a lot of air in that tea chest. Hee hee hee, hee hee hee. Didn't we think we were clever.

The sniggering bubbles started giggling and Tony and Bernard went overboard with the sea water practically up to their armpits. They lifted the tea chest and we hauled it on board the up and down boat. Water streamed from it. Tony scrambled back on board and started frantically to unpack the tins of film. They were all of them wrapped tightly at the seams with tape but we all know of the perniciously corrosive behaviour of sea water. You may be sure that any sensitive mechanical equipment like cameras or tape recorders will be stricken and useless if they are in sea water for only a matter of seconds.

The ghastly gloom that settled over the passengers of the up and down boat was truly dreadful. Bernard Bond was grief-stricken and stood silently in the cart like a mourner at a funeral. We tried to console each other. It was nobody's fault really, no one was to blame. We tried to smile and say goodbye to Bernard. 'We'll let you know how it turns out,' we said. The captain turned the boat in the direction of St Mary's. We had a few hand towels in our luggage and we dried the outside of every tin of film thoroughly. If the wretched sea water had got inside the tins, then that was just bad luck. It had got into one or two tins, but most of what had been shot was usable. The film 'Plapp' was shown round about tea time on Christmas Day.

I don't suppose Plapp saw the transmission. Tony took him in his cardboard box with his head sticking out to Dartmouth and there

Plapp was looked after by our friend and diving instructor Captain Trevor Hampton. Trevor's house and diving school were right on the sea and there Plapp was apparently happy to stay as long as he could pack away all the fish that he wanted. In due course he flew and mingled with the other cormorants of that part of the world. He came back now and again for a few bonus fish but eventually it seems he found that the wildlife where he could be self-sufficient was much better than relying on the daft antics of homo sapiens, up and down boats and backwards and forwards horses.

A freelance life

———— • ————

As a child I had been taught to play the violin and of course to read music. A little later in life I took singing lessons in Bristol. It did not occur to me that these two accomplishments blended perfectly to produce a speaking voice and rhythm of speech that many people found acceptable to listen to. It also did not occur to me at all to write for, or entertain, children. I was press-ganged into this in the most charming way by the Head of Children's Television. She was a very famous lady by the name of Freda Lingstrom, also known affectionately as 'Mum'. She was a most positive lady with ideas of her own, one of which was Bill and Ben the Flower Pot Men. She had an idea for me. She said, 'I have been studying the listener research reports and find much to my astonishment that a very high percentage of the people who listen to you are children. Now I have decided that you will work for Children's Television. You will be the Hot Chestnut Man. You will have a chestnut barrow on the street corner and every week you will tell the children a story. Now go away and do it.' 'Mum' did not mess about.

I was part of a magazine-type programme for children that was introduced by Eamonn Andrews. Also taking part with their own specialities were Tony Hart and Rolf Harris. In those days a freelance was expected to do everything and somewhere along the line I know Cliff Michelmore was allotted the job of producing the Hot Chestnut Man. No disrespect to Cliff, but with the Hot Chestnut Man there was very little to produce. Just one camera was used. It started way back at the end of the studio and then came creeping forward at the beginning of the story. It used to stop dead as it was about to run me down. Then the cameraman would lock the camera off and there it remained unmoved for the rest of the story. The cameraman was unmoved too. He used to go on reading a book. Well, he had heard my story twice before at rehearsals.

I had of course to learn my story by heart but I never found this a trial. As I had written it two days before it was pretty fresh in my mind and it was made all the easier by the fact that all the characters in the story had got something a little strange about them. A little boy once sent me a story he had written. It began 'Once upon a time there was a man and he had got something up with him'. He had got the right idea and he had no doubt got it through people saying to him, 'Hey, what's up with you?' When you come to think of it, pretty well everybody has got something up with them. I very much liked the idea of people who had something 'up' with them. Very true to life. So all the stories I dreamed up were about people who had something 'up' with them. They had various exaggerated regional accents. They had funny voices and kept strange animals as pets. Their pets were as peculiar as their owners. All the animals had something 'up' with them too. Some hated brown shoes, some loved music, some attacked people in uniforms and some, like their owners, had nervous tics. They had the qualities that as children my brother, sister and I used to mimic and laugh at. The permutations you could make of people that had got something 'up' with them combined with animals that also had something 'up' with them just went on and on.

And so the Hot Chestnut Man went on and on. Little did I know how close to the wind I was sailing, for it was a dictum of the BBC that you never made fun of people with disabilities. So what is a disability? Surely not people who had simply got something 'up' with them? I was never challenged about this, but I had a feeling at the time that dear 'Mum' was not altogether happy with the Hot Chestnut Man. She had, I thought, hoped for something a little more like fairy tales. Something just a bit more dinky, something that would appeal to the teeny-weenys. As it turned out, the Hot Chestnut Man seemed to appeal to the very young through to the very old. Life is much more interesting if it is peppered with people and animals that have got something 'up' with them, especially if you can set these characters in an unusual background.

I was most fortunate in knowing fairly intimately quite a bit about unusual backgrounds. In the radio programme 'Pass the Salt' I used to do a different job every week and report on what went on. I must have done over a hundred different 'jobs' altogether. Most of them were fairly lonely jobs. A pavement artist, a stop and go man, a newspaper seller, a taxidermist, a Turkish bath attendant, a steam train stoker, a street sweeper, a chimney sweep, a lavatory attendant, a window cleaner and a plumber's mate. In those days my face wasn't known, the various people with whom I worked thought that I was a genuine character really doing an honest day's work. I was building in my memory a hundred different sets of scenery, all absolutely authentic. I could fill in the background to most of the trades and professions in the British Isles and into those backgrounds I placed the animals and people who had got something 'up' with them.

I met a man who could not pronounce the letter s. If he wanted to say 'Stop that' it came out as 'Top that'. So I turned him into a plumber who had a mate called Tydney. They frequently stopped work for a mug of tea and when they had had their tea the plumber always said, 'Better make a tart, Tydney'. Now that plumber hadn't got a lot 'up' with him but he had got just enough 'up' with him to promote an interest and a mild smile. But then the golden age was also the age of simplicity. Television was honest, more or less true and certainly simple. Innovation was far from exhausted and producers and writers had not resorted to stunts and tricks to hold the audiences.

One very simple series of programmes for children came from Canada. It was called 'Tales of the Riverbank' – stories of a hamster, a rat, a guinea pig and other small animals living near a river. It was filmed using live animals and it was a charming idea and very easy to look at. But it was thought that the Canadian sound track would not be altogether acceptable to audiences of the Old World and so Peggy Miller asked me if I would invent voices for a hamster, a rat and a guinea pig and all the bit-part animals. I think that there were twenty-six programmes to start with and, as money was short, we had only a very limited time – three days – in the dubbing theatre.

There were scarcely any recording facilities. To record a television programme you simply stuck a film camera in front of the television screen and filmed that. The quality of the end product left a lot to be desired. It was found to be much better to perform a play twice rather than to watch the muzzy underwater replica of a filmed recording. The evening programmes were littered with breakdowns. Lights went out. Wheels came off. Scenery quite often crunched to the ground. Actors forgot their lines. It was a most nerve-racking business.

The really alarming business was not knowing when you were going to start. You might be scheduled to start at 8 pm when the weekly play had finished but all too often the floor manager would come over and say, 'Sorry, John, the play's broken down, you'll be at least twenty minutes late starting'. And the twenty minutes could become thirty minutes and on one occasion the play got into such a mess that they went back to the beginning and started again, so that I waited in a dreadful state of high tension for an hour and a half before delivering a single line. When I got the cue to start, my tongue had turned to solid lead and wouldn't wag. The floor manager had to cue me three times before I could utter a word. I had in a way suffered a new sort of stroke – a live transmission television stroke – and it had a most profound physical and mental effect. I delivered my lines well enough in a mechanical automatic way but for two days I had to lie still and say nothing except 'Pour me another one, please' from time to time. I suffered three or four live transmission television strokes until the system got used to it. Thank goodness I more or less developed an immunity.

So by the time Peggy Miller talked to me about 'Tales of the Riverbank', I was fairly well weathered and unafraid. Peggy had made a rough translation of the scripts and the dialogue but she told me not to take it too seriously and to put it into my own style and just say what I thought a rat would say and what a hamster would say. She carried with her such a casual assurance that this mammoth task became something of a giggle. I managed to keep one eye on the script and another on the screen. Peggy was so calm and collected I was able to ad lib quite a lot and the dear old Riverbank did become a most relaxed and attractive picture. The 26 films were ready well in time and to this day grown men and women ask me what has happened to them.

Light entertainment and far-off lands

— • —

Some time in the late 1950s Tony Soper decided to leave the BBC and become a freelance himself. In his place the BBC asked me if I would like to work with Brian Patten. Now that was jolly decent of the Beeb, but in those days the Beeb was jolly decent. I knew Brian only as a studio manager and liked him very much but now that he had been made a Light Entertainment producer he was qualified to produce my sort of light entertainment. We agreed to give it a go.

There is an old country saying that you never really get to know a person 'until you gets to live alongside them'. I didn't have to get to live alongside Brian for very long before I realised that I was living alongside a man of many unique and rare qualities. He had a truly blistering sense of humour. His brain worked with the speed of a laser beam. He could walk alongside you carrying on a conversation and yet do all sorts of physical conjuring tricks at the same time. Walking with me across the entrance hall of a hotel, he would, by the time we had reached the reception desk, have collected a wad of pamphlets and you wouldn't be aware that he had picked up anything.

Yet there were several qualities about him that were contradictory. He was terribly accident prone. It seemed as though most curbstones grew a few inches when they saw him coming and brought him crashing to the pavement. Not only curbstones. We were once walking in the tundra roughly 400 miles inside the Arctic Circle. The tundra is remarkably barren. Brian suddenly pitched forward as though he had been shot in the head. I could see no apparent cause of his awful collapse. Neither could Brian at once, but it was clear that he was attaching the blame to me. He lay in the tundra and from the prone position he glared at me with indignation. He sat up and he was obviously in some pain. He groaned and said, 'Oh my guts, my guts'.

I could see the cause of his discomfort. The bulge of his stomach had hit the ground first. Unfortunately he was wearing his camera around his neck and the rather long lens of the camera had been driven back through the camera case and into Brian's midriff. I helped him to his feet and then we discovered the cause of his collapse. There was a brass trip wire clutching at his ankle. The Germans had got him. The Second World War had penetrated far into the Arctic Circle and the place has been infested with trip wires and land mines. This trip wire had been waiting for Brian for over twenty years. Thousands of reindeer had passed this way and missed it. Hundreds of Lapps on their nomadic migrations had travelled through here and that brass trip wire had failed to catch one of them. But it had caught poor Brian.

And then the awful thought hit us both. If there were still trip wires hiding in the tundra there might possibly be land mines lurking there too. Our journey back to the guest house where we were staying would have made a cat laugh. We both saw what we thought were hidden land mines – a lump in the ground, a clump of pale moss, a dark patch of damp. The safe thing to do was to jump over these tell-tale markings. And so we both started jumping and leaping over these dreadful death traps. The trouble was we both read different signs in the ground and I would leap over things that Brian ignored and he jumped over things that I hadn't noticed. And in frantic barmy leaps and bounds we reached a gravel track without exploding one single land mine.

Brian's confidence was at a pretty low ebb when we went down to dinner that evening. But worse was to come. The guest house was very comfortable and well run and it stood quite attractively beside the gravel track in the tundra. The bedrooms were fairly large, the dining room was spacious but for some reason or other the builder had been very mean over the staircase. He had allowed very little room for the staircase. It was a big spiral staircase but spiral staircases carry with them their own particular form of danger. We reached the top of the spiral staircase together and Brian was telling me an involved story of the disgraceful behaviour of a person whom we both knew. I moved over to the broad outside of the spiral staircase but Brian was so absorbed with the story that he had to keep alongside me. The part of the spiral where he was trying to descend had tiny spiral treads the size of small pieces of cheese. Even for Brian he was trying to do the impossible. There was really no place for him to put his feet. In one tenth of a second he had assumed a sitting down position and, like a hundredweight of best coal down a coal shute, he arrived sitting down in the dining room.

Dear Brian soon became to me Tubby Foster, which is the fictional name I gave him. And the more we travelled the world together the more Tubby Foster cropped up in our radio adventures. We lived alongside each other for so many years we became identical mental twins. He knew what I knew and I knew what he knew. He certainly knew how to produce and to handle people. He never made that awful mistake that many producers make of trying to impose their own personalities on those they are producing. Brian left people alone. He could realise the extent and the limitations of a person's ability in a flash, and then he would guide them very gently to a better performance. It was a case of 'left hand down a bit, now right hand down a bit'. He did it when he produced me, for I am inclined to overdo things a bit. He would very subtly rein me in and check my impetuosity.

Our trips to far-off lands were commissioned by BBC 2. They were produced on a very low budget. We were usually away for about six weeks and we always came back with six half-hour programmes. They were filmed once again on a clockwork Bolex camera and the camera man on the majority of these trips was Jim Saunders. He was a remarkably fast operator. He could, as they say, put a square around a picture or a frame around a scene just about as quick as anyone I have ever worked with. He was most economical with the film and with his choice of criticisms of the scenes he shot. If he liked a shot it was 'quite delightful'. If he did not like a shot it was 'not very impressive'. We were usually able to present to BBC 2 six quite delightful films every year. We went out every day and shot what we liked and what we didn't like, we had no one to do research-ing.

Researchers are a comparatively modern convention. They had hardly been invented when Tubby Foster and I went spying in strange lands. Researchers and guide books generally lead you limply to cathe-drals, churches, art galleries and government buildings. We did take guide books of course but having flipped through them we discarded them. The guides of the New World were every bit as boring as the guides of the Old World. The best guides to any country are its postcard stands. Wherever you are, spin the postcard stand and in a few seconds you have a pretty good idea of what is worth looking at. Plough through a guide book and you'll simply pick up the potted history of the local cathedral and the archbishops therein.

The most remarkable thing we found on the postcard stands were the catacombs at Palermo in Sicily. Mount Etna, Sicily's great volcano, smoulders and spits, so it seems, all the time. The whole island smoulders, Palermo smoulders, but in the catacombs there hang those who have stopped smouldering and have withered into grotesque caricatures of death – shrivelled dead people in eighteenth-century costumes hanging on walls. The catacombs are a series of large caves and they are full of dead people of the past, all wearing the clothes of their respective times.

The caves lie under a monastery and people can come and go as they please. If you feel that you need to tell your great, great, great grandmother just what filthy tricks your cousin Antonio is playing, you pop down into the catacombs and tell her. There she is, in the third cave, hanging, supported on a binding under her arms, wearing a most beautiful blue velvet dress and long mittens. Her darling little lace mob-cap has tipped to a bit of an angle and there is a fair bit of dust on it. Her little brown eyes never were very good but now they are quite sightless. A great grin shrieks out of her sunken leather face. She seems to be saying 'I knew it, I knew it, serves you all right, serves you right, I'm glad I'm where I am, and you'll be here one day, won't you!' There they hang, hung under their arms. Ten thousand of them so 'tis said.

As a fashion museum it is quite superb. The luxurious clothes adorn the shrivelled bodies of the rich next to the coarse canvas smocks of the artisans. The clergy, however, seem to have a cave all to themselves. They hang there in their faded glory, a cardinal howling with laughter at an archbishop who has slightly slumped into the posture of the drunk and incapable. A quiet walk around the tombstones of an English churchyard will provide ample food for thought. A saunter around the catacombs of Palermo will all but destroy you. Tubby and I could not eat for getting on for two days. So perhaps the postcard stand did not help us very much that time. We did not shoot a single frame in the catacombs but we talked about them for the radio jaunts with Tubby Foster which were simply spin-offs of what happened to us while we were filming with our little clock-work camera.

Mexico

—— • ——

To plan a film about a country like Mexico would take years and
to film it, twice as long as that. It sounds therefore grossly impertinent
to say that we came back with six half-hour films about Mexico
which were 'quite delightful' and took six weeks to shoot.

Mexico is packed with pictures. Everywhere you look there is something going on that is colourful or dreadful or beautiful – sometimes
all at the same time. Tubby had little misfortunes wherever we went,
but the Mexican misfortunes were to say the least fairly original.
We were staying in a small town in the Yucatan whose name I have
long since forgotten. It was a picturesque whitewashed town drenched
in sun all day long. The heat in the middle hours of the day was
very intense and most of the population dozed in the cool of their
chunky houses or nodded on the doorsteps. A few scrounging scaven-
ging dogs loped the streets searching for something to eat. But there
is precious little to eat in certain parts of Mexico and what is chucked
away is instantly pounced on by the vultures that spend a good deal
of the day cringing on the rooftops waiting for something to die,
anything to die. They will even twist back an old, rotten tomato.
In Mexico it is forbidden to kill one of these vultures for they are
worth their weight in rates. You need no dust carts if you have vultures. They have an uncanny instinct about death and where it might
take place. A squeal of brakes will set them circling and plotting
as to where a corpse might stretch itself for dissection. The vultures
– the zopilotes as they are known – are a hungry and most efficient
bunch of undertakers. All estimates given free.

Tubby and I were walking along one of these picturesque streets looking for a cigarette shop. In those days Tubby was a pretty heavy smoker and he was down to his last cigarette and like most smokers he was getting fearful that he would not be able to get another fix for ages. He was very anxious. Now cigarette shops do not seem to exist in Mexico. Most cigarettes are hand-rolled, it seems, and in any case the strangest shops may have cigarettes. A vegetable shop will have cigarettes, a shoe shop sometimes may have a packet or two, but there are no signs to say definitely 'You can get cigarettes here'. They are simply not advertised. And so we walked along paying very little attention to where we were placing our feet. In Mexico this is an extremely dangerous thing to do as every footfall can be a pitfall. Small boulders can grow out of the pathway, large holes can excavate themselves any old where. Rolls of old barbed wire can fall from nowhere and lie waiting to scathe the unwary. Stumps of old lamp-posts lurk about here and there waiting to trip the careless walker. We were walking very carelessly looking for a packet of cigarettes. We were gawping.

Suddenly about a hundred zopilotes took to the air and circled above us. I turned towards Tubby. He was not there. He had gone. Down a manhole. Well, not completely down, for the top half of him was sticking out of the road. I simply could not believe it. Gags like this only happen in comics like the *Rainbow* or the *Beano*. But Tubby had gone down a manhole and what was left of him above ground was looking at me with the same sort of bottled rage and indignation that he had shown when he so neatly tripped over that wire in the Arctic Circle. I was the only person in sight that could have done such a dastardly thing. 'What a bloody rotten thing to do, what a bloody rotten thing to do.'

It was when I realised that he was all right that I completely broke down with laughter. I tried to lift him out but couldn't move him. The zopilotes came down to about fifteen feet above us to get a better view of what was going on and see whether there were any signs of life down below. I could not get Tubby out of the hole. I would have to get help. The streets were deserted. I would have to ask in the vegetable shop for help. How on earth do you say in Spanish, 'Could you give me a hand to get my friend out of a manhole, he's stuck in one'? Tears were tumbling down my face as I struggled once again to get him out.

It was my mad laughing that brought a man out of a house to

see what the dickens was going on. He came over and, as far as I could make out, explained in Spanish that only people of authority are allowed to go down manholes. Thank goodness he didn't think the situation a bit funny and so, being in possession of his full muscle power, he was able to draw Tubby out of the hole like a cork from a bottle. We thanked him as best we could and started to put the lid back over the hole but the man wagged his finger in that savage Mexican way and said that we were not to do that because the workmen were coming back next week. So we left it where it was and by then the vultures had settle back on the roof top and watched the English walk away extremely carefully.

But no matter how careful you may be you are liable to have all sorts of things happen to you in Mexico. In some of the bigger cities you hear explosions from time to time. Quite big bangs. It took us some time to find out where these big bangs came from. It seems that some of the high-rise flats have no lifts and amongst the things that are carried up the stairs are cylinders of gas. The valves of these cylinders are liable to get damaged as the carrier turns on the bends in the concrete stairs. A leaking cylinder valve is of course a pretty dangerous article and there are lots of them about in Mexico. The gas being heavier than air softly dribbles down the stairs and the first person it meets having a quick drag will certainly get his hat blown off, if not worse.

The casual and haphazard attitude to life is very apparent in Mexico and yet the struggle to keep alive is dogged and intense. It is a country where everything has a value. You will find people with a collection of empty tins at the road side. The tins are for sale and there is nothing in them. Just empty tins for sale. Well, someone might need them to put things in. The same applies to empty bottles. Very handy an empty bottle. Outside our hotel in Mexico City there stands a ragged sales lady. She is selling chickens' feet. She has a battered cardboard lid and in it are a collection of various chickens' feet. Could come in quite useful for a bowl or two of chicken claw soup, of course you've got to stew them for an hour or two. But they have a value. It is quite extraordinary what people will do to earn themselves a copper or two.

It was probably the need to make a few pence on the side that got Tubby Foster into his last and final misfortune in Mexico City. We were due to fly back to Britain in a few days. Our hotel was comfortable and conveniently placed. There was a strange system of booking hotel rooms in those days. Should you inquire if there was a room available the reception clerk would invariably say that he didn't know. He would know later in the day but he didn't know now. Why? When you take a room in a hotel, it is your room until you leave. You do not have to say when you are going to leave. It is your room until you decide to go. Sometimes a kindly reception clerk will send a bell hop to see if such and such a room is empty. It is a system that could be described as more than reasonable. But we had told our reception clerk that we would be leaving in two days' time and he handed us our passports just in case we went away and forgot them.

It was then that Tubby Foster discovered that his visitor's card was not there. In those days it was imperative that you had an official visitor's card. Without a visitor's card you could not get into Mexico and without a visitor's card you certainly could not get out.

Generally speaking it is much harder to get into a country than it is to get out. In the case of Mexico, without a visitor's card you let yourself into a sort of Kafka nightmare. Tubby had lost his visitor's card, and he had just two days to get one. He was advised to consult the emigration people at the airport. He went off in a taxi early in the morning and we decided to meet at our hotel for lunch. He didn't turn up for lunch but he did turn up for dinner. He had been messed about at the airport for a whole day. It was the old Spanish cat-and-mouse game – the goading of an animal that has but little hope of getting away. Large official leather-bound books are thumbed through. Cigarettes are lit, smoke blown in the air, cups of coffee slurped, high officials are consulted and after all that you are asked to come back in two hours. Tubby hung about for two hours and went back. Señor Gonzales has been called away, now what was the problem? Tubby was there all day and told to go back the next day. He went back the next day and the unbelievable happened. Señor Gonzales was sitting at his desk wearing his uniform. Yes, what was the problem? The problem we discussed yesterday about the lost visitor's card. You were never in this office yesterday, I was here all day, I never saw you.

Tubby couldn't believe it. Who could? Señor Gonzales appealed to his colleagues. Ever seen this one before? No. In this office? Never. You were never in this office before. Nobody here has ever seen you, what is the problem?

Poor Tubby got the jitters. Had he known then what we know

now he would have known what to do, for there is only one way to deal with the cat and mouse game and that is to lose your temper. Scream, shout, yell your head off, hurl your hat to the ground and stamp on it. Don't damage any government property, but behave as though you were on the point of murdering all the sons of bitches in sight. They'll stamp your card and show you out with a bow. Only too glad to be shot of you.

Tubby was totally demoralised and when I saw him that evening it took several stiff drinks before he could utter. He had to go back tomorrow two hours before our flight took off. They were 'looking into' it and cutting things as fine as they could. The next day we all went off to the airport with our luggage and checked it in. And then Tubby and I went off to see Señor Gonzales. He went into his act straight away taking long, long drags at his cigarette. Making telephone calls, going out of the room, coming back in again, sitting down, getting up, going to a filing cabinet, bringing a file over to his desk, finding it was the wrong file, putting it back, lighting another cigarette and repeating the whole ghastly charade again. This went on until I heard our flight called over the public address system. I pointed out to Señor Gonzales that our flight had been called and that surely we must go. Señor Gonzales simply flicked a finger first at me and then to the door. I got up to go. Tubby got up to go. Oh no, Tubby was not to go – the finger flicked again indicating that Tubby must sit down.

The cat and mouse game must be reaching its climax. I could see through the window the long line of passengers boarding our plane. I pointed to the queue of passengers. Señor Gonzales was enjoying this. He smiled and nodded gravely, took a long drag at his fag and blew a thunder cloud of smoke into the air. What were we going to do? There then followed one of those dramatic scenes which the British are most terribly good at.

Tubby said, 'You go on, never mind me, I'll get back somehow.'

'But I can't leave you alone in this damn Kafka hell hole.'

'I'm afraid that's how it will have to be, you'll see to all the gear, won't you, and ring the family when you get back, they can't hold me here for ever, good luck.'

We shook hands and on that touching note I left Tubby to the care of Gonzales. I was the last one to board the plane. Jim Saunders and Bernard Hedges were sitting there wondering what on earth was happening. The jet engines started and got into the hysterical frenzy that precedes the madness of hurling tons of metal into the air.

A man with a walkie talkie wheeled the boarding stairs away. He had got them a couple of yards away when he stopped and listened to his walkie talkie. He wheeled the stairs back into position. A tiny side door in the main passenger building opened, a plump figure shot out and scampered across to the plane. It was Tubby. It was then that it occurred to me that what Señor Gonzales had been looking for was a bit of a hand out, a tip, a dab in the hand. It had never entered our little English heads to drop him a couple of bob as we are taught from a very early age that to proffer money to a Government Official is totally unacceptable. To a waiter, taxi driver, postman or dustman, yes, but to government officials definitely No. Tubby had not offered a bribe to Señor Gonzales. And so in a way Tubby had won the cat and mouse game – just. For Señor Gonzales knew that if he had really prevented Tubby from boarding that plane there would have been hell to pay.

But the cat and mouse game had taken its toll on both of us. I had a bottle of duty free spirit in my hold-all. I opened it the moment we were airborne. We emptied it and slept all the way home.

Brazil

———— • ————

There is little doubt that in Mexico a bribe would have reduced the pain and suffering that a lost visitor's card imposed on us. But then, that was years ago, we were fairly green and innocent of the wicked ways of the New World. But should you ever wish to study the ethics of bribery I can most strongly recommend a visit to Brazil. For in Brazil you cannot do a thing without handing out a bribe. Did I call it a bribe? Tut tut. It's not a bribe in Brazil, it's a way of life, and should you require detailed information on the right person to bribe and how much, then you have an agent. They are openly available at the airport. You can pick one up as easily as catching a virus. It will pay you to hire an agent.

Our papers had been carefully prepared in London with all the numbers of the cameras, recorders, type of film, everything in detail. Did that help when we landed? Like heck it did. We were allowed to keep our personal luggage but the thousands of pounds worth of equipment was sealed up, wheeled away and impounded. We were all hopping mad. We were all going straight away to the British Embassy. This was no way to behave. Little did we know. The only ray of hope shone in the shape of a little man with crimpy hair and a pencil-line moustache. He had supervised the impounding of our equipment and he spoke a little English. He called a cab and told the driver to take us to the British Embassy. It took quite a time and I know we passed the same shops three times. What's going on? We eventually arrived at the Embassy and rang the door bell. The door was opened by a little man with crimpy hair and a pencil-line moustache. It was the same man who had impounded all our equipment. He wanted to get to the Embassy first to set things up and had told our taxi driver to hang about a bit.

A long flight in a big jet is bad enough. Arriving in a country which is so unlike home makes things worse. But to arrive and be confronted with such drastic confusion was enough to provoke a nervous breakdown in all of us. We were more than suspicious of what might happen to us. The big front door shut with an echoing clonk. We too, it seemed, were being impounded. I said to Tubby, 'I think the thing to do is cut and run for it. I don't think this is the British Embassy, it's just a posh thieves' kitchen. We are going to be held to ransom or something.' But Tubby had clipped his quick eyes around the entrance hall and he said 'Well, there's an English picture on that wall'. True enough, it was a large colour photograph of a set of lock gates made somewhere in the north of England. 'How about that – if you want a nice set of lock gates this is obviously the place to come, solid steel, perfect fit, not a drop of water will get through those lock gates until they are hydraulically opened. Now how many sets can I put you down for?'

In times of crisis Tubby was always remarkably buoyant. Within a few seconds of thinking we were being kidnapped we were both giggling over a set of lock gates. And then a very English voice said, 'Ah, welcome to Rio'. With his right arm stretched out to be warmly shaken there stood a tall Englishman. He was clearly a fairly high-up Under-something or other. The little man with crimpy hair and the pencil-line moustache came into the hall. He was smiling in the most affable manner.

The Under-something or other said, 'Tony got you here all right, then?'

'Well, yes he did, but he also helped all those geezers at the airport impound every bit of our gear.'

'Well, yes, that is true, but the trouble was, you see, your documents were made out in English and they have to be made out in Portuguese.'

I wasn't sure but I thought I detected the flicker of a wink in his right eye.

'Don't worry, Tony will get them translated for you all right. May take a couple of days, the translators are most awfully busy, but it shouldn't take more than a few days.'

Now this utterance was clearly arrant nonsense, that was where the wink came in. How can you translate the number of a lens from

English into Portuguese? A lens number B/S 44357 X translates into any European language as B/S 44357 X. Any fool could see that. No wonder the translators were busy, for they were literally translating Portuguese into Portuguese. It was all extremely interesting. At least we would be able to redeem our cameras and recorders but it took some little time before we could grasp the significance of the situation. The little man with the crimpy hair and the pencil-line moustache was clearly an agent, a despachante, a freelance despachante. Later we looked up the word in the dictionary and a despachante is clearly described as a customs house broker. Well, he had broken us up very nicely and there he was grinning and stretching his fine line pencil-line moustache right across his face until it was scarcely visible. Once more he had done a great job.

It was really a disgraceful state of affairs. And yet was it? The logic of the system, in a way, is quite sound. Basically it goes something like this. 'If people want to go dashing about the globe, moving from one country into another, you simply cannot expect the authorities to employ hordes of officials, who have to be paid wages, to bend and bow to their individual whims and wishes. In other words it is the traveller who must pay the wages of all the officials who have to inspect their passports and other documents. Some days there are lots of travellers, some days there are not many travellers. You simply cannot expect a government to pay armies of men and women in uniforms hanging about doing nothing except smoking cigarettes. The traveller must pay – he's doing business, making money, on holiday enjoying himself. And you pay right from the very beginning.

Our despachante, Tony, looked after us pretty well. First of all he knew where to get the right forms. The man who has the forms sits at a desk with nothing on it save a loaded ash tray. The forms are locked away in the drawers in his desk. The bribing starts here, then all he has to do is put his cigarette down, unlock a few drawers and hand over the forms. The forms were taken to the poor over-worked translators who had to translate the numbers of all our cameras and recorders into Portuguese. They had to have their cut. Then the forms had to be taken to the customs house where everyone expected a good dab in the hand. Baggage loaders, sweepers up, rubber stampers and professional impounders all got their whack. After a few days our despachante presented us with a bill for professional bribe services for a little under £100.

This was over twenty years ago and we thought it brazen extortion.

But if you go gadding about making money or enjoying yourself in Brazil then by jingo you have got to pay for it. But spare a thought for the unsuspecting American who turned up at Rio airport with a very large telescope. You could look at Mars through this one and it would show up as big as a hot air balloon. They whipped that into the impounding prison before you could say 'obrigado'. If you draw up a list of the rumours of what that astronomer is supposed to have paid and take a figure somewhere around the middle of those rumours then you fetch up with a figure of something like £5,000, give or take a heart attack or two. It was, even to an astronomer, a pretty astronomical sum of money to find when you are far away from home. The stars were just not with him that day at the airport at Rio.

The geography of Rio is beautiful and most dramatic. But what they have managed to build into that lovely landscape is perfectly horrible. It is a haphazard shambly mess. It is one of the few places to which we had no desire to return. It lacks any endearing qualities. Well, perhaps there was just one but it had such a slapdash element about it that it was only partly endearing. We met it first of all in our hotel bedrooms in Rio. There was a notice hammered to the wall. It was a direct translation from the Portuguese into English. It said in big bold letters 'Beware the furniture to damnify the walls'. It was translated literally from the dictionary. 'Beware the furniture to damnify the walls.' Damnify is clearly an Old Testament dictionary translation. It took us quite a time to translate the translation. We took it to mean something like 'Don't push the furniture about as you are liable to knock holes in the plaster walls'.

But it did not compare with an incredible pamphlet that we found in a shop which was a list of the goods they had on sale and the wonderful facilities they provided for the delivery of these goods. First on the list were two articles whose meaning we never discovered. One was called 'coops' and the other was called 'seepings'. Coops and seepings, it seems, were pretty valuable articles to possess. The nearest we got to 'coop' was that it was a cup, but 'seepings' really had got us licked. To satisfy ourselves we thought that 'seepings' might possibly be tea strainers. They were the only gifty things through which liquid seeped.

Trying to fathom out what was printed on that pamphlet was better far than Trivial Pursuits. How about 'Goods delivered on the Square proximity'? Well, it is of course 'Goods will be delivered anywhere near to this particular Square'. Or 'Petition to press'? We rather liked that and we got it fairly quickly, but then we had a little inside knowledge on that one. We had noticed that some doorways in the city had a certain type of door bell. They must have been supplied by some English-speaking firm, for on the bell button was printed the word Press. When you press you make a ring. That's where they got it from. Petition to press came from a plea to ring, which boiled itself down to Petition to press.

But the really funny one was 'Prigs of attacked'. 'Prigs of attacked' was difficult. Did it mean that they would have no prigs in the shop? Can you spot a prig as he browses over the seepings and coops and then attack him? No, that couldn't be it. In the end we decided that prigs meant prices, which ironed things out very conveniently. 'Prigs of attacked' must mean attacking prices, competitive prices, cut prices. The compiler of this pamphlet had grabbed a dictionary and had a stab at it, proving himself to be a sort of genius in picking the wrong meanings.

Prigs of attacked. Things are like that in Brazil.

Tubby's powers and misfortunes

———— • ————

Brazil was not our favourite country. Fortunately Tubby had no nasty misfortunes in Brazil apart from smashing up a chair or two. He never did it violently. But in his tubby shape he must have concealed the dreadful energy of a microwave oven. As you know, it can transform a soup that is 30 degrees below freezing to a boiling broth in a matter of a couple of minutes. And yet to look at a microwave oven you certainly would not suspect for a minute that it contained so awful a power. It was the same with Tubby, as far as chairs were concerned. He cooked them when he sat on them and they collapsed under him. I have seen him collapse oak, mahogany, yew, ash, several sorts of pine and one with a fair bit of padauk about it.

He took his devastating powers with him everywhere. Managers of hotels, clerks at reception desks, head waiters in restaurants couldn't possibly suspect that the happy laughing rotund man whom they welcomed so cordially could leave them at the end of the day one chair down on the last inventory. If only we had a reasonable basis for investigation but we had not. Sometimes a flimsy chair would look to me like a sitting duck for Tubby. But it would survive a four course meal, coffee, brandy and a lot of boisterous laughter. On the other hand, in a ponderous old hotel in Sofia, Bulgaria, we went into the lounge after dinner to think about the morrow and what we would do. The furniture was of the late Victorian period, each armchair looking as though it weighed half a ton. We had been sitting talking for about half an hour when Tubby's great throne let out a groan and with a ghastly crunch keeled over. There was

145

just no way of divining what chairs were resistant to Tubby's death rays.

On average Tubby's microwaves seemed to get to work on really tough, well-constructed chairs. During the thirty years we travelled about together he did notch up one or two frail-looking chairs but they were few and very far between. So I wasn't in the least concerned when we boarded a sampan in Hong Kong to ferry us across to one of the famous floating restaurants. I wasn't concerned at any rate about the chairs we were asked to sit upon as I had much too much to think about. I have mentioned before that the two things of which I have a profound mistrust are horses and boats. This ferry boat was a flat-bottomed punt and the ferryman was a very old and grotesque-looking Chinese lady. Like most ferry people she seemed grumpy, and she issued very stern instructions to us.

There were four passengers, two English and two American. None of us had much faith in boats and we all of us badly muffed getting aboard. Tubby took his life in his hands and took a mighty leap at the boat. He jumped too high and landed too heavy so that the sampan bucked and kicked just like a horse and jolly nearly had the old girl in the drink.

Didn't she ever carry on. It was Chinese, of course, I don't know what dialect, but it was very like the one that we used to listen to on the radio. A strange sing-song noise split into three syllables at a time. It sounded like that nursery rhyme 'Ding Dong Dell, Pussy's inner well'. That's how we used to sing it as children. The old sampan lady certainly gave Tubby the old Ding Dong Dell. Her scolding took on the tone of the Chinese radio announcer. They always sounded as though they were reading the football results. 'Bang gor durrr, Ko chay bar.' We always used to translate it as 'Bolton Wanderers two, Cardiff City four'. 'Por pend bee, Pooh ton pil' – obviously 'Southend three, Luton Town nil'.

We had no trouble at all understanding the football results but of course the wrath of the old sampan lady who was trying to get her sampan nicely balanced up wasn't giving out football results but still sounded as though it was. The American man mistimed his take-off, landed off-balance in the sampan and created much turbulence staggering about until he gained stability. He was told pretty firmly by the sampan lady that Tranmere Rovers were four and Stockport two. The American lady dropped her sunshade in the water and the sampan nearly capsized as the man leant overboard to retrieve it.

What by the Great Wall of China did they think they were doing? Didn't they know that Queens Park Rangers were seven and Southampton two? I managed to get let off pretty lightly. I only got my foot caught in a rope, not seriously, and the old sampan lady awarded me a goalless draw, Newport County nil, Hartlepool nil.

Life was not easy for her, she had to go through all the results of the Scottish Division 1 before she got us sitting on the very ordinary kitchen chairs on her sampan, the two heaviest on opposite sides beside the two lightest. Simple enough. She called out to another ferry sampan lady as she pulled alongside. You want to watch it, they're about today all right. It sounded like the result of two matches that had been postponed due to frost. The old girl pushed us slowly towards the floating restaurant, which seemed as enormous as an oceangoing liner. Magnificently decorated, hung with lanterns, snarling with dragons, ringing with gongs, it really was most impressive. We were spellbound. Suddenly there was a terrible crash as though someone had dropped a complete dinner service from a great height. I turned quickly to Tubby. He was in a heap on the deck of the sampan. His chair had disintegrated into matchwood. He'd done it again.

When the old lady saw what had happened to her chair her face contorted into one of those terrible dragons that they trot out at Chinese New Year. It was awful to behold. Poor Tubby, did he get a shower of football results for that: Aston Villa seven thousand four hundred and ninety three and Manchester City eighty-five own goals, six hundred and ten penalties and everybody was sent off by the referee. A little folding money helped to placate her but it was clear as we boarded the floating restaurant that she was thinking about retiring from the boat business. She had had almost enough.

During our meal on the floating restaurant we tried to fathom the mystery of Tubby's ability to destroy chairs. Tubby admitted he was just as nervous about boats as I was, but he swears that once he had sat down and received his ticking off he did not move. He didn't wriggle or change position, scratch himself or cross his legs. He sat rigid, upright and still. So, the worrying part of his deadly microwaves was that he did not know when they were on or off. We did come to one conclusion. He had never, as far as he knew, disintegrated a metal chair. His powers seemed to be effective only on wood. The only living animals that seemed to sense Tubby's microwaves were dogs. They never bit him but they put on a most ferocious demonstration when they saw or smelt him. Or it could have been that when we were together we seemed to meet a lot of difficult or bad-tempered dogs.

On one occasion I was not there. It happened in Bangkok in Thailand. It had been officially suggested that when we had completed our filming in Thailand we should go on to Burma. It was thought that as we were out there it would be a good idea if we visited the country. We weren't reporting politics, we were spreaders of goodwill. Not a bit dangerous. Could do a bit of good. Now we were not keen to be away any longer. We had been away for some six weeks, and living out of suitcases for six weeks is quite enough. All arrangements would be made and visas provided. All we had to do was to go to the British Embassy in Bangkok. Everything would be laid on.

Subsequent events showed just how ignorant the officials at home were of the state of affairs in Burma. I don't remember how many times we went to the British Embassy but I do remember that, to reach it, we had to walk through a sort of park in the centre of which was a large bronze statue of Queen Victoria. The sun beat down on the old Queen without compassion or respect. Every time we passed her she was in a muck sweat. Just her face, not her clothes. Perhaps it was the residue of the gardeners' early morning hosing, perhaps it was a trick of the sun or marks left by little birds. But the Queen was definitely sweating.

Every morning the dear Under-whatever had the same news for us. 'I'm afraid we have heard nothing from Rangoon, not a sausage, old boy, the folks in the UK have informed Rangoon and Rangoon promised faithfully to step on it and get your visas down here pretty pronto. Can't think what's happened.' Well, we could. Nothing. It was an extremely polite, make 'em wait, cat-and-mouse playtime. But this time, having passed the sweating Queen for four consecutive days, we told the Under-whatever that unless our visas were ready for us on the morrow then we were jolly well going to fly home.

Like the sweating Queen, we were hot, extremely bothered and not amused. The Under-whatever was caught a bit off guard. He strode up and down saying, 'Now hang on, hang on a bit, hang on a bit'. We pointed out that we were pretty well hung as it was. Suddenly he had an inspiration. He said, 'Now look here, there's obviously been a bit of a cock-up somewhere, why don't you go to the Burmese Embassy here in Bangkok and see them there?' And then he added rather undiplomatically, 'Take the bloody bull by the horns, beard them in their own den'. Suddenly the spirit of Sir Francis Drake seemed to course through his veins. But it didn't last more than a couple of seconds, for he added, 'In the nicest possible way, of course'.

That day as we passed the sweating Queen for what we hoped would be the last time, Tubby and I decided what we were going to do. Tubby would go to the Burmese Embassy as suggested and I would go to the airline office and confirm our tickets for the flight home in twenty-four hours' time. Nothing would happen at the Burmese Embassy.

We parted at the sweating Queen and went our separate ways, so that I was not to learn until that evening in the hotel bar exactly what had happened to Tubby. His story followed the surprising pattern of Tubby's misfortunes. He took a taxi to the Burmese Embassy. Yes, the taxi driver knew exactly where it was. It was adjacent to dozens of other embassies. They were all clumped together in a most beautiful part of the city, criss-crossed by canals with delicate pale mauve water lilies that send up fresh flowers every day. The taxi pulled up outside the Burmese Embassy. Tubby paid the driver and the taxi left. Tubby spent a thoughtful minute or two admiring these lilies. He knew he would never see the like of it again.

He was in a composed and philosophical frame of mind as he opened the small iron gate into the Embassy. It was rather rusty and let out a nasty squeaky noise which brought forth a most dreadful dog. According to Tubby it was as big as a donkey, its hackles were on end, it was slobbering from the jaws, its dog teeth were at least three inches long and it was baying and yowling in the most unholy way. Tubby realised that here again was another dog that hated the sight of him, or the smell of him, or the power of his magic microwaves. He stepped smartly back outside and slammed the gate. The horrible Baskerville hound tore away at the iron gate, making a noise like a pack of foxhounds opening tins of Chum with their teeth. It was a damn close call. But beside that iron gate was a similar iron gate that opened on a little path to the same building. Tubby had mistakenly gone through the tradesmen's entrance. This little path led him to a large expensive-looking door, outside which stood a dear little man of dark brown complexion, dressed in a very smart uniform. He bowed and opened the expensive-looking door and asked Tubby to please sit in one of the expensive-looking chairs in the expensive-looking hallway. And he went through a large door to inform someone that there was a man waiting to be dealt with.

Now you never go into an Embassy without a passport. Tubby had his passport and my passport, and he was determined to find out just what was going on. Either we got visas or we didn't. Well, the lovely calm that descended on him as he had contemplated the water lilies in the canal had been more than ruffled by that ghastly rabid animal at the tradesmen's entrance. He viewed the arrival of the man who had come to deal with him with some suspicion. The man was wearing a very well cut and expensive suit. His shirt was of the finest silk. He wore a gold wrist watch, his jet black hair was beautifully groomed, his good looking face was of an aristocratic well-polished brown. His manners were absolutely perfect.

'What can I do for you, sir, I am at your service.'

'I've come about the visas for these two British subjects.'

'British subjects?'

'Yes, British subjects.'

Tubby handed him our passports. He noticed a slight frown on the brow of the smooth official.

'Did you say you wanted visas, sir?'

'Yes, visas.'

There was a hint of violence in Tubby's voice. They could only say that they had them or that they didn't have them. The smooth official examined the passports carefully.

'They are in perfect order, sir.'

'I *know* that, I know they are in order, I have come for visas.'

'Visas?'

'Yes, visas.'

'But, sir, you do not need visas to get into my country.'

'Of course we need visas.'

'Please forgive me, sir, but I must correct you here, you do not need visas to get into my country.'

Tubby was almost dumbstruck. These tuppenny ha'penny officials were all the same. Give them a title, bung them behind a desk, and who the hell do they think they are? They play fast and loose with whom they like, they do it for bribes, to relieve the boredom, they like to watch their victims squirm and sweat. They site their embassies in the best possible places amongst the peace and beauty of the lovely mauve water lilies and they just lie in wait with the hounds of hell ready to tear you to shreds and make you suffer the torture of the damned. It's enough to make you blow your bloody top. And that is exactly what Tubby did.

'You steaming great git,' he said. 'You steaming great git, you're pissing me about, you know bloody well that we need visas, why do you think we have been calling at the British Embassy day after day after day only to be told that the visas had not arrived? You're doing nothing, nothing, bugger all. I don't care if we never get to your stinking, filthy country, you can keep it, stuff it, sod off. We were trying to help, you miserable bloody rat, you can rot in bloody hell for all I care, good day.'

Tubby had taken his revenge on all the passport officials and customs and excise officials in the world, not to mention the hound of hell that all but ripped him to pieces. The smooth official listened to Tubby's tirade with an elegant and beautiful diplomatic control. Whatever emotions that must have surged underneath his polished brown skin were held safely under lock and key by his stern and rigorous training. Instead of ordering Tubby out of his office at once, he smiled. He said, 'I think I understand the situation, sir. Forgive me for asking, but what country are you wishing to go to?'

Tubby still had a pretty good head of steam up. 'What country, what country? Well, bloody Burma, of course, bloody Burma.'

The smile on the diplomat's face stretched far and wide. 'I am most sorry to have to tell you, sir, that this is the Indian Embassy, the Burmese Embassy is next door. This is definitely the Indian Embassy and you will understand that we cannot deal with Burmese matters.' He was more than reasonable.

Tubby was a very good story-teller and he told me that story in the bar when he got back. He had not had a very good day. Fortunately, my day had been nothing like as arduous. I had no trouble at the airline office and our flights were booked and confirmed for the next day. We were all set to go home and we were looking forward to it. Tubby was not at all keen to give the hell-hound at the Burmese Embassy another whirl. He'd had enough. So had we all.

South Pacific

———— • ————

Tubby's misfortunes always had an original twist to them. Even a serious and dangerous misfortune could do a back flip and produce a surprise result. One such awful misfortune happened when we were filming in the South Pacific. The whole trip had been planned with a good deal of optimism, as they always were. We had planned to go to Honolulu, Western Samoa, Tonga, Tanna, Tahiti, New Hebrides and Fiji – all in six weeks. Of course it was barmy. But we always planned barmy itineraries.

The first hint of trouble came in Honolulu, after we had had a fairly hefty Polynesian dinner and were walking home. It was warm, there was a soft breeze, the islands were full of pictures, the beaches beautiful and the surfing was of enormous dimensions and made most dramatic pictures. We had no shortage of material here. There was nothing to worry about, until Tubby complained of a pain in the chest. He said that it was the heavy meal that had given him indigestion. This attack of indigestion was pretty severe but it eased off, went away for a time and then came back. And went away and came back. It was a pattern that was, to say the least, rather worrying. We were 10,000 miles away from home and some of the islands that we stayed on were not equipped to deal with cases of indigestion that came and went away. It wasn't until we got to our last port of call that I persuaded Tubby to go to the only hospital that we had been near. That island was Fiji. It had a sound old colonial hospital. The Irish doctor there confirmed that Tubby had a heart condition.

At least we knew for sure that it was not indigestion. But both of us had known secretly that it was something much worse than indigestion. Fiji was our last port of call. We were flying back home in a week's time. The Irish doctor gave Tubby a prescription to get some pills which he was to take the moment he felt a bad bout coming on. On no account was he to exert himself or worry and he was to notify his own doctor when he got back home. We left the hospital in the depths of depression and went to the chemists just around the corner. Yes, they had the pills but could we wait a minute or two. Surprisingly, there was a chair in the chemist's shop. Now, knowing Tubby's microwave potential, I was a little apprehensive when he sat down on it. I asked him if he thought that was a wise thing to do and he smiled wanly. And then we both started giggling as we thought of the many chairs that Tubby had shattered as we wandered around the world.

Perhaps his heart condition was not as bad as the Irish doctor had made it out to be. True, Tubby did look a little pale, but who wouldn't after being handed an ugly piece of news such as he had received a few minutes ago? The pills were taking a long time to materialise and, on the spur of the moment, I told Tubby that I just wanted to look at the electrical shop around the corner. I had noticed rather a good looking tape recorder there. Won't be a tick. I didn't go to the electrical shop but went back to the old colonial hospital where I found the Irish doctor and asked for his private telephone number. He hoped that I wouldn't need it, was almost sure that I would not, but gave it to me and added that if Tubby ever smoked another cigarette he would refuse to do anything for him at all.

When I got back to the chemists Tubby was talking to one of the assistants there. He had got the pills. Should he feel a pain he just had to put one under his tongue, let it dissolve and keep fairly still. He was feeling better already. We went back to our hotel. I must explain that we always shared a bedroom and bathroom wherever we went. It was much cheaper and we could do our after-filming paper work together. We never got in each other's way, we always agreed as to what we should do on the following day. Tubby wrote out the shot lists and, as he doubled up as a sound engineer, he wrote out the tape numbers as well. I made a few notes on this and that as, apart from the film commentaries, I knew that I would have to provide radio programmes.

We travelled all over the world sharing accommodation wherever we went. It was a first-class arrangement. Not only was it convenient, it kept us out of the hotel bars. You can waste a tremendous amount of time and money in hotel bars. We avoided that by taking our own drink with us. There is one commodity that you can buy anywhere in the world it seems and that is whisky. I didn't say Scotch whisky, although you can get that in most places, but whisky in some form is at hand wherever you are. I'm not saying how long a bottle of whisky lasted us but there was always one in our room and a bottle of mineral water. We could do our paper work and take a sip or two as we did it. We were both very contented men. We spent six weeks every year travelling the world deciding more or less where, how and when we went. The Beeb didn't worry about us at all as long as we delivered the goods. And we always managed to do that. It was indeed the golden age of radio and television.

But that golden age nearly came to a very sudden end in the early hours of the morning after our visit to the Irish doctor. I am a pretty heavy sleeper. The moment my head hits the pillow I'm gone, and it will take a furious thunderstorm to wake me. I was awakened just after two o'clock in the morning by Tubby. He was punching me, pounding me. He was in a dreadful state. He yelled at me, 'For God's sake shoot me, oh please shoot me'. He was suffering the terrible pains of a serious heart attack. It was too awful to behold. He was writhing and moaning and pleading with me to shoot him. I had the Irish doctor's home telephone number. I rang him. The instructions he gave me were clear and concise. Get him to take another of those pills, don't hurry him, but get him in a taxi and take him to the hospital as soon as possible. There the Irish doctor would meet us.

It's not all that easy to call a cab in Fiji at half past two in the morning but the hotel porter had a friend who had a taxi. A little money was all that was needed. The taxi arrived. We went to the hospital where, true to his word the Irish doctor was waiting. He examined Tubby and pointed out to him and to me that he would be in hospital for some time and once again added the warning that he would throw Tubby out of hospital if he ever discovered a puff of smoke in his room.

Tubby's recovery was steady but slow. There wasn't the remotest chance of him coming back with us to England. He would have to stay on in Fiji. Once again we had a touching farewell very similar to our parting in Rio when Señor Gonzales held Tubby prisoner and wouldn't let him go. But this time Tubby's custodian was his own defective heart and he couldn't escape from that for about three weeks. He made a very good recovery and was back home in Bristol a few weeks before Christmas. I live in Berkshire so I didn't see Tubby right away but we talked on the phone and he told me he felt fine, that he had been to the Bristol Infirmary and there they had confirmed that he was in pretty good shape but that they would be more than cross if he started smoking again. He had completely given up the weed and was looking forward to us both viewing the rushes after Christmas.

A few days later I had a phone call to tell me that Tubby had had another attack and was back in hospital and all wired up to one of those machines that send green lightning flashing about all over the place. But this time the forked lightning was really flashing messages that were both mysterious and very erratic. I was sure that Tubby's microwaves were playing up and that he would eventually smash up the lightning machine. But it was very difficult to get such a silly message through to the doctors and make it seem credible. The green lightning still played merry hell on Tubby's screen.

And then Tubby began to get hot. Very hot. His temperature began to climb into the dangerous hundreds. The doctors brought in fans as big as windmills and blew them at him to try to cool him off. He had already notched up 103 degrees and now everyone was getting very hot and bothered. They chopped up wheelbarrows of ice and packed it all around Tubby and checked their thermometers and studied the antics of the mad green lightning. The tropical heat of this frightening thunderstorm still raged through Tubby's ample body. The doctors had to tell Tubby that he would not be able to return to his work for many many months. His temperature they had managed to arrest at a steady 103 degrees. And the windmills blew and the ice melted.

There are times when a preconceived idea will stand you in good stead, when the information available to you will lead you confidently to the solution of a tricky problem. There are other times when a preconceived idea will lead you into a desert instead of taking you to a cool soothing river. The doctors in Bristol were absolutely justified in taking the steps they did in assuming that Tubby had suffered a very strong heart attack. The report from the old colonial hospital in Fiji was as clear as crystal. The Irish doctor in Fiji had reported Tubby's condition in terms that no doctor could mistake. The guidelines from Fiji were sound enough. But the preconceived idea of a heart condition had completely obscured the word 'Fiji'. Therein lay the vital clue that someone picked up after the windmills had been blowing and the ice had been melting for several hours. Fiji. What is so critical about Fiji?

You can pick up malaria in Fiji. Quite easily. The mosquitos go about their deadly business quite efficiently in Fiji. And there are a lot of them. Hotel bedroom walls are splattered with the smudges of dead mosquitos that have been slapped to death by visitors' folded newspapers. Tubby and I spent quite a bit of time in active exercise swiping at the little singing stingers every evening. One that we missed must have followed Tubby to hospital and got him there. In his anxiety Tubby forgot to take his malaria pills. As I remembered, the necessary dose was one pill per week. Tubby was in hospital in Fiji for about three weeks and that is where the rotten little fly got him. The malarial spasm passed away. They shovelled the ice away and turned the windmill off. Tubby recovered and we carried on with our travels.

I know it is entirely fanciful to talk about Tubby's microwaves, but he did break up inanimate objects like chairs because they restricted him – he did not like being still – and his magic microwaves so easily penetrated the sensitivities of the people around him. This friendly gentle person, with a quickness of wit that flashed past the winning post way ahead of the field, had a kindness and understanding that never varied or faltered. I tried to portray him as he was in the radio broadcasts. I only partly succeeded. It was impossible to reproduce his incredible qualities. When he appeared on the scene you felt a warmth smooth over you and within a matter of seconds you would be laughing and laughing. But our laughter came to an end, in this life at any rate, when his dear old heart and magic microwaves very suddenly stopped one fine July day in 1983.

Animal Magic and gags

———— • ————

The year 1983 was not a year one cares to think about too much. 1983 for me was the year when the Lords of Creation defected and the Devils of Destruction took over. Tubby Foster was no more. He was dead. Two months prior to his death the newly appointed Head of the Natural History Unit in Bristol told me that he did not like the 'Animal Magic' programme and that he was going to kill it. He had every reason not to like it for, as a producer in that unit, he had produced an alternative programme for children to elbow 'Animal Magic' off the screens. His programme, after a few series, flopped and was junked. And so that summer I attended two funerals of programmes with which I had been associated for more than a quarter of a century. One was tragic and the other comic.

'Animal Magic' was the name invented by Pat Beech, the former News Editor of BBC West of England. When the Natural History Unit was formed in Bristol it was thought that there should be an instructive and entertaining programme about animals for children. Pat Beech, who was a most inventive newsman, said, 'Children love animals and they love magic, call it "Animal Magic"'. The first programme went on the screens in 1962 in black and white. Television was very young, and so were we. We did not really know what we were doing. The happy marriage of education and entertainment is a very difficult state of affairs to bring about. You have on the one hand the purist educationalists, always predominant, and on the other hand the entertainers. There were precious few of them. The programme went in fits and starts like a T model Ford with a blockage in the carburettor, but it managed to jerk along and finally settled down when Douglas Thomas took over the production.

Douglas had been a film editor and I had worked with him in the past on a series of programmes featuring Hans and Lotte Hass, one of the first man-and-wife teams of divers who explored the depths of the oceans in various parts of the world. Doug was to cut and join the film and I had been asked to write the commentaries for Hans Hass as his English was a little ponderous. He liked to read the commentaries himself and was very happy for me to translate what he had in mind into a slightly lighter vein. He had the impression that I was a gag writer, for as I viewed the film he would say again and again, 'You are mekking some gegs, yes?' 'Can you mekking some gegs vis zis besking shark?' Well, making some gags was not easy as I am not a gag man. And making sentences for Hans Hass to wrap his tongue around was like forcing a handful of sausages into a kid glove. Some light-hearted asides would crash to earth like meteorites.

I remember that there was a shot which went on for rather a long time. It was of a young chick in a nest and beside it was an unhatched egg. What had to be said about this chick had already been said of lots of other chicks that we had been looking at for several minutes. The line I wrote was 'Here is another blue-footed booby, his brother there is still an egg'. Hans was not at all sure about this line. I explained that it was simply a 'throwaway' line. I should not have put it that way. Instead of treating it as a 'throwaway' line he took the matter literally and simply hurled it away like a twenty-stone shot-put giant. The line came out in a heavy declaiming guttural, 'Heeah is anuzzer blue-footed booby' and then with a military stand to attention command, 'His bruzzer zere is still an EKK'. To read convincingly in a foreign language is difficult enough but to make sense of slight innuendo is of course asking too much. I was very wary of putting in too many 'gegs' afterwards. The blue-footed Booby 'geg' didn't entirely fall on barren land. It was quoted in one of the Sunday newspapers in 'Sayings of the week'.

I worked with Hans, Lotte and Doug for quite a long time in the tiny cutting rooms in Whiteladies Road. Every ten minutes or so Hans would stride down the narrow corridor to Doug's cutting room calling out 'Dog, Dog'. We were soon calling Doug 'Dog'. And once again I was working with 'Dog' on 'Animal Magic'. 'Dog' was a family man. He had four young daughters who knew what they wanted and knew how to get what they wanted. Their little feet were firmly on the ground. Their criticisms of all television programmes were basic and all-embracing. You could not pull the wool over their eyes. They took after their Mum and Dad. And what Dad 'Dog' gleaned from their chatter simply confirmed that what he was doing with 'Animal Magic' was just about right. Like Tony Soper he was an original, ignoring most of the demands that administration imposed simply on the grounds that it was a waste of time. He hated meetings and always had a handy excuse for not attending them. Sometimes he would not even bother with an excuse – he just didn't go. As a freelance I was not asked to attend meetings, thank goodness.

In the light of what has happened to the administration, precious few meeetings have done much good. Meetings produce complications, as everybody at the meeting feels compelled to say something. Meetings gradually eroded the free and easy adventurous atmosphere that once blew like a following wind around Broadcasting House. The heavy stodge of meetings settled like the dead weight of a fat man in an armchair. Most meetings were followed by a slap-up lunch and lots of knock-down drinks in the board room where variations on the meetings theme were discussed and arranged. The clever invention employed at finding variations to the meetings theme was, to say the least, impertinent. First of all the travel variation was the best stand by. You never had meetings in the same old place. You chose a different city to drone in. This meant taxis, trains, aeroplanes and that stalwart standby, the overnight allowance. Everybody travelled first class. In fact it was a rule that had been thought up at one of the meetings. All producers travelled first class. Freelance artists who were asked to travel were graciously granted second class fares unless – and this is a very subtle distinction – unless they were travelling with a staff producer and then to save embarrassment he was allowed to apply for first class fares and accommodation.

There is little doubt that the travel variation was a very popular one on the meeting theme. It was very useful in evading productive work. Meetings saved meeting-goers from committing themselves to positive statements on the air or on the television screen. This evasive action skilfully permitted one television producer to trip in and out of Broadcasting House for over ten years without producing one single programme. He was of course a professional Swan. A brilliant Swanner at Swanning. I was asked some time ago to write a set of verses to go with the Carnival of the Animals by Saint-Saëns.

It was for a children's concert and it was thought that the original verses by Ogden Nash were a little out of date as they bore references to President Truman and the Andrews sisters whom modern children would not know. It turned out to be not a hard task at all writing a verse about a cuckoo or a donkey and I suppose I was pretty much in my stride when I got to the last-but-one verse which was 'The Swan'. I knew him!

The Swan

There are many ways of dodging work
It's really quite an art.
Apply for this, apply for that,
Do anything but start.
To run away from routine things,
To take a month's sick leave,
To fiddle a long sabbatical,
Or pretend you are bereaved.
But the master of this work-shy tribe
Who grandly glides upon
The shining waters of a lake
Is the glorious wonderful Swan.

In all fairness to that producer he must have attended thousands of meetings so he must be given credit for staying-power and stamina. The sheer boredom of all that yakkity yak must have been enough to blot out the sun. Doug Thomas consistently refused to attend meetings save for one or two here and there to prove that he was still alive and would not welcome advice or criticism as to what he should or should not do about his programme 'Animal Magic'. Like Tony Soper he was one jump ahead of administration and the meeting-goers. He needed to be.

Filming animals

———— • ————

A strong jealousy was building up against 'Animal Magic'. Some hated it because it was anthropomorphic. And anthropomorphism is one of the deadly sins. To make animals appear as though they were talking was totally and absolutely unscientific. Not only that, it was a cheap and facile way to entertain the boys and girls. To indulge in such worthless underhand tricks week after week was a disgrace. Not only that, the programme was becoming very very popular.

They had tried very hard scientifically to replace 'Animal Magic' and look where that had got them. There is but little doubt that as you walk sincerely along the road to success you sow all around you your own minefield. They lie waiting for you to put a foot wrong. They lie waiting for you at meetings, for at meetings there is a map of your own particular minefield. Do mind how you go. But we didn't mind how we went. Doug Thomas and I were born on the same day. I mention this simply because students of astrology might be interested. We were born on the same day and we treated television in much the same way. We were duty bound to entertain. Not only to entertain others but we simply could not work at anything that did not entertain us. Our mental ages, I always maintained, were about seven or eight years. We played out our childish daydreams around the zoos of Europe. I was the zoo keeper who was overlooked by a rather stern boss. You never saw the boss — he was a voice off-stage who shouted out from time to time, 'Morris, what do you think you are doing?'

It was an innocent little ploy but I was in fact in the same sort of situation as a child at school acting the goat and getting ticked off by the teacher. Morris was caught out in all sorts of silly situations. Balancing a broom on one finger when he should have been sweeping out the giraffe house. Playing hopscotch when he should have been cleaning the thick glass of the gorilla exhibit. I was in fact being naughty. Not very naughty – just a little bit. Added to this was the slightly bewildering but somehow magic way in which I talked to the animals and they talked back to me.

All the films we shot in those early days at the zoos were once again shot by a clockwork camera with a run of just over twenty seconds before you had to stop and rewind. The clockwork Bolex camera could be hand-held and this was invaluable when photographing unpredictable animals. It was by comparison with present-day cameras a dainty little lightweight. Although there was a tripod to go with it you only needed one if you were using a particularly big lens, for then the camera had to be absolutely steady. But generally, apart from extra large close-ups, the cameraman needed no tripod and it was a big help to be able to dodge about as the animal moved about. With animals you have to film things as they happen.

It is true that there were some cameramen who would not dare to take a shot unless the camera was firmly screwed on to a tripod. Their professional status demanded it and their pictures had to be rock solid and technically flawless. Doug Thomas carefully avoided such chaps as by the time they had composed their perfect picture and were ready to shoot, the animal in question had caught a number eleven bus and was on his way to Trafalgar Square. Except in certain circumstances tripods were not welcomed. The animals did not like them either. The more equipment you introduce into an animal's enclosure the more trouble you heap upon yourself. I have seen a young gorilla simply rip a tripod from a camera man's grasp and bash him over the head with it. He was not observing rule number one, which is never go into a great ape's enclosure with anything in your hand. It will first of all be taken from you and then you'll get it back with a vengeance. We shot film for years and years with a hand-held clockwork camera. No tripods and no microphones.

I think that most of the animals hated microphones, especially the microphones that were covered with a large windshield. They were most suspicious of these things that looked like airships. But they were more frightened than suspicious. And there is no way that you can make an agreeable and calm picture of an animal that is panic-stricken. You also stand a very good chance of being seriously hurt. So no tripods and no sound systems. Shoot mute.

Thank goodness Doug Thomas became fascinated in animals and in zoos. We were indeed fortunate that just a stone's throw from Broadcasting House was the Bristol Zoo. It is not a large zoo but it is extremely beautiful. It is also one of the oldest zoos in the country and to this day maintains a standard of gardens and gardening that cannot have changed all that much in well over a hundred years. They are of course formal gardens but their orderly beds are always most sympathetically arranged with bedding plants of beautifully blended colours. The blending, too, of animals and birds and plants was just what we wanted. The only time we used a tripod was to photograph the shrubs and flowers as a background.

It was quite amazing how the staff of Bristol Zoo took to the idea of a performer playing the role of a zoo keeper. It amused most of them and they were always careful to give you a detailed run-down of any particular animal that you proposed to handle. Without their help we would not have been able to present 'Animal Magic' the way we did. It was vital to know the character of an animal before you went into its cage. For, like horses, exotic animals vary enormously. Horses, as you know, all look much about the same, give or take a hand or two, yet one will come and nuzzle you for a lump of sugar and another will kick you right between the eyes for free. This applies to exotic animals too. They have their own particular characteristics and much depends on how they were treated by homo sapiens in their young days.

We took chances then that I would not dream of taking now. We were comparatively ignorant of the variations in animal behaviour and there were times when I could have been ripped to bits. Nowadays I do not think that I would enter an enclosure where a group of kinkajous lived. But I did just that, about twenty-five years ago. Kinkajous are most attractive animals. They come from Central and South America. They are about the size of cats with very muscular prehensile tails. They can, as they say, bite flashes. It is a largely nocturnal animal and so it has those lovely large goo goo eyes. Just the creature for the boys and girls to look at. I cannot remember who was looking after them at the time but when we asked whoever it was if we could go in with the kinkajous he said, 'Well, I don't know, they are all right with me'. That is of course a statement bearing a warning.

You hear it from owners of dreadful-looking dogs. 'He's all right with me.' It's a statement that can be made in foresight and later on in hindsight when you are dripping blood.

And so, taking a foolish chance, I went in with the kinkajous. They were absolutely charming. I sat on the floor of their cage. They viewed me with wonderment and with a little caution, but they knew I had a few bananas in my pocket. I sat fairly still and was sufficiently careful not to make advances towards them. They must come to me. And they did. In a matter of minutes I was covered in kinkajous. They wrapped their tails around my neck and hung from my arms. They drove their noses into my ears and then licked my face. Well, I was their banana Uncle and soon they were all covered in sticky banana gunge. They were having a lovely time, they were all over me and the cameraman with his little clockwork camera who also did not know what chances he was taking when he came into the cage with me. I remember looking out through the glass front of their cage and saw the head keeper Bert Jones watching everything with some concern. When we thought that we had enough pretty pictures of the kinkajous and their lovely prehensile tails the camera-man and I came out of their cage.

Bert Jones was more than relieved. He said, 'Well, you walked away from that one all right, didn't you? I thought I had better hang about a bit. I daren't go in with them, they'd rip me to bits.' It was a remark of some significance and I thought about it. Why would they go for Bert and not for me? Well, they knew Bert pretty well and no doubt he had done something to them that they didn't like – treated them for a cut or administered a pill or a drench. The memory and sensitivity of animals is so often underestimated. The kinkajous did not associate me with any unpleasantness in their little lives. But they did with Bert. They knew him.

But the opposite can be the case, although the factors are slightly more complicated. Our friend Terry Nutkins was assigned the task of looking after some otters. He adored his otters and as far as he knew they were always pleased to see him and showed affection. Until one day when he went to feed one of them. It attacked him. It bit the finger of his left hand and took it half off. Terry managed to push the animal away from him but as quick as lightning it did exactly the same to his other hand. Terry was left with two stump fingers, one on each hand. An otter is not a large animal but it has got a most effective bite – it can bite a conger eel in half – so a human finger is as a stick of celery is to us, no trouble at all. But why had this tame otter suddenly changed character?

The answer is that it had not changed but Terry had. The day of the attack was a cold day — very cold. Terry went out to feed his otters in his shirt sleeves and the cold air struck him rather hard. He went back for a pullover. He could not immediately find his own pullover and he put on someone else's. To the otter he was someone else. Now it may be said that the otter did not recognise Terry because of the strange pullover. But his contours hadn't changed so therefore one can only assume that his smell had.

Some animals are quick to notice the change of contours of a room or a person. My cats know immediately when there is a new bit of furniture. Once they happened to be out in the garden when a man came with a new wall cupboard and screwed it to the wall. When the cats came in they stopped and stared and looked at the cupboard and then at each other. They said, 'He's gone and got a new cupboard'. 'So he has, wonder what he had to give for that.' Their recognition of a new object is instant. I never wear a hat, not even in cold weather, as fortunately I still have enough thatch to keep the body heat in. But when the hurricane hit the south of England in October 1987 I was forced to dig out a battered old cap and put it on. When the cats saw me for the first time in their lives wearing a cap they were dumbfounded.

'Good heavens, what on earth has he got on his head?'

'God knows, he must be going off his head, hee hee.'

Sometimes it would seem that animals know much more about us than we know about them. Of course accidents do happen from time to time and they can always be explained away afterwards. But it takes years of experience to forecast what will happen twixt human and animal at any given confrontation.

Safety First

———— • ————

Fortunately I have never been seriously hurt by any of the animals that I have had dealings with. Of course I have been bitten, but not badly, and I have suffered a broken rib or two. There are some who say that I have been very lucky, and I would agree with that. But luck very often goes hand in hand with confidence, and it is very necessary to be confident. To approach any animal with timidity is simply inviting it to have a go. I would never dream of attempting anything with an animal unless I was confident. But then I had had a good start. I had dealt with thousands of farm animals for years and I knew perfectly well that they accepted humans who were relaxed and quiet, who talked softly and made no sudden movements. Never do anything that can be interpreted as aggression or attack. If you do, then you can expect the worst.

It is said by some that animals can smell the sweat of fear in humans. This may be so, all I can say is that any attack that any animal has made on me has been so sudden and short that I haven't had a chance to sweat in fear. A very famous old gentleman once said that the worst slogan that was constantly being dinned into the public was that of 'Safety First'. Safety First, he strongly maintained, spelt the death knell of the human race. If you considered Safety First before you did anything then you would never do anything. Safety First was killing the human race.

Strangely enough it was some years before the Beeb thought of insuring me against possible loss of earnings should I get beaten up by a gorilla or something. Safety First, in those days, was scarcely considered. As long as we enjoyed what we were doing, no thought was given to Safety First. Doug Thomas was very good at thinking up things for an amateur keeper to do at the zoo. And so were some of the other keepers. Donald Packham and Alf Elliot, both senior keepers, were always coming up with attractive ideas for things to do. Some of their ideas depended on the individual peculiarities of particular animals. A giant anteater turned up from South America and she was as tame as a cairn terrier. She followed me around the zoo, not quite like a dog but nearly. She persisted in disobeying the notices saying 'Keep off the grass'. Being South American she couldn't read English and the smell of the fresh grass persuaded her to think that any minute now she was going to come across a couple of million ants. She also went fossicking about in the flower beds, which the gardeners didn't like at all. If you can recall what a giant anteater looks like just fill in a choice background of polyanthus and aubrietia and you will get a good idea of what a barmy picture it made. The keepers at the zoo much enjoyed helping us make our programmes there as long as we didn't keep them away too long.

It is true that some animals can be coaxed a little by food, but an animal doing something that it does naturally is by far the most relaxed and happy way of making pictures. I can't remember who suggested it but the idea was put forward one day that elephants simply loved hosepipes. It could be that they had an affinity with hosepipes on account of the similarity with their own design of nose. Let's take a hose and wash down the elphants, they will love it. We arranged to wash down the two elephants out in the zoo, not in their enclosure but just outside where there was a hosepipe and there was enough pressure of water to spray around.

It was a lovely summer day. The children were on summer holiday. The zoo was very full. Frank, the keeper of the elephants and giraffes, arranged to have the elephants outside by mid afternoon. There were two elephants, called Wendy and Christina. They were not fully grown but they were getting on the big side. They must have been between fifteen and twenty years old. Both Frank and I had known them since they were little babies and they knew us. Even so, sincere Safety First people are inclined to shudder a bit when they see the film of the elephant washing. I must say they were very good elephants and they loved being washed.

It is true they were very used to people. When they were very little Frank used to take them for a walk around Clifton and one of their favourite stopping places was the greengrocer's shop where they used to fling back a cabbage or two as a mid morning snack. But the situation that we were creating was slightly different from a stroll around Clifton. The hose that Frank gave me was of the toughest rubber imaginable. It was elephant tough. We were soon surrounded by hundreds and hundreds of Mums, Dads, their little and big darlings, and tiny little pets in pushchairs and prams. The moment the water was turned on the situation started to get out of hand. I suppose I had that tough old hosepipe in my hand for a minute or so while I damped Wendy and Christina down, but Christina very gently but firmly took the hose pipe from me and damped me down. I was absolutely drenched and the boys and girls screamed with delight.

They screamed even louder and with more hysteria when Wendy took the hose from Christina and turned it on the boys and girls and kind friends one and all. The screaming mob was completely saturated. And they screamed and screamed with glee as Wendy calmly sprayed them again and again. It is true they retreated when they caught the full force of the hose but they came surging back screaming at the elephants to do it again. It was a classic Keystone Cops sort of scene. The concrete was swilling with water, people started slipping and sliding and falling about. The elephants sensed in a tick that a prone body was a sitting duck and those that slipped and fell were treated with another couple of hundred gallons to help them back on their feet.

It was a mad mad exhilarating half hour. Everyone was so wet they just did not mind this ruthless swinging hose. Little sisters pushed their big brothers towards the elephants who were trying to take the hose from each other. The water was going everywhere, anywhere, and the screaming was getting shriller and shriller. There was more than a whiff of madness in the air. Frank decided that the time had come to turn the water off. He was right, things had gone far enough. The crowd was dripping wet. Water was running out of people's pockets, picnic baskets sodden, the dyes of the pretty summer frocks were running down little girls' legs and yet when the water stopped the crowd went 'Ooooorrrhhhh'. They wanted more. I often think of that afternoon when I visit a zoo that provides amusements as well as exhibiting animals. A ride on the roundabout and a bash on the dodgems is quite good fun but turn on the hose in the elephants' enclosure at three every afternoon and you are on to a winner.

Another good ploy would be to put a heap of soft mud in the gorillas' pen. Gorillas love making mud balls and hurling them at passers by. Some gorillas are very good shots and you will hear yelps of delight when Uncle Fred gets his hat knocked off. But of course I am ignoring the Safety First factor. What would the insurance people say? The elephant washing that we did at Bristol Zoo must have happened some twenty years ago and a large number of the general public was involved and yet as far as I know not a single complaint was entered and there were no claims for damages. There were hundreds of people who got drenched and their clothes must have suffered. The people must have suffered too as they had to allow their clothes to shrink and dry on them. But thank goodness we didn't take much notice of Safety First in those days.

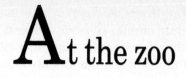At the zoo

———— • ————

As I have mentioned before it was many years before the Beeb thought it prudent to insure me when I went acting the keeper in zoos. And the zoos were most co-operative and pleased to grant facilities for me to show off their zoos and animals, for a screening of a zoo meant increased attendance. We were helped enormously by Bristol, who always let us know when something interesting had turned up. Other zoos took to letting us know of any new arrivals or of certain animals that are not normally handleable. Doug Thomas was always very quick to take up an invitation. We travelled around the zoos of Great Britain and we learned a great deal. And there was much to learn. To keep a variety of animals fit, well and reproducing is a most complicated business and you can produce a tragedy for yourself quite simply by doing the wrong thing.

We found many interesting items at many different zoos, items that could be amusing and interesting. We found a lot to interest the viewers at Twycross Zoo. We had known Twycross Zoo almost since the day it was opened. It was started by Molly Badham, who I soon realised knew an enormous lot about animals. She is also a human dynamo and full of ideas. It was at Twycross that we shot a simple sequence that fascinated many. We saw Keeper Morris going to a deep freeze and taking from the deep freeze a bunch of rose prunings. They had been collected when the roses were pruned. What was he going to do with a bunch of rose prunings? He was taking them along to the monkeys.

Rose shoots for the monkeys? It had been assumed for quite a long time that monkeys only ate monkey nuts and bananas. Oh dear, quite wrong. Different monkeys from different parts of the world have very different digestive systems. Some monkeys eat mainly leaves. They need leaves and as there are not many leaves about in England in winter time, as many leaves as possible were harvested in summer to feed the monkeys in winter. These rose prunings were fed to Molly's incredible group of Colobus monkeys. They are fairly shy monkeys but they allowed me into their enclosure without a lot of fuss. They were used to keepers but not male keepers, for most of Molly's keepers were girls and women. The whole zoo was as neat and clean as a well-ordered kitchen.

The animals were relaxed and clearly returned the affection that the girls bestowed on them. I am not saying that all female keepers are better than male keepers. Perish the thought. You have only to observe the dreadful animals that some lady dog-owners tow around the town. But there are certain aspects of animal care and training that some girls do far better than men. They have the maternal instinct and young animals recognise the maternal instinct. In my old farming days if we had a calf that had been rejected by its mother or was a bit of a weakling we always handed it over to Charlie's missus. She would soon have it on its feet and feeding. Within a week you just would not recognise it as the same animal.

Most of the girls at Molly's Twycross Zoo had the same qualities as Charlie's missus. It often happens in zoos that animals reject their offspring. It happens with the great apes from time to time simply because the mother simply does not know what to do with the little baby she has just presented to the big wide world. She does not know what to do because she has never lived in a group where babies are born and nursed for everyone to see. She is therefore ignorant. Not all the great apes in zoos are so afflicted but some are. A nursing mother in the ape world is worth its weight in whatever you like. Not only will the baby be happier and healthier but the teaching qualities of a nursing mother could spread to the other females who may not naturally possess strong maternal instincts.

The girls at Twycross were quite dedicated to fostering little gibbons, orang-utans, gorillas and chimpanzees. I often went into Molly's sitting room and found a gorilla there eating a stick of celery. This particular gorilla was very fond of taking a bath and Molly used to bath him in her bathroom. One day Molly suggested that I tried giving him a bath. He was about half grown and, like all gorillas, as strong as a team of shire horses. The same thing happened that happened with the elephants Wendy and Christina. I was the one that got the bath.

There was always something exciting and interesting going on at Twycross as there was at many other zoos. Edinburgh Zoo is noted for its large collection of penguins and every day they are taken for a walk around the Zoo. They have been doing it for so long they line up ready for the constitutional in the afternoon. One keeper strolls in front and one wanders along behind. It is a most unusual sight. Eighty penguins hopping and shuffling along with the crowds lined up either side of the pathways, acknowledging the clapping and laughing with a comic gracious dignity. It was also at Edinburgh that I first saw a pair of cassowaries and their chicks. The male cassowary looks after the chicks and a most extraordinary looking nurse-maid he is. He must be over four feet tall and looks to be wearing a funny twelfth-century soldier's helmet. There is a mad look in his eye and he has at his disposal a kick that will cleave a human right down the middle. It's a bird that is almost impossible to control or transport. It will kick the toughest crate to pieces.

As we travelled around the zoos we learned a lot about the incredible strength of some animals. At Chester Zoo somebody suggested we point out that the cuddly quality of bears meant absolutely nothing as most bears could kill you in a fraction of a minute. Teddy Bear is the loving little friend that we take to bed, he won't hurt you. Try and stroke and cuddle a bear at the zoo. Now it's not easy to demonstrate just how dangerous a bear can be, but at Chester they gave me an empty four and a half gallon wooden beer barrel. It was a new barrel and not a bit decrepit. 'Just throw that beer barrel to the polar bear and see what will happen,' they said. The polar bears at Chester have got a very spacious swimming pool and into this pool I tossed the barrel. One bear dived in. The barrel was sealed up and so it floated. The bear played with this barrel for a minute or two just like a water polo player. Isn't he sweet, the watching crowds said. Then the bear got the barrel and took it on to dry land. Just like someone tearing the cellophane from a cigarette packet he tore the iron bands off the barrel and within a minute or two that beautiful oak barrel was a heap of matchwood. The iron bands did not interest him. He had smashed up the barrel and he felt all the better for it. It was a fascinating demonstration.

Everywhere we went we found rarities and 'one off' animals. At

Basle Zoo in Switzerland we found a Komodo dragon. Not only one Komodo dragon but four or five. Not only four or five Komodo dragons but one was tame – if you can ever call a Komodo dragon tame. The director of Basle Zoo in those days was Dr Lang and a most original man he was. It was he who suggested that I should go in with the Komodo dragon. We had been at Basle Zoo for a couple of days and he was very quick to realise just what we were doing to provide entertainment and information for young viewers. This so-called tame Komodo Dragon was in an enclosure by itself and I went along to have a look at it. It seemed to me to be about the size of a Nile crocodile and just as attractive.

As always, I had to rely on the keeper to give me a run-down on its character. This dragon looked as though it would devour half a dozen damsels in distress for breakfast. But it was given a good character run-down. Like the crocodile at Paignton Zoo that loved having its teeth cleaned with a scrubbing brush. I simply had to take the keeper's word for it and scrub its teeth. It really liked it. This Komodo dragon, it seemed, liked mackerel and chicken. And he liked the chicken with the feathers still on. There is no mistaking the voracious intent of a hungry dragon. It is direct and positive. There is no messing about and it must not be thwarted in any way otherwise there will be all sorts of trouble. I went into the dragon's cage with a bucket of mackerel and a feathered chicken.

A Komodo dragon is a lizard, a heck of a lizard, and it moves like a lizard. It came at me with a quick wobbly lizard scuttle. It snatched the mackerel from me one at a time and then I bunged it a whole feathered chicken. Like a gecko with a fly, two gulps and it was gone. It looked into the empty bucket and then at me. Thank goodness I had no feathers about me. The expression on the dragon's face was of bored disgust. He wouldn't have me even if I had got feathers on. It sank down on its belly and lapsed into a dragon meditation for the rest of the day.

Dr Lang, as I say, was a most original man. He was very concerned about the boredom that descends on zoo animals. Rightly or wrongly he decided that any animals that could perform should perform. His troupe of elephants performed a couple of times a day. So did his sea lions. He said that they enjoyed it and really liked to hear the crowds laughing and clapping. He was extremely helpful and inventive as to what we could film in his zoo. Would I like to treat the elephants' feet. Yes, I would love to treat the elephants' feet. Quite simple with well-trained elephants. You have a set of blacksmith's tools – coarse files and sharp rasps and an elephant's footrest.

The elephants recognised the tools the moment I appeared, they knew exactly what to do and who was to be first to have the foot treatment. The big boss elephant ambled over and held up his front foot and I put the foot rest underneath. Elephants have beautiful toenails. I simply filed them down and polished them up. They seemed to enjoy it. I did get pushed about a bit but elephants are like that. What you have got to ascertain is whether the pushing about is good humoured and just a bit naughty or if you are being manoeuvred into a corner for a four-ton crushing session.

Elephants are remarkably subtle and sly. They never seem to hurry about their business and they need watching very carefully if you do not know each one very well. There was an elephant at Chester Zoo that I realised was out to get me. I was feeding them hay and there were seven or eight elephants altogether. This particular elephant was not interested in the hay at all and I realised that she was going to do me a mischief. The feeding was being filmed and so I positioned myself so that there was always another elephant between me and the calculating rogue. I managed to keep her away from me for a good ten minutes. But she won in the end and got me on my own. I had to jump for it into the big dry moat. She blew dust at me – that's all she could do, the rotten little coward that I was.

We went to Basle Zoo many times and to lots of other European zoos. Doug Thomas was always on the lookout for fresh items to film. He was a very good housekeeper as most producers were in the early days of television. He never overspent, which seems to be the fashion nowadays. He always had money in hand so that we could explore zoos that had not been investigated in our way before. We met animals that we knew existed but had never seen before. In Germany we came across a most amazing exhibit of shoebills. I knew what they were and I had seen pictures of them but to come face to face with a shoebill is quite something. And what a face it is. Just like a size eleven clog.

At Frankfurt we found a tame elephant seal. It took several days to persuade the director of the zoo to let me go in with this elephant seal. Well, he weighed three tons and had only had one keeper the whole time he had been at the zoo. How would he behave with a stranger? Apart from his colossal bulk he had a vicious set of teeth and, like all big animals that appear to move slowly, he could cover the ground at a deceptively quick speed. Like all male elephant seals he had a nose that looked like a big black sausage balloon. He was quite a terrifying spectacle. In the wild they can be most dangerous if you get too close to them. I had had some experience of them in Patagonia several years previously. The elephant seals there come ashore in the autumn to give birth to their young and mate immediately. It was estimated that there were about three thousand of them on the stony beach at the Valdes Peninsula. That is a considerable tonnage of seal.

The bulls have their own harems of cows and the number of cows in the harem is governed of course by the size and fighting prowess of the harem bull. Poor chap it is indeed a most busy time for him. He has no time to eat. He spends his days fighting to defend his harem, for all his cows are at risk as there are dozens of young untried bulls hanging around waiting on the fringe of the harem. They are only too ready to pop in and pull a fast one on the old man. The old man simply cannot let up for a second. He doesn't get a wink. The cows are absolutely tolerant of humans, you can walk about amongst them and their little ones. But the old man is totally intolerant. The whole huge bulk of him will come roaring blubbering after you, his blown up sausage balloon nose flapping and snorting. He will chase you until you are out of his territory. You have to be careful not to run into another bull's territory when he is not busy fighting one of the young bulls. The young bulls normally have to be dealt with first — he will attend to you in a minute.

The gigantic elephant seals on the Valdes Peninsula are a sight that you cannot possibly forget, and I thought of them when I looked at the big bull seal at Frankfurt Zoo. I went and talked to him several times a day. I was quite confident that he would not be hostile towards me. To start with, I was no threat to him because there were no attractive females about. And probably, like killer whales that become most docile in captivity, this elephant seal would be only too pleased to greet me if I had a bucket of herring. The director of the zoo made it quite clear that as no one else had been in with the seal except his one keeper, I was on my own. If anything happened I would be the one to blame. The only thing that might happen was that I could get squashed. The seal had a fine big lake to swim in but a very small shore on which to bask. I could get squashed on his seashore because with him on it there was no more room.

I had watched the seal's keeper feed him many times and he had a definite routine, a fixed pattern. Obviously I must follow that pattern. I got a bucket of fish and went along to the elephant's seashore. He was swimming in his lake, but as with all the seals in zoos all over the world the sight of a bucket sparks off frantic action. He came across that lake like a torpedo and landed with a great splat on the seashore just in front of me. He was ready for action. I couldn't help thinking of those great bulls on the Valdes Peninsula. I nearly turned and ran for it. There were three trembling spluttering tons of elephant seal towering over me. He rose to full height and placed his flippers over his great gut. He was going straight into his routine. He always did this and he always got a great roar of laughter from the crowd. He patted his belly with his flippers. He was ready for fish. This enormous quivering slug from the sea was ready to convert pounds and pounds of herring into more enormous quivering slug.

Basically we are all food converters. Everything has to eat something. But the elephant seal, on the surface, would appear to be a most crude food converter. Consider any of the little gazelles. They convert herbage into the most elegant shapes, the most delicate shades, the most lyrical stripes, the prettiest toes, barley sugar horns and a repertoire of gymnastics to make you gasp. But an elephant seal is just a stuffer, so it would seem. A crude converter. But even he has his delicate points. He is an excellent slip fielder. Every fish that I snicked at him he caught. No fumbling, no rolling over on the ground, every fish was taken neatly and cleanly and the crowd applauded every catch as the fish slipped down the gullet.

I saved a few fish for the last part of the act. He knew what to expect. I had to squeeze my way past him to get behind him. This was his finale. Standing by his tail, I called to him 'Come, come'. Very slowly and with surprising ease and grace he bent over backwards. This enormous animal was performing a contortion that would be a credit to a professional acrobat. He bent over like a hair pin – more than a hair pin. His great head finished upside down on his tail. Three tons of contortion. I dropped the last couple of pounds of fish into his upside-down mouth. That was the end. He knew it was the end. He unfolded himself very gracefully, rocked on his belly a few times to acknowledge the crowd's applause and then slipped into the lake. He was the great converter of fish into big sea slug, but he was a polite and very bendable slug. And everything has to eat something. As someone once said, 'Everything that Miss Brown eats turns into Miss Brown'.

Music for children

— • —

Way back in the fifties I had written a story called 'Delilah the Sensitive Cow' which had been set to music by Sidney Sager. It had been recorded by Decca and noted by the Northern Sinfonia orchestra as a possible piece for children's concerts. I was asked to go up to Newcastle upon Tyne to do this at one of their Saturday morning concerts. It was there that I met David Haslam the principal flautist and deputy conductor of that very fine band of musicians.

'Delilah the Sensitive Cow' was constructed to make the boys and girls laugh. Not only the boys and girls but also the mums and dads. Delilah is a contralto. Her husband Samson the bull is a bass, while the strong supporting cast of chickens, sheep and pigs all have soprano, tenor and grunty songs to sing. It is a most obvious and direct piece and it appealed to the orchestra and to David Haslam very much. Not only that, it needed just one soloist as I managed to ham my way through soprano, contralto, tenor and bass parts myself.

I must point out that the Northern Sinfonia is a very serious orchestra but they realised that to entertain children you must not be serious all the time. To set music on an altar and make it sacrosanct is simply asking for trouble. Music was invented by us so that we could be amused and entertained. Not that we should be rolling about laughing all the time, but we should be experiencing the other human emotions as well – sadness, doom, death, joy, elation and laughter. The trouble is there is precious little laughter about. I once went to a children's concert where the little pets were bored out of their minds by a whole

Brahms Symphony. At another concert where the kids had been press-ganged into attending a very modern piece of music I looked around and saw that they were behaving beautifully except that every little kid had got their fingers jammed in their little ears. Obviously this wasn't getting through to anyone and certainly wasn't making music a bit popular. It was making it something to be avoided.

David Haslam asked me if I had any more stories like 'Delilah the Sensitive Cow'. I told him that I hadn't but I could probably write one, and that while I could read I certainly could not write music. Writing music is for me one of life's great mysteries. So David said that I needn't worry about the music, he would write it. I was quite astonished when I heard the music that he had written to a story I sent him. It was called 'Juanita the Spanish Lobster', an unlikely tale of a most unlikely event. It called of course for quite a bit of flamenco singing, a lyric tenor, a singing seal and a chorus of lobsters singing as they knitted seaweed all day long. David was quite brilliant at imitating styles of music and slightly taking the mickey at the same time. He lived in Newcastle, while I lived in Berkshire almost 300 miles away. From time to time he rang me up to play to me what he had written. He simply put the telephone on the piano and played and sang to me. As an orchestral player he certainly made sure that the orchestra had plenty to do. He pushed them to the limits.

I went up to Newcastle on a Friday for the rehearsals for the Saturday morning concert. It was for me a very strange experience to hear something come to life that until then had only been typewritten words on paper and dots on printed lines. It was like taking a hyacinth out of a dark cupboard. It had only just begun to sprout and gradually before your very eyes and right into your very ears came the sight and sound of the Spanish Lobster clattering her castanets, stamping her feet and singing through her nose. It was most exciting because it was working and it was working very well.

I have already said that the writing of music is to me one of life's great mysteries. How David Haslam ever got this elaborate concoction on to paper was nothing short of a miracle. At times he imitated the style of de Falla, then Donizetti, then flamenco, then Handel. It was, as they say in Berkshire, 'one hell of a plate of dinner'. The boys and girls of the Northern Sinfonia sight-read it – just like that. Their professionalism left me gasping. There were one or two wrong notes here and there – a sharp that should have been a natural, a natural that should have been a flat – but generally the whole thing fitted together most neatly. 'Juanita the Spanish Lobster' worked.

Its running time was a little short of twenty minutes and we realised that this was just about the ideal time for a musical story. We realised that the ideal length of a children's concert should be no more than one hour. That's enough, with several short items at the start, pieces of varying emotions – fast, slow, loud, soft – and a fair bit of solo work for the different sections of the orchestra. Children are always interested in the machinery of an orchestra. They are fascinated by French horns, flutes, trombones and percussion instruments. They must never be allowed to think that they are on the receiving end of an arithmetic lesson.

Music is for enjoyment, even if it's on the sad side, because everybody feels better after a good cry. David had a wonderful knack of choosing short significant pieces. A movement from the 'Four Seasons' by Vivaldi, the trombone and double bass duet from 'Pulcinella' by Stravinsky. Oh yes, children are more than delighted with such pieces, because apart from the brilliance of the music they can watch the gymnastics of the performers. But no piece must go on for too long, no more than five minutes as the age of children at children's concerts nowadays is going down and down. As I remember, in the fifties and sixties the youngest ones were about six or seven. Now they are down to about two years of age.

So we adopted the formula for the concerts of several short pieces followed at the end by a musical story. The trouble was there weren't many musical stories. There was 'Delilah the Sensitive Cow' and 'Juanita the Spanish Lobster' and of course the incredible 'Peter and the Wolf'. 'Peter and the Wolf' is just a bit on the long side, its running time is around about thirty-five minutes, and children get really bored with it after the capture of the wolf. It should end there. There is no more plot to unfold, no more story to tell. That's it. But now each character in the story has to bow out slowly, one after the other, and that takes a good ten minutes. And so for the very young 'Peter and the Wolf' is not really suitable, brilliant though it may be.

I remember David saying after the first performance of 'Juanita the Spanish Lobster', 'I'm afraid that we will need some more stories, won't we'. And so I wrote some more stories. They were all about animals because animals, anthropomorphism, singing and music fit so beautifully together. The next musical story was 'Bouncer the Frog', the story of a new motorway and how it affected the animals on each side of it. Then 'Daggerlengro', which was about a gipsy, his lurcher dog, his ferret and a cruel gamekeeper. This collaboration went on at long range and by telephone and tape recorder. I would talk the story on to a tape and sing the style of song I thought fitted the part and after a few weeks David sent the tape back with what he had written.

David just would not leave things alone for long. He next suggested that we should write a musical story with orchestra and full choir as well. And so along came 'Cooey Louis the Racing Pigeon', who was sent to France to take part in the great 600 mile race from France to England. Unfortunately the pigeon Cooey Louis cannot remember the way home, which is a pity, but he does have some interesting adventures in France. Another piece with full choir concerns a racehorse called Lollopalong, who suffers from a hang-up and can never win a race. In the end of course he has to.

The writing of the stories was not a very taxing business for me but for David of course it was an enormous amount of work and I know that he really had to get his head down and concentrate as he was conducting the Northern Sinfonia and playing flute concertos. Professional musicians are, most of the time, extremely hard pushed. I have worked with many of the big orchestras of this country and although I consider that I have a fair bit of energy, I couldn't possibly keep up with these boys and girls year after year. I knew that sooner or later I would get a nasty attack of the screaming hab dabs. The boys and girls of the Northern Sinfonia are perhaps a little better placed geographically than the big London orchestras. They are but a few minutes drive from the beautiful Northumbrian countryside and the wild empty seashores. It is true it is a few degrees colder up there but at least you have a better chance of rearing a strong healthy family and enjoying your leisure time without the dreadful pressure of traffic congestion.

To be an orchestral player in London you need to have the constitution of an ox and the durability of its leather. You also of course need to have considerable musical ability. These qualities are supported and enhanced by strength of character, the backbone of which is determination. You will meet little slips of girls and slender lightweight little chaps who you imagine would be blown over in a southwest breeze. But you will find them deep rooted, steady and resolute in the awful gales that blow around the Barbican, the Festival and Fairfield Halls. And of course they are not simply playing tea time

Chelsea Bun music. Day after day they are rehearsing and playing thumping great works by Bartok, Stravinsky, Ravel and all the old masters.

The popular word now is 'Dedication' but to be dedicated of course means that you have to be very durable and totally believe in yourself. It is true that 'nerves' creep in. They are known as the 'pearlies'. There are some very noted 'pearly' pieces about and one of them is 'Peter and the Wolf'. It is full of solo passages and is very 'pearly' and so is the Classical Symphony by the same composer. I have heard it described by one orchestral leader as being 'unnecessarily difficult'. He said the same thing about 'Babar the Elephant' by Poulenc. The music to 'Babar the Elephant' is difficult but charming. I am very fond of it but in my experience children just do not like it. It is often included in a programme for a children's concert because a young elephant is involved and so it is bound to be suitable. Wrong. In my opinion the story and the music were written without children in mind at all. The result is a charming bit of self-indulgence by the author and composer. And the little pets seem to pick it up in a tick — one by one you will spot them nipping out to the loo. In no time at all you will spot great gaps in the rows of seats. In my opinion the formula of 'Babar' is not right.

The same cannot be said of Howard Blake's 'Snowman'. Howard Blake wrote the words and the music and he certainly had the little loves in mind. I have acted as narrator to the 'Snowman' many times and in concert halls that hold over two thousand there has never been one empty seat, a single cough or one little grizzle. Howard has got it right. And getting it right brings stimulation and elation which of course we all need, especially those hard-working, tough and talented musicians. Their concentration and perseverance absolutely shows that they love what they are doing and wouldn't want to do anything else. They work all day and half the night.

Musical performers

— • —

Another hard-working and talented musician was Douglas Coombes. I first met Douglas in the early seventies when he was a BBC producer of schools music programmes. He was a big man and versatile. As a youngster he had been a powerful and promising cricketer and was taken on to the ground staff of Gloucestershire County Cricket Club but his musical abilities persuaded him to follow a musical career. He had been to a concert at the Colston Hall, Bristol, when Sid Sager, the Paragon Orchestra and I had performed 'Delilah the Sensitive Cow' for the first time. Now that he was a music producer in London for children's programmes he was searching for material for children. Would I write a story to which he would write the music? So I wrote a story about a circus and an Elephant called Ting Tang.

Doug's music is powerful and direct and straight to the point, it can also be quite subtle but absolutely acceptable and understandable to children. Doug produced a thumping score. He score it for an orchestra of about a hundred and forty. He was going to get as many kids playing in that orchestra as he could. He got them. The piece calls for a sea lion playing the Bluebells of Scotland on the motor horns. It used to be part of the standard act of sea lions some years ago. The present-day kids had never heard of it and they fell about laughing when they tried to play it. It is a very funny effect and Doug knew exactly how to produce it. Doug's enthusiasm was quite remarkable. I worked with him quite a lot for the programmes 'Time and Tune' and 'Singing Together'. Nothing, but nothing, daunted him. If the programme was over-running by minutes he would make cuts instantly. There was no dithering, no doubt about what to do. He was supremely confident, extremely inventive and you instinctively did immediately what he told you to do. These qualities were extremely valuable when dealing with children and getting them to follow and sing the way he wanted them to sing. He was a power house of energy.

Energy is usually associated with smallish people. Big Doug was a big man and it was with big Doug that I first met Big Arthur Davison at Broadcasting House, London. Quite frankly, when I first met Arthur Davison I was quite frightened by his appearance. He was frequently mistaken for Orson Welles, such were his dimensions, and he had a predilection for impressive head gear. Arthur's hats always had brims that were much bigger than most hat brims and they needed to be to match up with his great height and his terrific width and breadth. I think he must have been a little apprehensive at meeting us both, for when he came into the listening room he had a surly half scowl on his face. It was Orson Welles in a very heavy role with a fair bit of doom and thunder in the background. But it did not last long. The thunder soon cleared and he was smiling like a sweet big cherub when we played him 'Ting Tang' the elephant.

Arthur was looking for pieces to play at his famous Christmas concerts at the Fairfield Halls, Croydon. Arthur has at his disposal many talents. He is first and foremost a fine musician, a beautiful fiddle player, a conductor with great authority and gentle sensitivity, and a wit that strikes like lightning. Not only that, he has the organising ability to 'put on' concerts. The combination of all these different qualities makes his concerts at Croydon so popular. And they are popular because Arthur is a personality – a great personality, for he's a very great man. We have worked together for many happy years now and no matter how many times we have done a particular piece Arthur always likes to go over the score with me before rehearsal to make sure that I agree with his tempi. This shows a consideration and concern that coming from such a big man I find touching. There are many conductors who say in effect, 'There is only one tempo and that is my tempo'.

There is quite a famous piece for family listening called 'Tubby the Tuba'. I had done it with Arthur many times and I was asked to perform it at a children's Saturday morning concert at Nottingham.

Arthur was not conducting, it was Rudolf Schwarz. I had worked with him before and he was known to everyone as Rudi, and Rudi called everyone 'My dear'. He is a very dear man. He had been booked to conduct a pretty heavy concert in Nottingham on a Friday night and stay over to conduct the children's concert on the Saturday morning. I turned up on the Saturday morning and Rudi said to me, 'My dear, what is this "Tubby the Tuba", I have never heard of it?' I said that it was a smart bit of nonsense, a bit tricky here and there but a bit of fun and the children really liked it. 'But, my dear, have you seen the score?'

I knew what he meant. There are many pieces the music of which has to be hired. Hired music goes the rounds and suffers the slings, arrows, cuts and thrusts of most of the musicians of Europe. The band parts and the conductor's score of this version of 'Tubby the Tuba' were quite shocking. In fact Rudi's score was practically unreadable. It was marked all over with signs, slashes of pen-strokes – pen-strokes when you are asked to mark only in pencil! It was marked in Norwegian, Dutch, French, German and English. It had been marked by the heavy-handed, the vicious and the spiteful. The real trouble was when it passed from one country to another. The French thought 'We'll fix this for those bloody Germans'. And the Germans thought 'We'll fix this for those bloody English'. Rudi's score looked like a tangle of rusty barbed wire in a fog. It was truly terrible. 'My dear, do you know this piece well?' 'Yes, pretty well.' 'Then, my dear, please do not worry, I will follow you.'

'Tubby the Tuba' was not in Rudi's repertoire at all, it simply was not his line of country. And he was asked to interpret pages and pages of ghastly musical mumbo jumbo. He had never seen it before. He showed not the slightest concern. We walked on to the stage of the Central Hall, Nottingham. Rudi had a serene, gentle smile on his face. It was a full house. He liked that, so did I. Whether he followed me or not I shall never know. He glanced at me once or twice and that is all I was aware of, save that from that dreadful set of parts and that awful score came a perfectly professional performance. My admiration of him and all those orchestral players was complete.

How had they done it? The world of music is full of such surprises – surprises that are so refreshing. Well, they are refreshing to me because I am only involved in the musical world from time to time. To the professional musician, who loves music but must find it at times rather boring, it must have been reassuring and reinforced their pride to have turned out a complete piece from such a muddle.

Squeaky gates

— • —

I have never been a serious musician. I bide by the rules and I can just about read the dots, but when the heavy affected intellectual mind descends like a slab of ice on to the warm emotional world of music I have to switch off or walk away. Such music is known as 'Squeaky Gate' music. Most orchestral players tolerate it because they find it easier to go with it than to fight it, but the name that they have given it speaks for itself. There are certain sounds that 'go right through you'. I remember a teacher at school often used to drag his finger nail on the blackboard as he wrote with a stick of chalk. It made a sound that would go right through you. Squeaky gates will do the same thing and certain music well deserves such a description. It could be said that this view is one of intolerance. It may be true but I was born into a world that did not know these sounds, there was no squeaky gate stuff about and since the first sounds you hear are the ones you hear even before you are delivered by the midwife then these sounds are not acceptable.

If you try to search for a meaning or a reason for this squeaky gate stuff you will find the answer to be much the same as that when you explore contemporary art. There is nothing there for you to find. You are too old, old man, too old. That is why I so enjoy working with youth orchestras. As a boy I went to a school where about four hundred boys were learning the three Rs. Of those four hundred, just two of us played the violin and jolly quiet we kept about it. Just two out of four hundred. Nowadays in schools a large percentage of the children play one, two, three and sometimes four instruments. The standard of playing is very high. There is nothing like strength in numbers. It is no longer a cissy thing to indulge in flute or clarinet or fiddle playing. It is now a competitive business. There is no fear of making a fool of yourself. You can do it. Ten to fifteen years ago when you listened to an orchestra on the radio you could tell that it was a youth orchestra. There was a certain diffidence and uncertainty in the playing. Certain sections were thin and unsure. Today you simply cannot tell the difference twixt a youth orchestra and one of the country's top professional bands. Well, I very often cannot.

When I was a boy music lessons were an expensive indulgence. Nowadays everyone can have a go. And don't they just. To watch and hear a little boy of eleven knock the stuffing out of a set of tymps will bring a lump to your throat as it does to his father and mother sitting in the stalls. Kids can learn anything if there is encouragement and competition about. A computer or a word processor will confound me. Just watch a little five-year-old manipulate one of these mystery miracle machines and you realise that he already qualifies to be a managing director who will attract a deal of interest from the Fraud Squad. I'm not saying that all children will learn everything but quite a number will learn a lot. And the standard of playing and the enthusiasm of the teachers is now quite remarkable. Not everything in this life is changing for the worse and these children will obviously benefit by the extra dimension that has been added to their lives. The more things you can do the more things you want to do. And it will stop you worrying. I never thought that I would spend a fair bit of time at a typewriter knocking out scripts for radio and television, performing at concerts, travelling the world and handling animals.

The easiest way to learn is through practical application and somehow or other I have almost blundered from one strange practical situation to another. My life with Willy and Gwen was a life of handling animals, growing crops, studying pictures, dealing in antique furniture and silver. Willy knew exactly what could be achieved in this life and he set about doing it. Away with inhibitions, there are no secrets attached to anything, it's all possible, now go and do it. He passed all this on to me and I shall always be eternally grateful to him for his instruction and the two thousand acres of his land that he allowed me to learn on.

The land of clip-on moustaches and lost marbles

———— • ————

I suppose that it was almost unavoidable that I should choose a clip-on moustache. Well, they were all the rage. Not all the clip-on moustaches were clipped on – but they looked it. Charlie Chaplin had one but that was painted on. Adolf Hitler had one and that was a real one. You could buy a clip-on moustache at the joke shop and I suppose I was about fifteen or sixteen when I bought one. Like Hitler's, it was a toothbrush moustache. A clip-on toothbrush moustache. It clipped on to that neat bit of gristle that separates the left from the right nostril. I dreamt up the clip-on moustache because I could think of nothing else and with Charlie Chaplin and Herr Hitler very much in the foreground I was sure that it would be a wow. I thought that it was, but looking back I can see that it was not. It used to get a laugh because I could wiggle it about. But it was not all that funny. A clip-on moustache is just not enough.

In those far-off days and of such tender years one knew but very little. I had been in a children's concert party called the 'Kiddiwinks' from about the age of ten. I suppose there must have been about thirty little pets in that party and we travelled by coach through the valleys of South Wales entertaining at Miners' halls and workhouses. I became quite well known in the workhouses and could always expect a warm round of applause when I appeared. The men and the women at the workhouse were segregated. The men sat on one side of the hall and the women on the other. They were all very drab and grey but to a troupe of children they were the best audiences we ever had. They were more than ready to applaud a

189

clatter of skinny tinsel fairies and a little boy extracting a wheezing agony from a concertina. Unlike the inmates, no doubt we enjoyed going to the workhouses.

Of course I outgrew the Kiddiwinks and was lucky to get a job as junior clerk in a solicitor's office. But during the Kiddiwinks period I met another John who was smitten by the world of theatre. He had every reason to be as his family were theatrical people. His mother had been a soubrette. Soubrettes were quite something. His grandfather was a theatrical agent. He knew all sorts of people in the world of variety. Grandfather said that if we two Johns could get an act together he could get us work. We were as good as made. All we had to do was to dream up an act. Straight man and funny man. Grandfather knew a gag writer who for a few pounds wrote a collection of gags for us. Grandfather's simple theory was that the more different things you could do, the more work you would get. He had special writing paper printed with the words 'The Two Johns'. The other John was a ventriloquist with a schoolboy doll. He also did dramatic monologues and was the straight man. I played the violin and sang and I was the funny man. That is where the clip-on moustache came in.

The funny clip-on moustache told the audience at once that with a bit of luck they were in for a bit of a laugh. Comedians had to look funny to start with. Funny hats, red noses, ridiculous eyebrows, exaggerated trousers, and unbelievable voices. The audience had to know that they could laugh unashamedly and not look silly, because up there on the stage was the silliest thing you ever saw. I don't think I looked all that silly but I did have check trousers, a tight frock coat, a floppy cravat, a trilby hat with the brim turned up, and of course that dear clip-on moustache. 'The Two Johns' got together an act that certainly had a lot of variety, for we both also took dancing lessons and learned to tap dance.

Grandfather got us lots of work at clubs and dinners and parties. He knew the artists that appeared at Moss's Empire each week. He took us to meet them backstage where we all drank Guinness. Drinking Guinness and we hadn't started shaving. Yet we had become adults in a matter of months. You learn so much back-stage and on-stage about the people out front. I still have my little box of make-up but the little clip-on moustache I seem to have lost. That catchy symbol of Charlie Chaplin and Hitler is no longer with me, that moustache which several nights a week used to change me from a junior clerk into something outrageous.

Clip-on moustaches are very much in fashion now except that you don't see them. You don't see them because they are only clipped on in the secrecy of the inner office. Follow most heads of departments into their inner sanctums and you will no doubt be very much aware that in a few seconds the mild well-dressed man has clipped on his Hitler clip-on. There then follows an hour or two of brutal slaughter, three hours for lunch, and what is left of the day is spent ordering plane tickets for the invasion of the Antipodes. The clip-on slips neatly into the ticket pocket and he's ready to smile sweetly at all he passes in the corridor. You cannot even spot the slight mark that the clip-on always leaves after a longish performance. The clip-on produces a technique that is not necessarily direct bombardment. There are pincer movements, dropping behind the lines, spying and all too frequently poison gases.

It is plain to see why the clip-on is active. An organisation slowly comes into this world to create things. In the case of television this organisation was quite tiny. It concerned itself with creating just a few hours television a day, starting late afternoon at about tea time and finishing well before midnight after late dinner. But like all organisations that are creative, they grow and are infiltrated by administrators who are not creators and insist on more to administer. From a few hours of creativity a day on one single channel we now have four channels, some of which spew out stuff night and day. Clearly that is going to take a lot of administrators and they hugely outnumber the creators. And once you have more administrators than creators then the bright light of creation gradually dims to a dull glow and eventually all but snuffs out.

I have known some creators who have become administrators and they are the best. For they know the conditions only too well, they have had practical experience, they understand. They generally are not interested and do not indulge in the intense power struggle that besots the administrative world. For administrators live in a dull world and the one way of geeing things up a bit is to organise a system that is governed by grade and status. That is the most important consideration. The fact that the viewing public are paying quite a lump of money to be entertained and informed is lost, forgotten, put aside. It has become a land of lost marbles. It is true of course that there are pictures on our screens, so we are getting something for our money, but when you consider if we are getting value for our money then the kindest answer would be a question mark. But a question mark is a very unsatisfactory sign.

Shall we go back a bit? When television grew from one channel to four in such a short time it soon became a target for careers. In the same way that students are persuaded that there are careers in banking, careers in the law, so there was added to the list careers in television. And very nice too. Good salaries, good careers for the students who are receiving their education. But education is very questionable stuff. To me it is like artificial fertilizer. Too much of it or too lavish an application and you are raising and supporting a plant that is in fact a phoney plant, a false plant. When I looked after Willy's farms we grew 1,000 acres of cereal crops. That was over forty years ago. Our average yield to the acre was about one ton. Artificial fertilizer was known and it was used, but only in very small quantities. Seed was sown with artificial fertilizer and the usual application was one to two hundredweights to the acre. There may have been a later top dressing but whether it was worth it or not was arguable. The crops were comparatively free of pest and disease since the strains of seed could look after themselves and were fairly resistant to sickness. Our yields were roughly one ton to the acre. The great monocultures of today produce three tons to the acre. But one wheat seed during its short lifetime will be sprayed fifteen times. It is sprayed with liquid fertilizer, herbicides and pesticides. This does not produce a true plant, it is a phoney plant, a plant that cannot look after itself, it is prone to disease and has to be sprayed again to counter that disease.

Life has become a life where we treat the symptoms. A land of lost marbles. The symptoms of our own body disorders are so often treated and the cause overlooked. Artifical fertilizers used to excess exaggerate the natural to produce the unnatural. This applies to a certain extent in education, where the amount of book knowledge and the use of electronic equipment reduces the natural abilities of brain and body. A row of qualifications will certainly get you a job as an administrator but will you appreciate the qualities of life that will let us live in peace and with a generous attitude to those whom we administer? I'm afraid that this is not the case. Administrators will deny this of course but they are all constantly at war, some more actively than others.

It has been said that there exists a 'dirty tricks' department. I do not know of it, but I know heads of departments who have their own special tricks to get rid of others and better their own shaky footholds. For the higher you go the harder you'll feel the clout. I think that the British Tommy of the First World War sniffed out the situation of promotion and power in the officer class. The object of the war, so they were told, was to create a land fit for heroes to live in. They soon realised that it was a quotation as hollow as an empty gasometer. They were soon singing of the officers –

> They were only playing leapfrog,
> They were only playing leapfrog,
> They were only playing leapfrog,
> And the fourth staff officer
> Jumped right over the third staff officer's back.

Further down the scale the Tommies sang with a certain amount of delight and spite –

> If you want the Sergeant major
> I know where he is,
> He's hanging on the old barbed wire,
> I've seen him
> Hanging on the old barbed wire.

The human animal doesn't change a great deal, which can be a good thing in many ways, for the danger is that it could get a good deal worse. The artificial fertilizer of education turns out so many brilliant but lopsided creatures, with a bulging cranium of book knowledge but far too often a lack of understanding of or sympathy for colleagues and friends. I paint a gloomy picture but we were taught as children to expect nothing from this life and you will not be disappointed. In fact, expect the worst. And if you expect the worst then you will quickly learn to appreciate the various quarters from whence the worst will come. For a freelance this is one of the most important ingredients for survival and surely television has helped us all to judge a character by its face. That big blown up close-up of a face will tell us immediately the nature of the creature that is talking to us. So you know what to expect from that one.

As a freelance I have been involved with many large corporations but have never been an employee as such. In many ways this is a good thing, for you do not get directly involved in the game of leapfrog. But the distressing thing is that the artificial fertilizer of education does not seem to increase the yield of decent manners or reasonable human behaviour. The rank rudeness and double-crossing at times is enough to blot out the sun. Freelances get their fair share of this, for in many cases the attitude is 'Well, they need the work'. But freelances, so it is said, can get used to anything except hanging, the real infighting takes place between the regular employees. Some of the stories are really rather funny. A third staff officer and a second staff officer were driving back after a meeting. The second staff officer said to the third, 'Have you ever thought about taking early retirement?' 'No, I haven't,' said the third. 'Well,' said the second, 'you had better start thinking now, you're sacked.' This true story brought sly smirks to the faces of many. And the sequel to that story brought stifled giggles some time later when the second staff officer was given the chop by the first staff officer and the general.

These stories make the clip-on moustaches in their lairs twitch a bit from time to time. It is often argued that a dismissal here and a quick chop there keeps people on their toes. I would that it were so. The land of lost marbles gets bigger and fuller of marbles than ever before. It is proposed to pay someone to read an autocue £100,000 a year. This is something that the thirty-odd thousand members of Equity could do – I almost said blindfold. It is indeed sad to stand behind a row of pensioners in the post office and as they draw their pensions they hand some of the money back to buy television licence stamps. So much of that money is simply squandered. The old children's programme 'Animal Magic' was broadcast live for about seventeen years. That meant it took just one day in the studio. The replacement programme now takes three days to record and a further three days to edit. And no one in the land of clip-on moustaches and lost marbles says 'This cannot go on'. But it is going on, for the licences are going up by almost a fiver. It is all very like the Army now and so very different from the golden era when we were experimenting and exploring. I know it will be said that I sound like an old Blimp bemoaning this and that and complaining and acusing. I feel that it must be put into writing. It's true that I owe so much to so many who gave me my chances, checked my impetuousness, offered advice, and adjusted my steering. The difference between then and now is of course enormous. The individual is fading away and most of the originality has been used up. But I may be wrong. There is much that I do not know. And you don't know how much you don't know until you're told.

Some years ago, on account of my interest in steam trains and my recordings of 'Thomas the Tank Engine', I was made a vice-president of the Bluebell Railway. The President in those days was the Bishop of Lewes. He loved steam trains. There was a celebration lunch at the Bluebell Line station at Sheffield Park. I sat next to the Bishop, who was an extremely gentle and understanding man. We talked of steam engines for a long time until we both ran out of steam on that topic. The Bishop was very quick to cover fresh ground. He said to me, 'Tell me, where do you live?' In those days I lived in Wiltshire and told him so. He said, 'Ah, Wiltshire, lovely county Wiltshire'. I said I thought it was. And then he said again, 'Ah Wiltshire, lovely county Wiltshire, do you know Salisbury?' I said that I knew Salisbury fairly well. He said, 'Ah, Salisbury, delightful man Salisbury, isn't he?' I was, as they say, more than somewhat took aback. I could only nod in agreement while I tried to collect my thoughts. My ignorance was incredible. No, I didn't know York. Nor Bradford. I'd seen Bath and Wells on the telly but never met him. Surely I knew Truro and Exeter. Oh dear, what an ignoramus. I knew nothing. The dear Bishop's world was his own and he knew it well.

He must have been a very happy Bishop. He observed the Christian rules and he was sure that those to whom he talked did likewise or tried to. Of course it took the Church many hundreds of years to establish its code of behaviour and adjust its set of rules. During this development thousands were put to death by fire, hanging, the sword and the gun because they were deemed to be unbelievers or defied their elders and betters. There were quite a lot of Cardinal Richelieus knocking about and still are. And of course persecution is one of Homo Sapiens' favourite pastimes. We feign horror and disgust at the treatment meted out by a pussy cat on a mouse. What hypocrisy. We are much better at persecution and torment than pussy cats, for pussy cats do not torture their own kind. We do. All the time. We spend a lot of time and energy in telling others what to do and how to behave. It is in our muddled cussed natures to do so.

I think that the internal combustion engine was deliberately invented by us so that we could get at each other. Imposing speed limits, penalties, no parking, clamping (Oh, that's a lovely one), breathalysing, double yellow lines. And indeed we encourage individuals to practise their own personal persecution on others in the shape of traffic wardens. We just cannot help twisting others' arms and making them scream and it will not get any better. It seems to be bred into us from childhood. From early age we are victims of the diet dictators. Eat that – it's good for you. You can't have that, it's bad for you. New fresh bread is bad for you. Very bad for you. That was simply a law invented to save on the housekeeping, for as you know new fresh bread disappears much quicker than stale bread. My dear Dad was a very kind and understanding man but he invented his own little persecution. You must admit it was quite original. His three children and his wife were made to drink two spoonfuls of pure neat olive oil every morning. Now that takes a bit of twisting back. I knew they swill it away in the Mediterranean, but they have done it for centuries – we haven't. The sight of a bottle of olive oil still makes me heave a little. The diet dictators will always be with us commanding us to eat either brown or white bread, denouncing butter and mutton fat, extolling margarine, cursing and forbidding sugar and salt.

I like salt, I love to create a small pyramid of salt on the side of my plate. Not so long ago I did this at lunchtime and a lady who was present said to me, 'It is my solemn duty to warn you that salt is extremely bad for you'. I like that. My solemn duty. We will practise our persecution under all sorts of disguises. The worst one is very much like 'It is my solemn duty'. It is 'In the name of the Lord'. Whenever I hear one of the clergy intone 'In the name of the Lord' I long to ask the gentleman if he has got a chitty from the Lord to say that he has that authority. Authority over others dresses itself up from a very large wardrobe.

So it is not difficult to appreciate that in the world of television and radio our unpleasant inherited afflictions will manifest themselves and cultivate their own particular viruses in the comfortable broth of success. I have said before that if you are even moderately successful you sow a minefield around yourself and you do not know where those mines are. But the longer they lie in the ground the more power-ful they grow. I know that I sowed a lethal crop of minefields around me. They were the scientists. Mind you, they were beautifully con-cealed. You just would not know they were there. But they were all primed with their clip-on moustaches. They were all scientists who could not tolerate my anthropomorphic approach to the animal world. Anthropomorphism was a Cardinal Richelieu sin. It must be put down. Trouble was the anthropomorphic approach was a very popular approach, it produced consistent and high viewing figures.

But I was well aware of the antagonism of the scientists and I was not all that surprised when I was told that my programme would be killed after another two series. But there was considerable surprise when I said that I had no contract with the BBC nor they with me, that a quick execution is preferable to slow strangulation, and that the programme was finished now. No doubt some people put away their clip-on moustaches with a certain amount of satisfaction when they picked up their brief-cases that evening.

The natural history programmes now are very dependent on the brilliance of the cameramen – and their patience. The films are still watchable but the lecture-type commentary persuades me to turn the sound off and just watch. And even just watching is tarnished by the amount of material that is shot in the studio. Much of what we are led to believe is natural is quite simply 'set up'. Tricks and stunts are taking over, not only in the natural history films but elsewhere. Natural ability is simply fading away and so tricks and stunts have to be created to attract our attention – by the 'Graphics' people.

But all is not lost. Every now and again there comes shining such a ray of hope. One of the finalists of the 'Young Musician of the Year' competition was a charming thirteen-year-old sprite who played the flute. She had the confidence of a top barrister, for she admitted that her favourite pastime was 'arguing'. But she didn't argue with her flute, she played it like a fairy in a sunny woodland glade. She was worth every penny of the licence fee. She no doubt will go on dancing and fluting in the sunshine of the glade and be tempted to test the shadows deeper in the forest. I only hope that she has the great luck and good fortune that has fallen on me and comes out the other side on the calm seashore in one contented piece.

Entertainment

— • —

Entertainment is as old as the hills and in certain parts of the world it still carries on in the form of the storyteller. In the great square in Marrakesh in Morocco the acrobats, the jugglers and the story-tellers perform every evening. The storytellers always seem to attract a lot of listeners. I used to go and listen to them. I had no idea of course what they were saying but even so they held my attention. They used all the tricks in the book as they went to work on the audience. The audience simply had to listen as the storyteller altered the pitch and tone of his voice, carefully planting one fact and then another as he built the story bit by bit. The audience loved it and so did the storyteller. He was extremely sensitive to his audience, he knew exactly how he was 'going over', for like all good performers he had the humility to know that he had to give the audience what it wanted. He had to hold them and interest them and please them. It is a skill that some people have and quite a lot do not have but would dearly love to have.

It is so understandable that there are so many who would want to hold the centre of the stage – the ones who are 'stage struck'. I was such a one. I was absolutely stage struck, but any thought of making a living or career on the stage I had to put firmly in the margin. To start with, my looks were against me, my size was against me. Everyone said, 'For goodness sake forget it'. And so I did. I was going to follow a nice conventional life doing goodness knows what. There were certainly no openings for me on the stage, so don't be silly. That was a nice way of putting it. There are no openings.

And in the days before the Second World War there certainly were no openings. But now there are plenty of openings since the enormous growth of radio and television. And countless are the numbers of people who are now attracted to those openings. There are thousands who now wish to be in on the act.

The vision that so many have of appearing on television shines very bright and promising indeed. Unfortunately the opinion that so many have of themselves far exceeds their ability. Not only that but all ability needs controlling, training and experience. The story-tellers in the market-place have the ability to entrance their audiences but they were not able to do it overnight. They had to learn how to capture and hold a critical crowd. They learned from their fore-fathers and their own experiences. Like all the crafts it was a tradition. It was inherited. You simply cannot be a performer or a director just like that. Oh, but you can now because the openings are there. There are thousands of openings and the openings are filled by the intelligent, the clever, the smooth and the glib, the placid, the ex-citable, the honest and the frauds.

And so a television industry has come about in the space of a short lifetime. In the beginning it groped carefully along just feeling its way, guided by people who knew the theatre, who knew how to write, who knew what people liked. There was just one viewing channel and it operated for just a few hours a day. Now we are told that we can expect satellite television offering goodness knows how many channels to choose from. I only hope that the old story-tellers of Marrakesh keep their traditions going for as long as they can, for in America, so I am told, there are some very popular tele-vision shows where the entertainment is provided by the host of the show screaming obscenities at the audience. The audience screams back and the obscenities get worse and worse. It is rather like the hysteria that afflicts football crowds – football hooliganism. Can we be on the verge of developing a sort of television hooliganism? If that be the case all that can be added is, as they say in Wales, 'Well, there's lovely, isn't it?'